# Discovering Kindness

*A Collection of Modern-Day Fables*

**Kevin J. Smith**
*with* **Laura Sherman**

M&B Global Solutions, Inc.
Green Bay, Wisconsin (USA)

# Discovering Kindness

*A Collection of Modern-Day Fables*

ISBN: 978-1-942731-37-5

Published by M&B Global Solutions Inc.
Green Bay, Wisconsin (USA)

# Dedication

*To all the courageous individuals who continue to question their limitations until they discover they are not real. These are the people who can truly help themselves and the world.*

# Contents

# THE TACO MAN

STORY 1 IN THE "DISCOVERING KINDNESS" SERIES

## Kevin J. Smith
### with Laura Sherman

# *Felipe*

Felipe Alvarez smiled at all the passersby as he weaved in and out of the throng in the outdoor market in the heart of Mexico City.

He closed his brown eyes for a moment and enjoyed the lilting voice of the woman singing *Feliz Navidad* accompanied by twin guitars. The music blended into the cacophony of the background chatter perfectly, as if the people were, in fact, part of the song. Almost on cue, a hawker called out to patrons, adding to the percussion section of the symphony.

Felipe loved the smells of the spices and meats, along with the push and flow of people moving in and out of the stalls. The busier the better. He especially adored the Americans. Everything about them fascinated him.

"Por favor," he heard a man with a distinct Southern American twang say to a vendor.

Felipe turned to his right to take a good look at the man. He was tall and elderly. Felipe guessed he was from Texas because he was wearing a large, leather cowboy hat. Felipe paused and waited to hear what he'd say next.

The vendor gave him a big smile and greeted him.

"Si," the Texan said, pointing to a pile of shredded beef. "Uh . . . I'd like . . . punto cinco pounds of that meat there."

The man behind the table looked confused. "Punto cinco?"

Felipe smiled, "Excuse me, sir," he said to the cowboy in perfect English. "May I be of assistance?"

"Oh, son," the man said in a gush of relief. "Your English is real good. I want a half pound of that stuff there."

"Ah, punto cinco. Point five is a half," Felipe said more to himself than to anyone else. "OK, well a half pound is about a quarter kilo. Is that what you want?"

"Yeah, that's right. Not pounds. Kilos. We're not in Kansas anymore, are we?" he said with a wink.

Felipe tilted his head to the right and said slowly, "No, sir, you're in Mexico City in Mercado de la Merced."

The cowboy laughed and said, "Can you tell him what I want?"

"Sure," Felipe said. He turned to the man and gave the order.

The vendor immediately looked relieved. "Gracias, Felipe," he murmured.

"De nada," he said to the vendor. Then he turned to the American and said, "Enjoy your stay in Mexico City."

"I will," the man said. He reached into his pocket and pulled out a few coins. "My way of saying thanks."

Felipe took the coins without counting them. That would have been rude. It was a gift regardless of the value of the money. Felipe bowed.

"Thank you!" he said gratefully.

"De nada!" the man said, looking proud of himself.

When Felipe was out of sight of the man, he looked down at the three coins. There was one peso and forty centavos. He ran a hand through his curly brown hair and pocketed the money. He was grateful for anything.

He turned left, then right, and stopped when he heard the sonorous voice of Juan, one of his favorite tour guides.

"As you know, this market has a rich history. Traders have always come from all over to visit and sell their wares. In 1860, this permanent market began on the site of a proud and ancient monastery that once resided in this very location.

"You can find everything you want in La Merced. The freshest and ripest fruits and vegetables of all shapes, sizes, and varieties are available. Anything your heart desires."

Felipe could hear his stomach growl and hoped it wasn't so loud as to disturb Juan and the Americans surrounding him.

Juan looked around the group, and his eyes settled on a girl who looked to be about eleven. She had long, twin blond ponytails with bright red ribbons on each end. He leaned down and said, "Did you know that you can even find fried grasshoppers within this amazing market?"

Felipe grinned and waited for the girl's response.

"Ew!" she cried. "No way!"

Juan laughed and said, "I know, I know, it is a delicacy here, but not for everyone."

Felipe glanced over to a nearby stall that had a large basket filled with delicious grasshoppers, lightly fried in oil and sprinkled with chili and lime. Again, his stomach growled.

Juan's eyes caught Felipe's for a second, then he said, "Would anyone care to purchase some grasshoppers for my good friend Felipe here? He looks rather hungry, and I'm sure he'd love to eat a few."

A dozen sets of eyes turned to face Felipe. He grew red as they looked him up and down. There was an awkward silence until the little girl turned to her mother.

"Mommy, please?" she whispered. "I'd like to see the boy eat a grasshopper."

The woman looked at Felipe and said, "Really? You want to do this?"

Felipe grinned at her. "I love *chapulines*," he said. "They are tasty. I like their crunch and flavor."

The woman shelled out a few dollars and gave them to the vendor, who was very happy. He gave Felipe a small handful of the treat. Felipe raised an eyebrow and looked at Juan, who smiled and said, "I never developed a taste for them myself."

Felipe shrugged and crunched on the bugs, eliciting a collective gasp of disgust from the tour group. The little girl watched in horror, then buried her face into her mother's long, gray sweater.

"Delicious," he said with a grin, knowing that bug parts were sticking out of his teeth. Anything to entertain the Americans.

The mother handed him a dollar bill. "For your troubles," she said with a shudder.

Felipe took the money. He tried to remain calm, but knew that his feeling of awe was probably transparent on his face. He pocketed the crisp bill, swallowed, and quickly ran his tongue across his teeth. "Thank you, ma'am. That's very generous of you."

As the tour moved forward, the little girl looked back at Felipe and waved. He waved back and smiled. There was no doubt about it. He was lucky. After all, most days he couldn't afford breakfast. He could really only count on one meal a day, huddled around the small table with his grandparents and siblings in their one-room studio apartment. However, today, he'd been given not only the gift of protein, but a whole American dollar as well. He couldn't wait to show it off.

\*\*\*

Later that evening, Felipe waited for his *abuela* to put a spoonful of beans and rice on his plate. His grandmother always knew how to spice up the plain dish, and it filled his belly nicely. He watched his younger siblings, Mateo and Teresa, wriggle in their shared chair, vying for a little more space. He wished he could bring some meat home to add to the dish.

"How was school?" his grandfather asked Teresa.

"Good," she said. "I like math."

His grandmother smiled. "Smart girl." She turned to Mateo. "And how did you do today?"

He reached into his pocket and pulled out ten pesos. "Not bad," he said. "I helped sell mangos at the market."

"Good boy," she said. "And you, Felipe?"

He brought out a handful of coins and the dollar bill. He grinned when his grandmother clapped her hands and the others expressed their astonishment. "Amazing! What a help you are." She kissed him on both cheeks.

Felipe grinned. "And I was given all kinds of snacks, too."

After the meal, the children cleaned up and set up the room for sleeping. As Felipe put Teresa to bed, he felt a pang of sadness. Tucking her in should have been his mother's job.

Sofia had been such a beautiful woman, with her long, black hair and soft smile. He could muster up her scent of honeysuckle and chilies if he concentrated. A single tear fell from his eye. Then another. He was grateful that Teresa had begun to softly snore so she couldn't see his grief.

His parents had been killed on the way home from work two years ago. They'd been in the wrong place at the wrong time. Everyone who lived in the area knew to stay indoors after it got dark, but Sofia and Alberto had been asked to stay late at the factory to work on a last-minute order that was needed the following day. There was no getting around it; when an employer asked for your help, you gave it.

The police determined they had been caught in the crossfire when the drug cartel came into the city in a convoy. Ten innocent civilians were murdered, including two Americans. Nothing was done about it; no one could stop the cartel.

The incident had made the papers because of the two American lives that had been lost. Otherwise, the tragedy was all too common to have been of interest to anyone outside of the city. Felipe stood up and paced the small room. Would that he could go outside and take a walk, get some fresh air, and escape his deep sorrow and growing resentment.

He took a few deep breaths and looked over at his grandmother, who was watching him. She seemed to understand his mood and simply stood up and gave him a long hug. Felipe sagged into her embrace and let another tear fall.

\*\*\*

Six months later, Felipe was following Juan's tour when he spotted a new vendor selling tacos. He was a stocky man who had lost nearly all his hair. His warm smile was as inviting as the tantalizing aromas from his street tacos. Most vendors sold a variety of different treats to the tourists and locals, but this man chose to stick with one item.

As Felipe inched closer, he noticed each taco cost only ten pesos, much less than the other vendors in La Merced. The food smelled so good, and although this man was new, he already had a line snaking down the aisle.

Felipe drifted toward the stand as though caught in a current. His stomach growled so loudly that the other patrons turned to look at him. He blushed, but couldn't move away from the magnetic booth. Was it possible to gain nourishment simply by the smell of good food?

As Felipe approached the side of the booth, he could see the vendor was completely overwhelmed by the surge of patrons. The stocky man wiped his brow and glanced up at Felipe.

"Hey, kid, can you give me a hand?" he said in a low voice. "I'll give you three tacos for lunch if you can start now."

Felipe couldn't believe his luck. "Sure!" he replied. "Of course!"

"I'm Miguel."

As if he'd been doing it for years, Felipe slipped behind the table and began taking orders. He watched Miguel double-wrap the corn tortillas and fill them with a variety of spiced meats, black beans, and cilantro salsa. "It's my grandmother's recipe," he whispered to Felipe.

"What is?"

"All of it," he said with a laugh. "She was a brilliant cook."

For the next three hours, tacos flew out of the little stand at a steady rate. Felipe and Miguel took a late lunch break when the crowds died down. The moment Felipe bit into the first street taco, he moaned with pleasure. He had never tasted such amazing pork and beef. The spices the street vendor used in combination with the salsa were delectable.

Miguel laughed. "Like it? Good. That's important if you're going to work for me."

"Really?" Felipe said, momentarily forgetting he had a mouth full of *carne asada*. He quickly swallowed and wiped his mouth. "You're going to hire me?"

"I need help. And you're a quick study. To start, I'll pay you what I can. Then as the business grows, I'll pay you more."

"I'll take whatever you offer," Felipe said quickly.

"And I'll throw in leftovers each day. How does that sound?"

"Sounds amazing!"

After they finished their lunch, people started coming up to the booth again, clamoring for more food. They served tacos all afternoon until the meat was nearly gone. Finally, Miguel closed shop and handed Felipe a bag with a dozen wrapped tacos. "For you and your family. I made sure to save these for you."

Felipe grinned. Adrenaline raced through him as he thought about how excited his siblings and grandparents would be about receiving a real meal. "Thank you!"

"And here is your cut of today's sales," Miguel said, handing Felipe three hundred pesos.

Felipe gasped. He reeled as he stood there clutching the six pink 50-peso bills. He'd never had so much money. "I-I- . . ."

Miguel clapped him on the back. "You deserve it. I need a hard worker by my side. Look, I promise I'll be able to pay you more than this. Eventually. Right now, I have a ton of start-up costs. Give me some time, and I'll show you how we can make some good money."

Over the next few months, Felipe learned how to make mouth-watering street tacos. He met Miguel early each morning and stayed until they sold out the food. Sometimes they sold out in the early afternoon, sometimes only late at night. It didn't matter to Felipe. He loved the job.

One day, it was nearly ten at night when he and Miguel finally closed down the stand. Miguel looked as if he was about to fall asleep on his feet. Good thing he lived around the corner.

Felipe was glad it was only a short walk to his home as well. The market was nearly deserted by this time; only a few street cleaners were there, sweeping up the trash from the day's transactions. Felipe waved wearily at a vendor as he passed. The man looked as tired as he felt.

Suddenly, a car squealed to a stop at the edge of the market, just at the end of the aisle from Felipe. He watched as a burly man jumped from the passenger seat and ran over to the vendor. The thug grabbed the vendor and muscled him into the back seat of the car, jumping in beside him. With another squeal of the tires, the car tore away into the night.

It all happened so fast that Felipe barely had time to register the shrill cries of the vendor as he begged for mercy. Felipe shook himself and slowly resumed walking.

*** 

Felipe was making enough money with Miguel after a few months to allow his grandparents to switch to part-time hours at the shoe mill.

"Do you think it's wise to do this?" his grandmother asked her husband.

"Yes," he responded. "It sounds like the taco business isn't going anywhere but up. I know you're worried it won't last, but you've worked hard your whole life and deserve this break."

"Miguel promises to pay me as much as he can afford," Felipe said. "So the money I bring home will just get better as the business continues to grow. We have big plans in the works."

"You're such a good boy," she said, giving him a hearty hug. "Bringing home food and money to your *abuelos*."

"This is just the start," Felipe said. "When I get to America, I can send you much more money."

His grandmother's shoulders slumped. "You know I don't think that going to America is a good idea."

"*Abuela*, you know how I feel about this. America is the land of promise, where hopes and dreams all come true."

"You sound like an advertisement," she said.

He shrugged. "It's how I feel."

"But it's too far away!" she cried.

"I'll send for you."

She shook her head. "I don't want to leave my home."

"*Abuela*, be reasonable! I can make so much more money there. Then I can take much better care of all of you." He paused and ran a hand through his hair. "And we'd never have to watch our backs and worry about the drug cartel shooting us down in the street."

Once the words escaped his lips, he wished he could take them back. They had a tacit agreement not to talk about the dreadful night that took the lives of his parents. "I'm sorry," he whispered as he saw his grandmother's face become wet. "I didn't mean . . ." He reached out to touch her hand.

She waved his hand away. "I don't want to talk about this anymore." She got up and went to her little wooden chair in the corner of the room. Felipe watched her pick up her knitting and ignore everything around her.

*** 

Felipe handed change to a customer. She thanked him with a big smile and carried away her tacos. He glanced around and noticed no one was lining up, so he quickly put up the sign indicating that the booth was closed for lunch. Miguel turned off the grills and wiped the sweat from his brow. They emerged from the heat of the booth and sat under the umbrellas they had recently bought to provide shade to the four small tables in front.

"So you want to go to America, huh?" Miguel said. "Smart boy!"

"Not according to my *abuela*," Felipe grumbled.

"She doesn't want to lose her grandson. Once you go, you'll probably never come back."

"But I plan to send for her."

"You think she'd leave Mexico?"

Felipe shook his head sadly. "I don't understand it."

"This is her home. Her heritage. Everyone and everything she knows is here. She probably feels she's too old to move to a country where everything is foreign and different."

Felipe gave him a small smile. "It's like you're channeling her. Those are pretty much her exact words." Then he paused. "What about you?"

"I like it here. Mexico City is my home, too."

"So I'll be going alone then."

Manual clapped him on the back. "You'll do great there. Sell my tacos on the streets of New York. They'll be a huge hit."

"You'd be OK with that?"

"Of course. Why not?"

# *Gabriel*

Thump! Thump! The rhythm of the basketball pounding on the pavement melded with the angry car horns and the rumble of the traffic. Staccato bursts of curses and cheers wove through the background noise. Gabriel closed his eyes for a moment and let the music of the city wash over him as he took slow, deep breaths. He felt inspiration grow, opened his eyes, and trained them on the lithe bodies in front of him as they seemed to glide across the court. He watched one tall boy fake left and drive right around the point guard. Then he leapt gracefully into the air and slam-dunked the ball with ease.

Gabriel's pencil flew across the sketchpad as he raced to capture the moment. He enjoyed testing his ability to catch vitality in freeze frame. He looked at his work and smiled with satisfaction. If only he had a nice set of graphite pencils. His sketches would be a lot more professional.

Sitting cross-legged on the cold cement wall, he fell into deep thought. His eyes lost focus on the basketball game in front of him as his mind drifted back to thoughts of home.

Home would always be Paris.

\*\*\*

He and his mother, Aimee, had shared a tiny flat on the top floor of an antiquated apartment building. Rooftops of all the other buildings in the area cluttered the view. You always flushed the toilet twice and prayed it would go down. But it was home, and he wished he could teleport himself back there.

*Why did we have to leave?*

*Because Father was a jerk.*

That was the simple truth. Gabriel couldn't stand to see his mother with another blackened eye or bruised arm. Moving out had proven to be useless in protecting her. After all, Victor had known the hair salon where she worked and found it easy to follow her back to her home.

The day he found them, Gabriel received a broken arm when he'd attempted to protect his mother's frail frame from his father's brutish strength.

The only real solution was to move far away.

"America," his mother said when they left the emergency room that night. "He can't follow us there."

"But *Maman*," Gabriel cried. "I don't want to leave."

She sighed and put an arm around his shoulders. "I know, I know. It's just the way it is."

Gabriel continued to try to talk her out of her decision, but couldn't.

In the end, he realized that he was tired of constantly looking out for the ogre behind every tree and alleyway. She was right. He just didn't like it.

***

He heaved a deep sigh and stretched his back, relieving the cramp that had settled during his recollections. Looking out at the kids playing ball, Gabriel wondered if he'd ever find friends like he had back home. Probably not. He wrinkled his nose at the pungent smell of rotting vegetables and industrial exhaust that assailed his nostrils.

Brooklyn.

Why Brooklyn?

That was easy. It was the place where his mother could get a job cutting hair. Her friend, Francois, had agreed to sponsor her at his posh hair salon on Atlantic Avenue.

"You're the best stylist I know, Aimee," he'd said. "I always loved working with you at the old shop on *Rue Tandou*."

His mother had jumped at the offer without exploring other options. After they'd arrived, Gabriel was overwhelmed by the cultural differences and could think of nothing except flying home. If he'd had the money, he would have boarded the next plane.

Out of the corner of his eye, he saw a dark-skinned hand reach toward his sketchbook. "What are you drawing?" Dawn asked.

Her question sharply brought his attention back to the present, and he pulled the notebook close to his chest. He glared at her. "Nothing."

How he wished he had a music player like most of the other kids had. Then he could generate inspiration whenever he wanted by immersing himself in his favorite bands. At the same time, wearing headphones would make it clear to others that he wanted to be left alone.

"Don't be like that, Gabe," she said. "Let me see."

"It's not finished."

She folded her arms across her chest. "So?"

He looked into her chocolate brown eyes for a moment, then sighed and gave in. He let the sketchbook drop to his lap face up. "Whatever."

She sat down next to him and delicately pulled the book from his lap as if it were a treasured find. After she studied the latest drawing for a few moments, she looked at him. "That's amazing. That's Terrance and Mo shooting hoops!"

"Yeah, I know," he said, his lips quivering slightly at the corners.

She hit him playfully. "I mean, it's really good."

"Thanks," he said, taking his book back.

"How did you get them jumping in midair like that? I can never draw action."

He shrugged. "I don't know."

"Can I see more?"

"Maybe. Sometime." A shrill bell tore through the noise. He stood up. "I've got a Spanish test." He trotted off to class, feeling a little better about himself and life in general.

*** 

The roar of the four o'clock train dampened the sound as the twin deadbolt locks opened to a basement apartment. Gabriel entered and locked the door behind him. He threw his black backpack on the worn corduroy couch and took two steps into the kitchenette.

As usual, a yellow sticky note greeted him when he opened the refrigerator. He stared at the plate covered in plastic wrap resting on the middle shelf.

"Meatloaf for my growing boy. Love you, *Maman*!" the note read, along with her trademark heart with a swirl under the words.

He touched the paper gently before he scooped up the dinner and put it in the microwave. As he watched the plate of food slowly spin, he considered walking to the salon to say hello to his mother, but knew he had too much homework to do.

After dinner, Gabriel opened his antiquated laptop and finished his homework by eight. Determined to stay awake to see his mother, he set up the couch as a bed and propped himself up with a Tom Clancy book he'd borrowed from the library. However, he lost the battle with his eyelids and didn't even hear the rumble of the eight thirty train. It was only when he heard the locks open hours later that he bolted up, his heart beating fast.

When Aimee walked in, it was as if a member of the folk punk rock band *Chats Noirs* had entered the room. "*Maman*!" he shouted, hurling himself shamelessly into her arms.

She playfully exaggerated the groan as his five-foot-nine frame hit her petite body. "You're getting too old for this," she said, but returned his hug with gusto. After a few moments, she pulled away and looked at him. "Did you like the meatloaf?"

"Yes," he replied. "Thank you."

"It's after your bedtime," she said, giving him a reproachful look. "You need your sleep if you're going to continue to get A's."

"I wanted to talk to you," Gabriel said with a shrug. "Would you like some chamomile tea?"

She nodded her head. "You know me too well. Sure, let's have a cup of tea, then it's off to bed. For both of us."

He put the kettle on and pulled out two tea bags, placing them in two red mugs. He drizzled a spoonful of honey into each and yawned as he waited.

"So what's on your mind?" she asked.

His back still turned to her, he shifted his weight from the right foot to the left. "I hate that you're gone all the time."

"You know I have to work two jobs. We need the money."

Gabriel nodded, but still didn't turn around to face her. When the whistle blew softly, he poured the water and stirred the honey. He clanked the spoon against the side of the mug and deposited it into the sink.

Finally, he turned around and brought his mother one of the mugs and sipped on the other. "I want to work," he said.

She knit her eyebrows. "Why?"

"Living in this city is expensive. And you're working so hard just to pay for rent and groceries. I want to help out. Besides, there's nothing left over for other things."

"Like what?"

"I really want a music player. And better art supplies."

She let out an exasperated sigh. "Yeah, I get it. I'm doing my best."

"I know, *Maman*. Let me find the money for it."

"Honey, your most important job right now is to study and get good grades. Then you will be able to get a good job and be successful."

"But I am getting good grades."

"How long will that last if you start working and take attention off your studies? I mean it, Gabriel," she said.

He watched his mother sip her tea for a moment. "I just want to earn money so I can help buy the extra stuff."

Aimee gave a long, drawn-out sigh. "I know. But you shouldn't have to work. It's my job to take care of you. I want you to get into college and earn a degree."

"Maybe I don't want to go to college," he said. "What I really want to do is be a professional artist."

"We've had this conversation before. Professional artists wind up poor. I don't want that for you."

He folded his arms across his chest. "And you know that I don't agree."

"Get a degree and do your art on the side. It's got to be a hobby, not a career."

"A hobby?" he whispered.

She stood up. "I'm tired. It's late. I don't want to have this conversation right now. It's time for you to go to bed. I need sleep. We both need sleep."

Gabriel watched his mother shuffle off to the bedroom. He wanted to call out after her to say something, but didn't. Now wasn't the time to convince her of anything.

***

Gabriel wasn't eager to face the empty apartment, so he took the long way home. As he walked by an overpass, he noticed a taco truck parked underneath. The fact it was painted to look like the Mexican flag captured his interest: broad bands of green and red ran along the right and left side, and a white field ran across the middle, where a man with curly brown hair leaned out of a window and handed food to customers. Several small tables were scattered in front of the food truck, covered with brightly colored tablecloths and topped by red plastic flowers. People sat at the tables, relaxing, talking, and laughing. It seemed to Gabriel that they had forgotten they were in the middle of the city under a gray underpass. They were enjoying themselves in this little oasis.

From his position, Gabriel couldn't make out any words. The overhead traffic was too loud. Still, he could see that the man was very animated and his patrons were listening attentively. Gabriel inched closer and hid behind a column. He didn't wish to be observed, but he was intrigued and wanted to find out what was going on.

"See you tomorrow, Taco Man," a large-bellied man shouted over his shoulder.

"Don't forget to ask for a raise. You'll never get one if you wait around," replied the vendor, pointing his finger at the man.

Gabriel watched the man bounce down the street with a huge smile, munching on his taco.

The next man placed his order, and the Taco Man chatted with him about his daughter, who had apparently fallen ill with a virus.

"It's just a cold, I think," the man said with a heavy German accent. "It's just not improving, and we can't afford a doctor."

The Taco Man pulled out a glass jar and handed it to him. "It's a combination of onion, garlic, ginger, jalapeno pepper and fresh horseradish, all mixed with apple cider vinegar."

The man looked dubiously at the concoction. "I don't think she'll drink it."

"Mix it with apple juice. Trust me, it'll help. It's a good tonic."

"OK, I'll give it a try. How much do I owe you?"

The Taco Man pointed at the big glass jar marked "Tips" to the right of his window. "Just pay me what you like."

The man dropped some bills into the jar, then paid for his tacos. As he walked away, the next man came up and purchased three tacos.

Gabriel's stomach grumbled as he watched patron after patron order and eat their food. Even from his distance, it smelled incredible. He wished he had a few bucks, but knew there wasn't any money in his pockets, so he turned around and walked back down the street. As his stomach rumbled, he wondered what his mother had left for him in the refrigerator.

Felipe watched the sullen boy with the black backpack trounce off down the street. He knew that look; the boy was hungry. If only he'd hung around a little longer, Felipe would have happily given him a few tacos.

He ran a hand through his hair in frustration. There was no way he could leave the truck to run after the boy.

\*\*\*

When Gabriel opened the apartment door, he immediately noticed his mother sitting at the small kitchen table. His heart raced as he took in her bent head and quiet sobs. He dropped his backpack and rushed to her side.

"*Maman*, what is it?" he whispered.

Aimee looked up at her son with tears spilling out of her eyes. "Francois fired me."

"What?"

"I was so tired," she said. "I really messed up. It was one of his best clients. I butchered her hair. I have no excuse. No reason. She immediately went onto every review site she could find and gave Francois one star."

"I'm so sorry," Gabriel said, feeling cold creeping up his spine.

Gabriel looked into his mother's eyes and saw a new level of exhaustion. "I need to go to the restaurant soon. They'll be expecting me," she said.

He shook his head. "Absolutely not! You need to get some sleep." He picked up her phone, dialed her boss, and explained that his mother was too ill to come in. Then he ushered her to her bed and tucked her in.

She closed her eyes and instantly fell asleep.

Gabriel tried to focus on his homework, but he couldn't think straight. What would they do without his mother's job? She'd need a new sponsor, or they would have to return to Paris and run the risk of being found by his father. Not only that, but they would run out of money soon. *Maman's* part-time job at the Burger Barn wouldn't support them.

He had to convince her to let him get a job to help out. They wouldn't make it otherwise. He felt a lump in his throat as he realized that getting a music player was definitely out of the question now.

# The Taco Man and Gabriel

By the time Gabriel woke up the next morning, his mother was gone. She'd left a note saying she went out to look for another full-time job. He sighed and wondered how that would go without a reference.

After school, Gabriel followed the same path he had the previous day. He wanted to see if the taco truck was parked under the overpass again. He wondered if the magical sight was a daily occurrence. He smiled when he saw it and inched closer than the day before. He counted three men standing around eating their tacos as they listened to Mariachi music trumpeting from the radio on the counter of the truck. He jammed his hands into his pockets and debated leaving. He had no idea why he was there. He was just drawn to the brightly colored truck.

Felipe spotted the boy and was delighted he'd returned. The child seemed troubled. And today he looked like a stray dog ready to bolt down the street. Felipe felt a strong urge to help him. He turned off the radio. "Hola!" he called out with a huge smile. "I hoped you'd come back."

Gabriel froze. Was the curly-haired man actually talking to him? He scrunched his brows and turned around. The guy couldn't possibly mean him. He hadn't even met the man. Still, no one was behind him, and when he turned back, the Taco Man continued to smile at him. The man seemed to be patiently waiting for him to respond.

"Me?" Gabriel finally said.

"Of course, you," Felipe replied, softening his voice so as not to startle the boy. "Come, have a taco."

Gabriel felt a rush of understanding. The man was a typical hawker, selling his wares. Gabriel was just another mark. He stood rooted to his spot and muttered, "I don't have any money."

"That's OK. It's on me."

Gabriel's head spun. What was this guy's game? No one gave away things for free. There were always strings. Still, the delicious aromas of the meats and sauces reminded Gabriel that it was dinner time. It smelled so good.

"No, thank you," Gabriel said half-heartedly. His traitorous feet moved closer to the truck. "I'm not hungry." As if poking fun at him, Gabriel's stomach chose that moment to give a loud grumble. Felipe and the others around the truck began to laugh.

Gabriel scowled and stopped moving forward. His shoulders sagged as he turned to leave.

Felipe stretched his hands out in front of him. "No, wait!" He fumbled with the words in a desperate attempt to keep the boy from running away again. "Please, I'm sorry. I didn't mean to laugh. It was just kind of funny, no? I mean it was, wasn't it?"

Gabriel turned back. "Why do you care what I think?" he bit out. "You don't even know me."

Gabriel couldn't fathom why he was still there. Maybe it was the kindness he saw in the Mexican man's eyes. Maybe it was the aroma and his lowered blood sugar. Whatever it was, Gabriel couldn't bring himself to walk away.

Felipe watched a variety of emotions flit across the boy's face. "I just do. My name is Felipe, but people call me the Taco Man."

"I heard," Gabriel muttered. "Why's that?"

Felipe shrugged. "Maybe because I make tacos?" He glanced up at the boy and saw that he had inched closer. Good, he looked as if he felt a little more comfortable. "Do you like pork, beef, or chicken?"

"Chicken," Gabriel said. Then he thought about it and said, "Or pork. Beef's good, too."

Felipe suppressed a laugh. The last thing he wanted to do was to offend the boy again. "All three it is!" he said. "You don't mind cilantro, do you?"

Gabriel shook his head and took another step closer. He watched the Taco Man build three tacos for him. It was mesmerizing to see him create the food with speed and dexterity. The odd man obviously loved his work.

Felipe handed the three wrapped tacos to the boy and waited for him to take his first bite. By then, the other customers had left. He was glad for the break. Now maybe he could figure out what was going on with the boy.

Gabriel sat at the table closest to the truck and bit into the chicken taco. Instantly, he felt the most delicious sensations course through him. The flavor combination was unlike anything he'd tasted before. And that was saying something, because between Paris and Brooklyn there were a lot of tasty treats available. There was no doubt, hands down, this was the best taco he'd ever had.

"*Mon dieu!*" he exclaimed when he could find his voice. "They're incredible."

Felipe grinned. "Good, no?"

"Yeah," Gabriel said with his mouth half full. He didn't care. "These are the most flavorful tacos I've ever eaten."

"Good, eat up." Felipe said as he began to clean the counter.

Gabriel was grateful that the man was allowing him to eat in silence. Suddenly, it occurred to him that he'd never introduced himself. "I'm Gabriel," he said.

"Good to meet you," Felipe said. He'd wanted to ask for the boy's name, but felt it was better to wait for him to feel comfortable enough to offer it. "You're from France, no? How long have you been in the US?"

Gabriel stiffened. He wasn't sure how much he should tell this man.

Then he shrugged and figured that a free meal was worth a little trust. "I came from Paris about six months ago with my *maman*."

Gabriel shoved the last few bits into his mouth, then said, "Thank you."

"De nada," Felipe said with a wave of his hand. "When I was your age, a man was kind to me." Felipe's eyes misted as he thought of Miguel.

Gabriel noted the emotion in his voice and wondered at it. He nodded in response.

Felipe wiped an eye. "I miss him."

"I'm sorry," Gabriel murmured. "What happened?"

"Miguel, he died," Felipe said. "Back in Mexico City. I worked with him, and he shared everything he knew with me."

"How'd he die?"

"He had a heart attack. In his sleep. Then his two brothers took over his business and ran it into the ground. They didn't want me around." Felipe released a ragged sigh. It had been a difficult time, but that was behind him.

"That's horrible!" Gabriel muttered. People all over the world could be so nasty.

"Yes and no," Felipe said with a small smile. "Honestly, I don't know that I would have left for the United States without the push. Just before Miguel passed, he gave me a nice bonus. He knew I wanted to leave Mexico." As Felipe shared his story with his new friend, he felt a rush of love for his old mentor. He gave a silent prayer of thanks to the heavens.

"How long have you been here?" Gabriel asked. "I mean in America."

"Ten years."

Gabriel whistled low. "That's a long time."

They fell silent for a bit, then Felipe stopped cleaning. "So, how are things going for you?" It was a bit direct. However, if Felipe was going to help the boy, he needed to understand Gabriel's situation better.

The last thing Gabriel intended to do this afternoon was pour his heart and soul out to this total stranger under the large overpass. But his belly was full, and the man had just confided in him. Gabriel raised his voice to be heard over the droning traffic overhead. He told the Taco Man all about how his father, Victor, had abused him and his mother for years. He didn't leave out any details. Then he described coming to America, and how hard it was to adjust to his new life.

"I miss Paris," he said with a sigh.

"You'll go back one day," Felipe said with a warm smile. "I'm sure of it."

Gabriel shook his head. "You don't understand. I can't leave my *maman*, and she will never return as long as that monster Victor is still there." He shuffled his feet back and forth for a moment, then said, "Besides, I could never afford the plane ticket."

"Things will get better, my friend."

Gabriel folded his arms across his chest and glowered at the man. "Well, I'm not sure how. *Maman* just lost her job, and I don't know if she'll be able to find another. I wish she'd just let me work, but she won't. And she's exhausting herself every day."

Felipe held the boy's eyes with his own. "Ah, I am sorry. That's rough."

Gabriel sighed. "Yeah, well, there's nothing anyone can do." He felt the hot pricks of tears in the back of his eyes and turned away.

Felipe watched the boy struggle with the weight of the world and politely turned his back to clean the stove. It looked like his customers were winding down for the day, so he started in on the heavy-duty cleaning. It would give his new friend time to collect himself.

Gabriel watched the Taco Man scour his stove for a while. He was throwing himself into the task. It was then that he noticed a large glass jar spilling over with money. The thing was stuffed with bills of all denominations. A slow anger burned up inside him as he considered how unfair it was that this man from Mexico City had so much money while he and his mother had nothing.

In the blink of an eye, Gabriel grabbed the jar and took off. His heart hammered in his chest as he ran down the street. As he increased the distance between himself and the truck, the jar's weight increased. It felt as if it were made of lead. His arms felt like jelly, but he couldn't slow down. Gabriel's chest began to ache, and his legs burned, but he kept going.

He knew that the Taco Man was probably right behind him, chasing him down. He had no idea how much money he held, but it was a lot. He couldn't turn back, or he'd be caught. Gabriel imagined the Taco Man's face twisted in a furious expression, betrayed by the teen he'd so generously fed.

The weight of the jar was getting to be too much, and his feelings of guilt started to eat away at his resolve and strength.

Maybe he should return the money.

No, that was impossible. He couldn't go back now.

What if the Taco Man put him in jail? He'd have every right to do so. Then they'd be deported for sure. He and his *maman*. Gabriel wondered how much money he was carrying. Judging by the weight, it was probably enough to cover *Maman's* lost wages and the rent that was due in two weeks.

What would his mother say when she found out that her only child had become a thief? A new wave of fear coursed through him, worse than the thought of the police being on his heels.

Finally, out of breath, he stopped and looked back. No one was behind him. No one was chasing him. There were no police sirens and no angry Mexican man with curly brown hair. He sagged to his knees, still clutching the jar. His lungs burned, and his whole body ached.

Gabriel realized he couldn't stay where he was, out in the open. When he could, he pulled himself up again and half-jogged, half-walked home. He wondered if his mother was back from a day of job hunting. It was so hard to get work in this city. It could take her weeks to find employment.

*Maman* would probably be getting ready to leave for the restaurant soon. He madly tried to think of reasons he'd be carrying a large glass jar filled with American money. He paused outside his apartment door and finally settled on the most plausible explanation he could come up with: he'd found the jar of money. Gabriel ran a hand through his hair and convinced himself that it was something that could have happened.

When he opened the door to the apartment, he tentatively surveyed the small space. It was empty. Relief flooded through every pore of his being.

Gabriel placed the jar on the kitchen counter. He opened the refrigerator, which doubled for a mailbox. He saw his mother's beautiful scrawl stuck to a plate of pasta and meatballs.

"Found a job at a gym. Start at 5 am tomorrow. Left for restaurant early. Love, *Maman*."

He sighed. They always needed people at the restaurant at all hours to fill in at the various stations. She usually manned the cash register and sometimes flipped burgers in the back. Sometimes she ran the drive-through.

Gabriel closed the refrigerator, flopped on the sofa, and groaned. He'd stolen the money for nothing. His mind burst with conflicting thoughts. He closed his eyes and pushed away the gurgling guilt that threatened to surface. Then he reminded himself that they would always need money. It was a good thing he took it. And now at least *Maman* would never have to know what he did.

After a few minutes, Gabriel got up, brought the jar back to the couch and tipped it upside down. The thing was packed full of money. Fascinated, he watched the bills spill out. Most were ones, but there were fives, tens, and even twenties. He wondered how much there was.

"Three hundred and seventy-four," he breathed after he finished sorting and counting all the bills. He gave a low whistle. He was pretty sure that was just a few days' haul for the Taco Man.

"He doesn't need it," Gabriel said resolutely to the empty room. "And I do."

He put all the money back into the jar and hid the jar at the back of the linen closet, under a few old towels. After taking a long shower, he put his sheet on the sofa and did his best to fall asleep.

***

"Can I see your latest drawing?" Dawn asked as she sat down next to Gabriel.

Gabriel didn't look at her and continued to gaze out at the school-yard. It was buzzing with activity. Just a few feet away, a group of girls played with a hacky sack, bouncing it back and forth between them. In the far corner, three boys stared intently at their phones, barely notic-ing anything around them. Then a cheer rose from the basketball court as a tall boy sank a free throw and shouted, "Nothin' but net!"

"I haven't done anything in a while," Gabriel said.

"Why?"

He shrugged. "I don't know." He pulled his backpack closer and picked at a loose thread.

"Come on."

Gabriel stood up and slung the pack over his shoulder. "Look, I'm going to skip last period. Can you tell Mr. Severnson that I threw up and went home?"

"You know he won't take that from me," she said. "He'll need a note."

"Yeah well, I'll deal with it tomorrow." He shuffled off without a backward glance.

Gabriel walked out of the schoolyard and down to Flatbush Avenue where all the pawn shops were. He was plagued by the idea that he should just return the money. But he pushed it away, scoffing loudly as he walked by a couple. The man pushed a stroller, while the wom-an walked a reddish-brown miniature dachshund. They turned a con-cerned look in his direction. Gabriel blushed and murmured an apolo-gy.

Returning the money just wasn't an option. How would that con-versation go?

"Here, Mr. Taco Man, I've come to give you back your tip jar!"

"Oh, good. I'd hoped you'd be stupid enough to return. It just so happens that the local police love my tacos. They've been waiting here to take you in."

Gabriel wiped his brow and shuddered. No, he'd never be able to return to the taco truck. His stomach immediately protested with a loud grumble, and his mind filled with the memory of the best tacos he'd ever tasted.

"And never will again," he murmured. He quickly looked around to see if anyone had caught him talking to himself. He sighed and shook his head in an effort to remove the unwanted thoughts.

The street was crowded with people as well as vendors trying to sell what Gabriel imagined was stolen merchandise. He briefly watched a middle-aged woman bargain with a man for a Gucci knockoff purse before moving on. He glanced up at the bright yellow sign that announced many things for sale and walked into the shop.

He'd been in this pawn store a few times, but had never had the money to buy anything. Well, today was different. Today he was going to get the music player he'd been wanting for so long. After perusing the various glass cabinets, he finally asked the shop keeper to show him an older iPod sitting on the top shelf of the case. It cost $75. He talked the man down to $70 and walked home.

Gabriel downloaded music from his laptop and spent the evening listening to his favorite bands. It succeeded in distracting him from thinking about the Taco Man, the police, and his new life as a criminal.

*** 

The bell rang and Gabriel was one of the first out of the stuffy classroom. It was a sunny spring day and he wanted to be outside. He was grateful for the afternoon break.

He opened his backpack and pulled out his sketchpad and pencils. After laying them carefully on the top of the wall, he opened the side pocket to pull out his iPod. It wasn't there. Panic welled up as he thought about the last time he'd had it. It was the previous night, on his couch. He'd put the music player in the little pocket at that time. He was sure of it.

Gabriel dumped all his books and supplies out of the bag, but couldn't find it in any of the compartments. His heart hammered in his chest as he remembered leaving the backpack under his seat when he'd used the bathroom during fifth period. Did someone really steal it? He sighed. Yes, five minutes was enough time.

His shoulders sagged while he slowly put everything back into its place in his bag. He didn't feel like drawing. He didn't feel like doing anything.

He spent the free period propped up against the wall, watching the other kids playing hoops and joking around. Dawn spotted him from across the playground and walked over to him. He groaned and started to stand up, but realized he had no place to go, so he slumped back down again.

"What's wrong?" Dawn asked tentatively.

"Nothing," he muttered. He wanted to tell her to go away, but couldn't bring himself to be that rude to the only person he could possibly call a friend in the United States. Well, Taco Man might have been one, but he'd blown that out of the water. After all, who'd want to be friends with a thief?

Dawn put her hands on her hips. "I don't know you very well, but I can tell that something's wrong. I'm not going anywhere until you tell me."

Gabriel glared at her, then softened. He shook his head. "It's embarrassing."

"It can't be that bad."

"It is," he said with a sigh. "My new iPod got stolen. I think. I can't find it anywhere."

"I'm sorry." She sat down next to him.

"Thanks," he said. For some reason he felt a bit better.

"I had a Game Boy I'd gotten for Christmas last year. Someone swiped it, so I know how that feels." Her shoulders slumped as she talked. "It feels like such a betrayal, doesn't it? Like you can't trust anyone."

He nodded. A cold feeling crept up his spine. Is that what Taco Man had felt when he realized his tip jar was gone? What would Dawn think of him if she knew he had betrayed someone the same way she had been betrayed? Gabriel put his head in his hands and moaned. "It's awful."

"It just makes you feel unsafe, you know? Like, what else could they take?"

"Yeah, I guess. For me, I don't really have anything else. That was it." Then he thought about the remaining money sitting in his linen closet.

That was his.

Or was it?

He had to go home to make sure the money was still safe. He knew he'd feel better if he could just touch it.

The bell rang. Gabriel looked at Dawn. "I'm going to take off."

"Geez, Gabe. Again? They're going to kick you out of school if you keep skipping."

"What happened last time?"

She shrugged. "You got lucky. I don't think the teacher noticed. He seemed distracted. Didn't even call roll. You're not going to get that lucky again."

"Don't rat me out, OK?"

"I won't, but maybe you should stick around. It's just one more period. And it's Friday. You'll have plenty of free time over the weekend."

Gabriel thought about it and nodded. "Yeah, you have a point. It's the right thing to do."

As soon as he got home, Gabriel took out the glass jar and counted the remaining money a few times. Just holding the bills made him feel a little better. However, that feeling dissipated quickly. He knew the money would never truly be his. He really only had one choice, and the consequences just didn't matter. He needed to return the cash the next day. He hoped the Taco Man wouldn't be too harsh with him.

He slept better that night than he had in three days.

\*\*\*

Gabriel watched the Taco Man work with a wild flurry. There had to be at least a dozen people waiting in line for tacos. He shifted the jar from his right hand to the left. Would Felipe notice that it was lighter than when he'd stolen it three days ago?

He stood there watching the scene in front of him for thirty minutes, debating the wisdom of approaching. Certainly, he didn't want to walk up with a jar full of money. The customers would likely glower at him, knowing that he was the one who took their tips.

Finally, when the crowd thinned, Gabriel walked slowly to his death sentence. Many scenarios went through his mind. None of them ended favorably. The last few feet were the toughest. He imagined this must be how someone on death row would feel.

Gabriel froze midstride when he locked eyes with Felipe. His heart leapt into his throat, and he nearly gagged on it.

So be it.

When Felipe caught the hazel eyes of the boy, he was momentarily stunned. He'd come back. He'd actually returned with the glass tip jar. Not many people would have done that. He smiled. He knew the boy had a good, kind soul. Felipe held his tongue for fear his voice would be enough to scare Gabriel away. He also purposely kept still, as if watching a doe in a meadow.

Gabriel couldn't read his expression, but was relieved that the Mexican man wasn't hurling choice words at him. The curly-haired man just continued to look at him. And he didn't appear to be reaching for a weapon of any sort. Sensing he wasn't in immediate danger, Gabriel moved closer. He quickly glanced around at the remaining two customers. Neither seemed to care about him or the large glass jar.

Finally, with a shrug, Gabriel lifted the jar back to its rightful place. He pushed the temporary plastic bucket Felipe had on the counter back to make room for the glass one.

"I'm sorry," Gabriel muttered.

Felipe dumped the contents of the small bucket into the glass jar. "What's done is done," he said with a smile. "Hungry?"

Gabriel shook his head and stared at the jar. He had put the few dollars he'd saved from his birthday into the jar to try to compensate for what he had spent. It wasn't enough. Not nearly.

Felipe ignored the boy's answer and made him two pork tacos. "Look, I have extra today. If you don't eat them, they'll just go to waste."

Gabriel suppressed a smile at the man's lie. "OK," he said.

The other customers ambled away down the street. Gabriel watched Felipe work a while, then noticed a note pinned to the side wall of the window frame. The writing was a neat cursive and said, *"If you realize that you have enough, you are truly rich."*

Felipe went to hand the boy the tacos and paused. He could tell Gabriel was trying to work through the quote to understand it.

"It's from the Tao Te Ching. Have you heard of it?" he asked.

Gabriel shook his head.

"How about the philosopher Lao Tzu?"

Gabriel nodded. "Yeah, I've heard of him. He founded Taoism, right?"

"That's right," Felipe said. "Not many kids would know about that."

He shrugged. "I read."

"That's great. Well, the Tao Te Ching was written by Lao Tzu and lays out the Taoist fundamentals. Anyway, what do you think of the quote?"

"I'm not sure," Gabriel said, shifting from one foot to another. "I mean, it's good and all, but I'm just not sure what *enough* is, you know?"

Felipe nodded. "Most people struggle with that."

"Maybe it means that if you convince yourself you have enough, you'll be happy," Gabriel said, but then shook his head. "No, you've got to *believe* it. But how do you believe it when you don't? Truly and completely believe it, that is."

Felipe smiled. "It took me a while to get it, too. It's not an easy concept."

Gabriel looked at the wrapped tacos in Felipe's hand. "So you gonna give those to me or what?"

Felipe laughed. "Of course. Sorry. Here you go."

Gabriel lowered his head in a little bow. "Thanks. I missed these."

"Eat up," Felipe said. He noticed that Gabriel's eyes went back to the sticky note before he sat down to eat his tacos.

Felipe recalled the day he first encountered the quote himself. He had just arrived in the States and was feeling lonely. He'd walked the twelve miles to Manhattan, an island densely packed with people who seemed unhappy. He'd tried to connect with them, but no one returned his greetings and most had permanent scowls on their faces. Still, Felipe was happy to be there. He knew that somehow he'd find the opportunity to make his dreams come true.

As he walked, a small piece of black paper stuck in a crack in the sidewalk caught his eye, and he leaned down to pick it up. On it was the quote: *"If you realize that you have enough, you are truly rich."*

The truth of it hit him. He knew that if he could fully live by its truth, he'd find what he was looking for. Felipe felt as if the note had been left for him. When he flipped the card, there were the words "Thank you!" and a smiley face.

He memorized the quote and left the card on the street where he'd found it for the next passerby. The wisdom of the ancient religious leader had helped him that day, and he hoped it might guide another who happened upon the same card in the future.

"You know," Felipe said after a few moments, "for me this quote really turned my life around. I realized that I needed to stop focusing on everything I didn't have. I lost my parents when I was young. I had so little money. And I had to scramble to find a place to live. These things were smacking me in the face every day when I first arrived in America. It took stepping back and looking at what Lao Tzu said over two millennia ago in order for me to see what I *did* have."

Gabriel swallowed the bite he'd been chewing and looked at the man skeptically. "And what was that?" It sounded to him as if Felipe had about as much as he himself had when he arrived. Nothing. Everyone else always seemed to have so much more than him.

"Well for one, my dream of coming to this country had come true," Felipe said with a soft smile. "I'd wanted that for so long. And there I was on the streets of Manhattan. I was grateful for that. I also had the knowledge of how to make the best tacos in all of North America."

"Probably the world," Gabriel added.

"Thank you. Yes, I think so, too," Felipe said. "When I realized that I had everything I needed, I felt a certain peace. I stopped trying so hard and just breathed and lived. Everything came together after that."

Gabriel sighed. He took another bite and looked to his right, then to his left. No one else was there. "I need to tell you something," he said after a minute.

"Yes?" Felipe said, keeping his voice calm and cool. He really wanted to help this boy, but that could only happen if Gabriel trusted him. He held his breath and hoped that the boy was ready to confide in him.

"I . . .," Gabriel began before flashes of his father slapping him hard across the face overwhelmed him.

He remembered Victor charging at him with hatred in his eyes.

"How dare you?" he'd spat.

Earlier that day, Gabriel had borrowed his father's moped and banged it up pretty badly when he'd taken a turn a little too fast. Already weakened from the accident, Gabriel had crumpled to the ground from his father's blow.

Playing dead hadn't stopped Victor from kicking his son a few times. Finally, he'd walked off, leaving Aimee to pick up her son and clean him up.

Felipe watched the boy struggle with his personal demons. He held his tongue, but when Gabriel didn't continue speaking after a few moments, he said softly, "You can tell me anything. Trust me."

Felipe's gentle tone pulled Gabriel from his waking nightmare. "I took your money," he said in a rush.

"I know," Felipe said, tilting his head. "But you returned it."

Gabriel closed his eyes, wincing in anguish. Then he opened them and looked into Felipe's soft brown ones. "Not all of it," he said, as unwanted fear assailed his senses. He took a deep breath and really observed the man in front of him. Felipe didn't look angry. He didn't even seem upset. How was that possible? Maybe Felipe didn't understand. "I bought an iPod with some of the money. It's not all there," he clarified in a measured voice.

Felipe held his gaze, then nodded. "I understand."

Gabriel held his breath, waiting for what he had done to register. But Felipe didn't say anything else. Finally, Gabriel burst out, "Is that it? Aren't you mad?"

Felipe smiled at him. "No. I'm very happy. You felt safe enough to tell me. That means everything to me. We can work out the rest."

Gabriel shook his head. "I don't get it."

Felipe waited for the boy to look up at him again. Then he said, "I realize I have enough."

"But . . ."

"I'll help you with this. Where is the iPod now?"

Gabriel's shoulders slumped. "It was stolen. Right out of my backpack. I'm sorry. I can't even give it to you."

"How much was it worth?"

"Seventy bucks."

Felipe nodded. "Why don't you work with me after school? You've seen this place. I could use an extra hand."

Gabriel's heart beat quickly. "Really? I mean, yes!" he cried out, realizing that he shouldn't question this generous offer. "That would be great."

"And after that, if you want, you can continue to help out, and I'll pay you."

"Wow," Gabriel said. "No way. That would be incredible."

That night, Gabriel couldn't stop grinning. He wished his *maman* was there so he could share his good news. She'd just have to understand. He could work and earn money.

Gabriel pulled out his art supplies and began writing out the quote that Felipe had on his truck. He'd mastered calligraphy a few years ago and enjoyed using his fountain pen to practice the letters.

It was then that a thought hit him, and he began to work on a project in earnest. He was still working on it when Aimee came home at midnight and insisted he go to sleep.

\*\*\*

The following day, Gabriel nearly ran to the Taco Man after the final bell rang. He couldn't wait to give the man his gift. The place was packed, so Gabriel waited for Felipe to notice him.

Seeing the boy, Felipe waved him inside. "You can put your backpack over there," he said, indicating the corner with the boxes of tortillas. "It'll be safe there."

Gabriel nodded and washed his hands. Felipe showed him what to do to assist him, and he spent the next hour serving the dozens of customers who came to the window. Gabriel liked being on this side of the taco truck. There was a certain power to it.

Having the boy there gave Felipe the opportunity to talk to more of his customers. He was even able to step out of the truck and get into deep conversations with some of them. They each had their own problems and needed to confide in someone. Felipe loved giving advice along with the nourishment. It was food for thought along with food for the body.

When things slowed down, Felipe went back inside the truck. He looked at Gabriel, who smiled at him.

"I have something for you," Gabriel said.

"You do?"

Gabriel washed his hands and reached into his bag. He pulled out a book and opened it. Inside, stuck between the pages, was a beautiful sign the size of a postcard. It featured the quote from Lao Tzu in calligraphy next to an ink line drawing of Felipe's taco truck under the overpass.

Felipe inhaled sharply and felt the pricks of tears behind his eyes. He silently accepted the drawing, unable to find the right words. Then he looked up at Gabriel. "You made this? For me?"

Gabriel had been watching him intently and grinned. "Yeah."

"It's the most beautiful drawing I've ever seen."

"I don't know about that," Gabriel said.

"Well I do. I'm going to get a frame for it and hang it right here," Felipe said, indicating a spot by the window. "In fact, you know what? I happen to have a frame here."

Felipe pulled out a simple black metal frame, which he'd had tucked under the counter. Gabriel's picture fit perfectly. "I'd been saving this for a photo of the truck, but this is better."

Throughout the rest of the afternoon, many customers commented on the image and quote. Each time, Felipe gave credit to Gabriel, who blushed from the recognition.

At the end of the day, Gabriel peeled the original note from the wall and said, "Can I have this?"

"Sure. You want it?"

"Yeah." He stuffed it in his pocket. "See you tomorrow!"

Later that evening, Gabriel excitedly greeted his mother when she came home. He made tea and explained everything that had happened. She listened quietly and shook her head. "You're lucky. You know that, don't you?"

He nodded. "*Absolument.*" Then he pulled out the slip of paper with Felipe's handwriting on it.

"This is the note?" she asked.

"It is," Gabriel said. He stood up and pinned it under a magnet on the refrigerator. "We need to keep this in mind."

"Maybe you can make me a sign like you did for the Taco Man."

"Yeah, I can do that." He came back and sat down on the couch next to her. "So, you're OK with my working with him?"

She tilted her head to the right. "Do I have a choice?" she asked with a small smile.

"Not really. It's what I need to do."

"I can see that," she said with a nod. "Sure, you can work for the Taco Man. Bring me home a few, will you? I need to try them for myself."

"You got it," he said, throwing himself into her arms. He felt so much lighter now that he had his *maman*'s stamp of approval.

***

The next day, Felipe asked to see more of Gabriel's sketches. He was in awe of the boy's talent. "You should sell these."

"Yeah, right," Gabriel scoffed.

"Don't do that," Felipe said. "You're good. You need to own that."

Gabriel nodded slowly. "OK. It might take some time."

"Time we have," Felipe said with a grin. "Look, do you have any more that are finished?"

Gabriel flipped through his book and pointed out a few. "I'd like to put a few finishing touches on these, but yeah, they're pretty much right."

Felipe nodded. "Bring them back tomorrow and I'll find some frames for them. Sign them, will you? We can sell these for sure."

"Where?"

"Here!" Felipe said. "All day people have been asking me about your sign. Some asked where I bought it. I think they'd buy ones like it if they were reasonably priced."

Gabriel didn't need to be told twice. The next day he came back with three of the sketches and a few more that he'd drawn the previous night.

Felipe framed all the drawings and hung them on the outside of the truck. When he was done, he smiled. "It's like we have a little art gallery."

By the end of the day, all the sketches had sold.

# JOANN

STORY 2 IN THE "DISCOVERING KINDNESS" SERIES

## Kevin J. Smith
with Laura Sherman

Alexandra Devon checked herself in the mirror. Her silky, long black hair glistened as she moved her head back and forth. Not a hair out of place. Of course, no grays. Her eyes roamed up and down her form. No bulges, no wrinkles. She had the perfect body.

"There," she breathed.

It was a work in progress. She was always tweaking the angles of her face and the contours of her shape. Everything was just so.

Alexandra slipped on the gold dress she had just purchased with real money. She chose a pair of matching shoes and exited her apartment. Strolling down the street, she was surprised to see so many people out and about. One couple was making out under a streetlamp.

Despite the late hour, many shops were open. She poked her head into a millinery for a moment to admire the hats on display. Further down the road, she smiled at a pub's flashing neon sign that welcomed residents of *A Better You* inside. Alexandra was drawn to the window and looked longingly at the people inside. They seemed to be enjoying themselves. With a sigh, she turned away and continued her stroll.

People flowed in and out of the stores, and some greeted her casually. Usernames flashed above the passing avatars. Antonia Vermillion walked by, and Alexandra admired her sleek platinum hair. She wondered what her name outside *A Better You* was. There was no way of knowing.

"Maybe I should go blond?" she murmured as she moved forward.

Bobby Sheridan approached and winked at her. He always wore a tank top to show off his pecks. So cute. She wondered what he looked like in real life.

\*\*\*

*Real life.*

Joann glanced at her watch. It was nearly two in the morning. She had to sign off and go to sleep. Alexandra Devon might not need rest, but her real-life body sure did.

She groaned as she stood up. All her muscles protested the sudden motion. She shuffled over to the bathroom and stared at her face in the mirror.

*Certainly not the same as Alexandra's.*

Joann's dull, brown hair curled in all the wrong places. And every time she looked, there was a new gray strand popping up. It was like an invasion. She was only thirty-two. It wasn't fair.

As she continued to study her flaws, she brushed her teeth with a long, drawn-out sigh. Would that she could make instant adjustments to the face and body that reflected back at her.

She looked at her cheekbones and wondered what she'd look like if they were a little higher. Of course, she'd drop thirty pounds, maybe thirty-five, and the grays would go. She was putting off using hair dye for as long as she could, but knew it was nearly time.

And her eye color. She'd considered getting contacts to give herself a darker jewel blue like her avatar, but it was too expensive.

"What I'd do to have your perfect vision," her mom had said just last week.

"I know," she'd said. "I just wish they weren't so watery blue."

"What does that matter?"

*It just does.*

Joann cast her eyes to the scale. It seemed to mock her. She knew she shouldn't weigh herself more than once a day. But she couldn't help herself.

One hundred fifty-five pounds.

She frowned. *It's the clothes. And people always weigh more at the end of the day.*

She crawled into bed, closed her eyes, and hoped she would shed a few pounds overnight. Wouldn't it be great to wake up and be down to 152 or even 150?

***

The next morning, Joann opened her eyes and yawned. Her clock radio played Bon Jovi. A classic rock star playing on an antiquated contraption. She was pretty sure she was one of the few who still owned a radio like this.

*It's probably an antique by now.*

A former boyfriend had given it to her when he'd worked at Radio Shack. She wondered where Frank was now. Static soon drowned out the song, and she shut off the radio and stood up.

*Time for the morning weighing.*

Her heart beat a little faster.

*Good. Maybe it will burn a few calories.*

As she approached the scale, she glanced at the mirror. Same old Joann. She opened the drawer to the right of the sink and pulled out a little black notebook. The last three entries had been consistent. 154.

Today would be different.

She shrugged out of her PJs and put down the notebook. Every ounce counted.

Stepping onto the scale, she held her breath as she waited for the digital readout to proclaim today's weight. 153.8.

She smiled. It wasn't much, but she'd finally broken through the 154-pound barrier.

"Thank you, scale," she whispered, nearly bending down to kiss it.

Joann skipped back to her closet and pulled out her jogging sweats. She was out the door in five minutes.

*Thirty minutes of exercise. That's all I need.*

*Maybe twenty-five, because I'm down in weight.*

She jogged, then walked, then jogged, then walked until she'd circled the block around her apartment three times.

Her knees creaked as she climbed the stairs to her bathroom. She was tempted to step on the scale again, but didn't. All the books said to only weigh yourself every other day so as not to get frustrated, and she'd already broken that rule. As she waited for the water to warm up, Joann gave in to temptation. Same reading. It seemed to her that twenty-two minutes of jogging should have resulted in some drop in weight. She slumped and shuffled into the shower.

Afterward, she quickly got dressed and made her lunch. Joann carefully weighed five ounces of turkey and put it between two slices of thin, whole wheat bread. Then she grabbed an apple and some raw carrots and headed in to work.

*** 

Joann stared out the window into the office space across the street. There was her counterpart, speaking animatedly on the phone as she watered the plants that threatened to overtake her desk. With a sigh, Joann turned her eyes back to her own cubicle. Gray walls, gray carpet, gray furniture. Her cubicle was bare, save for the furniture and computer. Her supervisor despised clutter and had banned all expressions of personality. Joann rolled her neck to relieve the tension and resumed typing. After a few moments, she glanced at her watch. Smiling, she hit save and gathered her belongings.

*Lunch time.*

The medium-sized breakroom, with its yellow walls and white curtains, was filled with people. Joann gratefully hurried over to Stacy, who had arrived early to secure their favorite table by the window, which had a much better view. It was fall, so all the trees in the park below were showing off their yellows, oranges, and reds.

Joann took a seat and opened her lunch. She carefully placed the sandwich and carrots on the table before she began eating.

"Up late again?" Stacy asked as she took a bite of her chicken salad.

"Maybe," Joann said, casting her eyes downward.

"That game's addictive."

Joann pursed her lips. "How many times do I have to tell you? It's not a game."

"Isn't it, though?"

Joann rolled her eyes. "I like it."

"I know," Stacy said with a chuckle.

Joann recoiled as a plate stacked with cupcakes was pushed under her nose. She looked up to see Linda, a middle-aged woman who loved to organize all the office celebrations.

"Have a cupcake," Linda said. "They're left over from Stephanie's birthday party yesterday."

Joann swallowed hard. "No thanks."

Stacy helped herself to a chocolate cupcake topped with a tower of fudge frosting. She took a bite, then said, "Have you considered e-flirting? It's kind of new."

Joann shook her head. "Online dating? All those sites are the same. I'm just not into that."

"Really? That doesn't make sense."

"Why?"

"Because you like *A Better You* so much."

"That's different."

Stacy giggled. "Yeah, you might actually meet a *real* guy and go on a *real* date!"

Joann chewed carefully. Twenty chews per bite. She swallowed, then said, "Maybe."

"I'll take that as a yes," Stacy said with a cheer. "Come over after dinner and we'll set you up."

"I don't know."

"OK, I'll come to you, then."

Joann laughed. "That's not what I meant, and you know it."

"I know," Stacy said, "but let's just get you set up. You don't have to do anything with the account."

"I guess."

Stacy looked excited and pumped her fist. "Yes!"

\*\*\*

Joann regretted tacitly agreeing to her friend's meddling in her love life. As she watched Stacy click through all the pages required to set up an e-flirting account, she yawned.

"We still need a profile pic," Stacy said, her eyes never leaving the screen.

"I don't have one I like," Joann replied grumpily.

Stacy scrunched her eyebrows and glanced over at her friend. "Don't be like that."

"Sorry."

"Come on, what photos do you have?"

Joann perked up. "I have my avatar!"

Stacy rolled her eyes. "You mean that cartoon from *A Better You*?"

Joann crossed her arms and pouted. "Alexandra's not a cartoon!"

"OK, but she's also not real. Neither is that name."

"I like it better. Not like Joann. I hate my plain Jane name."

"Don't get any ideas. You can't use it," Stacy said, giving her friend a sideways glance. "And you can't use the avatar."

"Why not? It's not like everyone on this site is using a realistic photo. I'm sure most are Photoshopped. That's kind of like using an avatar."

"No. It's not."

"Fine," Joann said. She brushed Stacy's hands away from the keyboard. "Here are a few photos." She clicked through various folders until they located one that she didn't find completely objectionable.

"That's not bad," Stacy said, wresting control of the keyboard again. "Let's stick that in. You can always change it later. In fact, you really need a few photos. They suggest four, but allow up to ten." Then she looked back at her friend. "But *not* the avatar."

Joann shrugged and said, "I really should be getting ready for bed."

"You're not fooling anyone," Stacy murmured.

"Come on, we made good progress today," Joann replied. "Let's finish it tomorrow. Or the next day. It's been hours."

"It's been forty-five minutes."

"Really?" Joann said, looking at her watch.

"Uh huh. Look, we're almost done." Stacy clicked through the last few pages. "In fact, now we just need a credit card."

"What? This costs?"

"Of course, silly. What did you think?"

"That it was free."

Stacy laughed. "You can poke around for free for a few days, but they won't let you talk to anyone until you set up an account."

"How much is it?"

"Twenty-five dollars a month. But look here," she said, clicking to a new page. "They have a special. Three months for fifty bucks. That's not bad."

"I don't know," Joann said.

"Come on," Stacy coaxed.

"Fine, but only because Mom still owes me a birthday present. She said I could pick anything I want."

Stacy grinned. "Your mom will like this. She wants grandkids, right?"

Joann laughed. "Yeah, she does."

As soon as Joann had subscribed, they checked out the different guys who lived in the area. Joann shook her head at most of the candidates. Then one guy, Terry, caused her to pause. She read over his profile and liked what she saw.

"Look here, his favorite movies are on my top 10 list. And he likes

80's bands. Just like me!"

"That's cool," Stacy said, leaning in. "And it says that he likes art museums and baseball. Same as you."

"Plus, he's kind of cute."

Stacy grinned. "Sounds like a match! Wanna send him a wink?"

Joann instantly blushed. "No. I mean, what's that?"

"It's a way to show interest and get noticed."

"Isn't the guy supposed to make the first move?"

"Not anymore. If you want to get to know him, you have to go for it."

Joann thought for a moment. "Is there something less obnoxious than a wink?"

Stacy clicked a few buttons and paused over a page. "It says here that you can send a micro message. Kind of like a tweet."

"A what?"

"How can you be so into a virtual world and not know about social media?"

Joann folded her arms across her chest. "I'm on Facebook."

"Posting a reply once a year to your ten friends who wish you a happy birthday doesn't exactly count."

"Whatever. So, what do I send Terry?"

"This article suggests you read over his page and find something you have in common. Then you can construct a little two-line message to say hi."

Joann crafted a short message for Terry and sent it. Then they both stared at the screen for a moment.

Stacy laughed. "It's going to take a while."

"How long?"

"Days, maybe. Who knows how active he is."

"OK," Joann said, stifling a yawn.

"Fine, fine, I get the hint. I'll let you get back to your other world. Just promise me to check in every day to see if anyone writes you."

Joann grinned. "Sure!"

\*\*\*

The next few days went by in a blur. Some might call the type of work Joann did boring, but she found peace in the predictability and logic that numbers provided. No drama. Her job in accounting was the exact opposite of her friend's. Stacy was in HR, which was perfect for her. She could chat with employees and seemed to love interviewing new candidates.

On Friday, during the afternoon break, Joann's phone pinged. She glanced down and gasped. Then she looked up sharply at Stacy.

Joann's heart hammered in her chest. "Someone from e-flirting is asking me out for dinner," she said.

"First one?" Stacy asked.

"Yes."

"Let's see." Stacy grabbed the phone. She clicked and swiped a few times, then handed it back to Joann. "Check him out. His name is Benjamin. He seems OK."

"OK?" Joann asked nervously. She glanced down at his profile. He was cute. He had a nice smile. He liked books and board games.

"What do you think?"

"I think I don't know anything about him. Not really."

"Yeah, well, you'll find out more on your first date."

"So you think I should accept?"

"Why not?"

*Because it could be a complete disaster?*

"I don't know," Joann mumbled.

Stacy grabbed the phone and clicked a button. Then she turned the phone back over to Joann. "Done."

She looked down in horror and saw that Stacy had accepted the invitation.

*Now what?*

As if reading her mind, Stacy said, "Now you go on a date."

"When?" Joann asked, reviewing the invitation. Scanning the message, she found that Benjamin had suggested they meet at Alfonzo's the next evening at seven.

"I have nothing to wear."

"You'll figure it out," Stacy said, standing up. "Don't stress too much. It's the first date of many. No biggie."

"Easy for you to say," Joann said with a sigh.

***

As Joann approached the small Italian bistro, she slowed. Why had she agreed to go on a date? And why Italian food? Most dishes would exceed her quota for carbs. She didn't want to push past 154 pounds again. It had been such hard work to get down to 153. She hoped they'd have something other than pasta on the menu.

Joann looked down at her plain blue pants suit and wondered if she'd dressed properly. It was the only thing she had in her closet that made any sense for a blind date. She'd tried on three dresses, but they all looked frumpy. Well, that was Stacy's word. She had texted her friend photo after photo of different outfits until finally Stacy had stopped answering.

Her cell pinged and she looked down.

"Are you here?" it asked.

"Yes," she answered out loud. "Or at least I'm thinking about it."

It pinged again. "I'm inside."

She texted back, "I'm walking in."

*Am I?*

She walked to the front door, opened it, and looked around. She wished that people's names would hover over their bodies like they did in *A Better You*. However, she was able to recognize Benjamin without too much trouble. He looked as clean-cut in person as he did in his photos.

After the two exchanged the usual pleasantries, the waitress brought the menus. Joann nervously looked over it and spotted a large Caesar salad with chicken and smiled.

"I'm in the mood for a big plate of lasagna," Benjamin said with a grin as he closed the menu. "No one does lasagna better than Alfonzo—I'll say that much."

She nodded and fiddled with the pages of the menu.

"I sure hope you're not one of those girls who orders a small salad and calls that a dinner."

Joann turned beet red and stammered, "I-I . . ."

Benjamin's smile faded slightly, then he nodded. "No worries," he said.

The waitress came, and Benjamin ordered the lasagna along with an appetizer of fried mozzarella. When the waitress turned to her, Joann closed the menu.

"I'd like the Caesar salad with chicken. Dressing on the side." She mentally did the math and realized the calories in the dressing would be too high. "And no croutons," she croaked, barely above a whisper.

"And to drink?"

"Water. With lemon."

When the waitress left, there was an awkward silence. Joann found herself fiddling with the tablecloth. The waitress returned with a basket of rolls. Benjamin grabbed one, slathered it with butter, and then munched happily on it for a moment.

"How long have you been on e-flirting?" he asked as he took a second roll.

"Four days," she said.

He laughed. "So I'm your first?"

She smiled. "Something like that. How long have you been on it?"

"Three months, or four. I can't remember."

"You like it?"

"Sure," he said. "I get to meet a lot of people."

Joann felt her shoulders relax a little. She hadn't realized how stiff she had been. She leaned back in her chair. "So you like board games?"

"Yeah," he said. "And you?"

"When I was a kid."

He winced. "Really?"

She laughed. "I didn't mean it like that. I just haven't played one in a while."

"What do you like to do?"

"I'm a resident in *A Better You*," she replied. She tore a bite-sized piece off the roll and took a mouse bite from it. "I'm there a lot, actually."

He nodded. "So this is a new thing for you then. Venturing into the real world?"

"Ouch."

"Now it's my turn to apologize," he said with a grin. "Actually, I have a lot of friends who love that game."

*It's not a game.*

"I wonder if I know them," she said.

He reeled off several names, but she didn't know any of them. They probably used different names in that world.

Just then the waitress brought out their dinners. Benjamin rubbed his hands together, picked up his fork, and scooped up a large chunk of lasagna. He rolled his eyes in delight as he chewed. Joann watched him with envy as she speared her lettuce.

They chatted about the virtual world, then veered off into books and movies until Benjamin's flourless chocolate cake arrived.

"Wanna bite?" he asked.

She shook her head. "Well, maybe a tiny one."

Joann relished the piece and sighed. Would that she could just eat like Benjamin and not have to answer to the scale in the morning.

When they left, Benjamin gave her a polite kiss on the check. "Don't stress about dating so much," he said as he pulled away. "Enjoy yourself."

She nodded and watched him walk away.

\*\*\*

Joann fell back into the chair in the breakroom and rubbed her eyes. She had spent the last three hours staring at her computer screen. It was a relief to look at the white clouds scudding across the sky. She took a sip of her coffee, enjoying its warmth as it traveled down her throat. She relaxed.

"So how did it go?" Stacy asked.

Joann took another sip of her coffee, then shook her head. "Not great."

Stacy gave her friend a sympathetic look. "Was he obnoxious?"

"No," she said quickly. "He was really nice."

"Were you obnoxious, then?"

Joann giggled. "No."

"Are you sure?" Stacy asked with a grin.

"Yeah, I'm sure."

"Did you talk about your virtual world?"

Joann sniffed. "Yeah."

"Well, that date must have been fun."

"Actually, it wasn't bad," Joann said, taking another sip. "I mean, it could have been worse. He was a nice guy. I'm just not ready, you know?"

"What do you need to become ready?"

Joann ran a hand through her hair. "A better body, for one thing."

Stacy looked at her watch and stood up. "Sorry, I forgot I have a meeting. Look, let's talk more about this after work, OK?"

Joann gave her a small smile. "No problem. I'll be fine. I'm just not cut out for dating."

Stacy looked as if she wanted to say something else, but bit her upper lip instead. When she left, Joann looked at her watch. She still had another five minutes of break left.

"Joann?" a female voice said from her right. "Did I get your name right?"

Joann turned her head to look up into the brown eyes of a wiry, middle-aged woman with snow white hair. "Yeah," she replied slowly. She remembered talking to her at the Christmas party and then again at Stephanie's birthday party last week. She was pretty sure she was in accounting, too. "You're Tammy, right?"

The woman nodded and sat down in the chair Stacy had just vacated. She leaned forward. "I'm sorry. I couldn't help but overhear. I hope you don't mind."

"Uh, no. I guess not," Joann said with a shrug.

"I don't normally do this, but I just had to say something. I think it's important. I wanted to tell you that you have the perfect body right now."

Joann flushed red. Maybe she hadn't heard correctly. "What did you say?"

Tammy looked her in the eye. "All I'm saying is that you have a perfect body. Right now."

Joann's mouth opened and closed a few times before she stood up abruptly. Frowning, she said, "I've got to go."

She left without looking back. She wasn't sure, but she thought Tammy had called after her. The blood rushing in her ears made hearing difficult.

When Joann was halfway down the corridor, she groaned. She'd left her half-drunken coffee cup on the table. She stopped and turned to look back at the open door of the breakroom. She debated going back, but then thought better of it and moved on.

***

That evening, Joann stood in front of the mirror and looked at her body. Really looked at it. She took in her puffy tummy, the saddlebags that bulged from her thighs, and the flabby arms.

*Perfect body. Hah!*

She looked at the magazine photos of actresses and models she had taped to the edge of the mirror.

*I'll never look like them. No matter how much I diet.*

She stomped over to her laptop and logged in to *A Better You*. When Alexandra appeared, Joann looked at her critically.

*Not good enough.*

She spent the next few hours adjusting her body, face, and hair in a desperate attempt to achieve perfection. Exhausted, she fell asleep on the couch, her laptop balanced on her knees.

The next morning, Joanne awoke with a headache, called in sick, and went back to bed. She woke up a few hours later feeling refreshed and logged back in to *A Better You*. Finally satisfied with Alexandra's hourglass figure, Joanne took her avatar for a walk.

Alexandra strolled past Tony's Pasta Palace and felt her stomach rumble. On impulse, she turned back to look at the menu displayed in the window, then entered the establishment. Finding a table in the darkest corner, she ordered a lasagna and devoured it quickly.

She paid the check, then grinned as she passed a virtual mirror. Still perfect.

***

The next evening the phone rang, jolting Joann. Her attention had been fixed on the large piece of wedding cake that Alexandra was about to dive into. There were always so many weddings to attend in *A Better You*.

"Are you all right?" asked Stacy without preamble.

"Sure," Joann answered. She paused, then related what had happened with Tammy.

"And then she said I had a perfect body. Can you believe that?" Joann said. She had the phone on speaker so Alexandra could eat while she talked to Stacy.

"Honestly, I don't think Tammy meant anything by it," Stacy replied.

Joann could tell she had her on speaker, too. "What are you doing?"

she asked.

"My nails. I figure if you can play your game while you talk to me, I can give myself a manicure." She paused. "I know, I know, it's not a game."

Joann smiled. "So what am I going to do about Tammy? It's so creepy."

"I don't think she meant to be creepy."

"I don't know, Stacy. I mean, who walks right up to someone and says something like that?"

"Maybe she was just trying to empower you."

Joann frowned. "You think?"

"Yeah."

"What did she mean by that, then? A perfect body. What the heck, you know?"

Stacy sighed. "I sometimes think it's weird that we can't all just say what we think. It would be nice if we lived in a world where people didn't have to be so guarded all the time."

Joann laughed. "You don't sound much like an HR rep right now."

"I know, I know. Look, why don't you just ask Tammy what she meant. I'm sure she'll be happy to explain."

Joann shuddered. "I could also go on my next date naked."

Stacy barked a laugh. "I wouldn't recommend that."

"Me and my perfect body," Joann muttered.

***

The next day Joann avoided the breakroom, opting to eat at her desk. She continued to do so for a few days until Stacy burst in on her one afternoon break.

"You can't keep avoiding the whole world because you're afraid of Tammy," she said.

Joann frowned. "I'm not sure in what universe the *whole world* consists of a breakroom, but whatever."

"Whoa," Stacy said.

Joann could tell she'd hurt her friend's feelings. She sighed and said, "I'm sorry."

"It's OK. I know you're under some stress. So you'll meet me in the breakroom at three?"

Joann chewed on her lower lip, then said, "Sure."

As if on her way to the executioner, Joann reluctantly put one foot in front of the other and forced herself to meet Stacy for coffee. As she approached the breakroom door, her heart began to hammer. Her mind was flooded with "what ifs."

*What if Tammy yells at me?*

*What if she just ignores me?*

*What if everyone else calls me out for being so rude?*

*What if I'm just being silly?*

She took a deep breath and entered the room. She immediately sighed in relief when she saw it was nearly empty. No Tammy. And everyone else was doing their normal routines. No judgmental ogres.

Joann looked at Stacy, who rolled her eyes. "Has anyone ever told you that you're a drama queen?"

"Never," Joann said with a giggle. She felt a surge of happiness and realized how much she missed the breakroom and the companionship of her friend. "Well, maybe a few times."

***

When 4:30 pm rolled around, Joann packed up her few belongings and hefted her large, brown bag over her shoulder. It wasn't too heavy.

As she exited the elevator, she checked her Facebook notifications that had collected throughout the day. Clicking through the messages and comments, she smiled, glancing up now and then to make sure she didn't run into the person in front of her.

"Joann?" a female voice came from the left.

Frowning, she wondered who was calling out to her. The voice sounded familiar, but she couldn't quite place it. She looked up and scanned the dozens of people in the area until her eyes settled on Tammy's.

She froze and quickly sifted through her choices.

*Run!*

That was definitely her first impulse, but as she looked at Tammy, she realized the woman didn't look particularly angry. She also wasn't moving toward Joann. She realized Tammy seemed to understand what she was going through and was giving her space.

Joann made her choice. Her shoes felt as if they were made of lead as she made her way over to Tammy. She weaved her way through the throng to get to her, like a salmon swimming upriver. When she was in front of the slight woman, Joann looked her in the eye.

"Thank you," Tammy said.

"For what?"

"Not walking away."

Joann nodded. "I thought about it."

"I understand."

Joann let out a pent-up sigh. "Look, I need to apologize. I was rude to you."

"No, no," Tammy said. "I made you feel uncomfortable. I should be the one to apologize. I was trying to help, but I put my foot in it. Didn't

I?" She gave a nervous laugh.

Joann smiled. "I overreacted. I just didn't understand. At all. But I'd really like to know what you meant. Maybe we could grab a cup of coffee sometime?"

"Sure. How about right now? My treat."

Joann thought for a moment, looked at her watch, then said, "Sure. Now's good, I guess."

They walked over to the Starbucks across the street, and Joann ordered a black coffee while Tammy got a mocha with extra whip cream. They found a table with two leather armchairs next to a large window. Joann sipped on the brew as she watched the passersby.

Tammy smiled. "Enjoy people watching, too?"

"Yeah," she said with a grin. "It's peaceful. Like looking at a fish tank."

Tammy nodded. "I feel the same way."

They sat in silence for a few minutes, then Tammy said, "So do you know why I said you had a perfect body right now?"

Joann shook her head. "No clue."

"Sounded a bit out there, right?"

Joann laughed, feeling relieved that Tammy had voiced her exact thoughts. "You nailed it! Because, honestly, I don't have a perfect body. Far from it! It's not at all what I want it to be."

"If you'd permit me . . ." Tammy began, looking hesitant.

Joann nodded. "Go on. I promise not to run away this time."

"Good!" she said with a lopsided grin. "So, what you just said. That's the problem."

"What did I just say?" Joann asked, knitting her brows.

"You said your body isn't close to what you want it to be."

"Well, it isn't."

"When you say that, when you even think that, it puts you at war with your body. I mean, don't get me wrong, most people are. And that's the problem."

Joann slowly shook her head. "Sorry, I'm not tracking."

"OK," Tammy said. "Let me back up a bit. Do you have siblings?"

"Yeah, a sister."

"Younger or older?"

"Younger."

"Perfect!" Tammy said. "Did you two fight when you were kids?"

"All the time."

"Right. Do you still fight?"

Joann paused and thought. "No, not really. I mean, we have disagreements, but I wouldn't say we fight nowadays. Nothing like when we were little."

Tammy nodded. "So if you were to get together to share a slice of cake, for instance, there wouldn't be a problem, right?"

Joanne laughed. "No, because I'd let her have the whole thing. I can't afford the calories."

Tammy grinned at her. "Sorry, my mistake. OK, let's say you're sharing a veggie platter. Carrots and celery. And you're hungry. Would there be a problem? Or would you both get what you wanted and be pretty happy about it all?"

Joann thought about that for a minute. She closed her eyes and remembered the last time she and her sister went for lunch. They had shared some appetizers. She opened her eyes. "Yeah, there'd be no fighting. My sister's generous. And I want to make sure she's happy, so it would all work out."

Tammy nodded. "No strife?"

Joann shook her head.

"Right," Tammy said. "That's because there's no battle. No war. You and your sister are at peace."

Joann exhaled and thought about it. "Definitely."

"It's a little like playing tug of war with someone who is pushing the rope toward you instead of pulling on it. There's no conflict. No resistance. Nothing to fight about."

Joann leaned back in her chair and thought about it. "You know, when we were kids, I always felt like I had to get my way. I felt . . ." Her voice trailed off.

"Did you feel a little at war with your sister?"

"Yeah, I did!" she said with a laugh. "That's weird, isn't it?"

"It's actually quite common."

"I suppose so."

"Did you ever get what you wanted?" Tammy asked.

"Sometimes. But sometimes I didn't."

"My guess is that you and your sister were rarely happy with what you got. If you're anything like most siblings, you both wanted what the other had. Does that sound familiar?"

Joann nodded. "We were always jealous of each other. I remember that. Neither of us were happy."

"So now look at your situation with your body. Are you at peace with your body right now?"

Joann shook her head vehemently. "Not even a little."

Tammy laughed. "And that's the problem. I've noticed that every time you go to a company party, you eat very little. How many diets have you been on in the last year?"

"Dozens. I've tried everything."

"And let me guess, you weigh yourself all the time?"

"How did you know?"

"My cousin did the same thing," Tammy said. "And what happens when the number isn't what you want it to be?"

Joann looked sheepish. "I get mad," she whispered.

Tammy looked around the coffee shop and pointed at the display case of sweets. "And would you like one of those?"

"Of course," she said. "But I can't."

"Right. Is that a pleasant feeling?"

Joann thought about it. Denying herself things was so commonplace she didn't even think about it anymore. But when she looked at it, she noticed that her body sort of tensed up. "No," she said quietly.

"Now, I'm not suggesting you binge on sugar," Tammy said. "And I'm not saying you can't lose weight, if that's what you want to do. You can. It's just that by fighting with your body, it won't go the way you want. It's a hard battle to win."

"So I've got to learn to push on the rope?" Joann said, looking over at Tammy.

"You got it," she said, grinning. "Life gets much easier when you're not in the middle of a war."

Joann nodded. "And I'd imagine it might be a little more fun."

***

Later that evening, Joann watched Alexandra roam around the virtual city. She looked at the other avatars and noticed for the first time that not all of them were perfect.

Thomas 245 had a little paunch and Stardust Sally was a little taller than normal. Becky Anne had pinkish hair. And Stan Frootloop had a tattoo on his right arm.

Suddenly, she gave a little gasp. The people behind the residents had actually selected these flaws.

Were they flaws?

Maybe not. Maybe they were marks of personality. Of individuality.

One thing was certain, they were intentional.

Firstgirl walked by with her blond hair and classic Barbie doll looks. Joann scrunched her face critically as she watched her pass. Odd, that would have seemed ideal to Joann yesterday, but now this look seemed too fake. It just wasn't appealing anymore.

Joann sent Alexandra home and had her stand in front of the mirror. Why not put a little plump in her hips and turn her eye color back to a light blue? She made a few more adjustments, then sent her avatar back outside and waved greetings to everyone as usual. No one treated her differently, and Joann liked the way Alexandra looked now much better.

*She's perfect.*

*Right now.*

The next morning, Joann stretched and headed into the bathroom. She stepped on the scale. 154.3.

*What?* She clenched her teeth.

She frowned and stepped off and back on the scale. Same number.

She glowered into the mirror, and then stopped herself. Was she really at war with her body? It seemed so. She sighed and tilted her head to the side.

"I don't want to be at war with you," she said to her reflection.

Although there was no response, Joann felt and saw her body relax a bit. As she continued to look in the mirror, she realized she no longer felt complete disgust. She relaxed a little more.

*I have the perfect body right now.*

*No, I don't,* came another thought immediately after.

She shook her head. *I have the perfect body right now.*

Before she could disagree again, she bent down and picked up the scale.

"You will live in the closet for a while," she said as she put it on an empty shelf.

***

A week later, Joann poked her head into Stacy's office. "Wanna go out for lunch?"

Joann shrugged. "Why not? I'm not feeling my turkey sandwich today."

Stacy grinned. "OK. Where to?"

"I'm in the mood for a juicy burger."

"Me, too. Been craving one all morning."

"Let's go!"

"You sure? I thought you were counting calories," Stacy said hesitantly.

"Nah. I'm not worried about it anymore."

Stacy grabbed her keys. "I'll drive."

"Let's walk," Joann said. "It's a nice day."

"Do we have time?" Stacy glanced at her watch.

"Sure."

"It's exercise, though. Thought you were against that sort of thing," Stacy said with a grin.

Joann laughed. "No, I've changed on that. Didn't I tell you I've been biking to work each morning?"

"No," Stacy said with a low whistle. "Are you kidding? That's like ten miles or something, isn't it?"

"More like twelve."

"Don't you arrive all sweaty?"

"I use the gym shower downstairs."

"Maybe I should try that," Stacy said.

*\*\*\**

Days slipped into weeks and weeks into months. The scale stayed in the closet. However, Joann knew she was losing weight because her clothes had become baggy.

Joann glanced at her watch. She had about five minutes before she had to leave. Opening her closet, she selected a lilac dress. She got dressed and smiled when she looked into the full-length mirror.

*I have the perfect body right now.*

Joann could honestly say that she liked the way that statement felt and how she looked. In the beginning, she had to trick herself into not hating her body. She'd find things she could like. For instance, her ears had always been pleasing, and her ankles were trim despite the additional weight she'd collected.

Then, bit by bit, she discovered more things she liked until she could like her body, as a whole, at that moment—every moment.

She'd kept her account with e-flirting and had gone on a few dates. No magical connection yet, but she'd enjoyed each encounter. She'd even given Benjamin a call and asked for a second chance. No love match, but they'd become good friends. Pasta buddies, as he called them.

Joann winked at herself in the mirror before trotting down the stairs to the parking garage. She picked up Stacy and headed out to the suburbs to attend a baby shower for Kari and Doug.

"Aren't baby showers the best? I just love the games." Stacy pulled on the pink ribbon on her gift.

"Mmm," Joann said noncommittally.

Stacy swiveled to face her. "You know, I don't think I've ever seen you go to a work party. I mean outside of the office."

"It's been a while."

"What changed?"

Joann glanced over at her and shook her head. "I don't know. I think I relaxed a bit about the food."

"Huh?"

"Well, fattening food is always served at these things. Especially cake," Joann said as she turned on her right-turn blinker. "I'd get stressed out about all the calories."

"Really? I didn't know. You never said anything."

Joann shrugged. "It seemed silly. I don't even think I realized it was an issue. I just remember thinking that I didn't want to eat cake, but it was rude to refuse. Then I'd want the piece of cake, but would worry what the scale would say."

Stacy laughed. "If scales could talk, I think they'd say 'Ow!' a lot."

Joann joined in the laughter. "Mine's living the life of a retired scale in the closet."

"Haven't stepped on it in a while?"

"Nope."

"Well, whatever you're doing is working. You look great! I know I keep saying that, but it's pretty cool."

Joann grinned. "Thanks!"

"Going on a date this weekend?"

"Nah, I don't want to push it."

"Still no word from Terry?"

"No," Joann said with a sigh. "I know it's silly, but I really like him. I mean, I like his profile. I think we'd be a good match. I wish he'd respond."

Joann pulled into the driveway, and the two hopped out and walked up to the house. Inside, a couple dozen guests were milling around the small house decorated with pink and yellow streamers. Joann and Stacy put their presents on the gift table and chatted with various people. One for one, everyone commented on how healthy Joann looked, asking her what she'd done.

Joann glanced over at Tammy, who gave her a small bow. She returned it with a grin.

\*\*\*

Joann was curled up at home with a good book later that evening when she received a notification ping on her phone. She glanced at it, expecting it to be a text from Stacy. Her heart leapt into her throat when she saw that Terry had sent her a message from e-flirting.

"Been out of the county for a few months. Forgot to cancel my membership. Would love to talk soon," the short message read.

"Wow," Joann breathed. She sat up and wrote back that she'd love to meet up when he was ready. Something about him seemed right. She was glad he hadn't responded to her message when she first sent it. She hadn't been ready then. Now she was.

It was perfect!

# MALLORY

STORY 3 IN THE "DISCOVERING KINDNESS" SERIES

## Kevin J. Smith
### with Laura Sherman

Mallory's eyes popped open at the gentle vibration from the Fitbit on her right wrist. She glanced at the time. 4:45 a.m. It was precisely the right time. She hit a button and located her sleep score: 84.

*Good* the Fitbit told her. Mallory frowned.

*Good? That's not good enough.*

She sighed and gingerly climbed out of bed. Jonathon wouldn't be up for hours. No Fitbit on his wrist. "I can't sleep knowing something is watching my every movement!" he'd told her when she offered to buy him one last Christmas.

She had shrugged and purchased a new recliner for the living room instead. Black leather. It had been a big hit.

Mallory quietly slipped into her gray jogging suit, put her long, brown hair into a ponytail, and tiptoed down the hallway. She didn't want to wake her three children. Their alarms were set for much later.

As Mallory descended the stairs, she carefully avoided the center of the fifth step down, knowing it would creak. She made it to the bottom and closed her eyes, relishing the complete silence. Just the way she liked it. This was her time.

Entering the kitchen, she smiled as the silver coffee machine was finishing up her single serving French roast brew right on time. She had ten minutes to enjoy her fresh cup before she had to leave to meet Maria.

Mallory had first met Maria in line at Starbucks after she'd finished a jog. They had struck up a conversation about running and had instantly decided to become running partners. Of course, that was back when Mallory used to run before her first cup. Then she had read an article in *The New York Times* about how caffeine helps a runner's performance. Studies showed it made a real difference, so who was she to question it? She'd switched to drinking her coffee before her run, but she sometimes missed the trips to Starbucks.

\*\*\*

It was 5:09 a.m. when Mallory arrived at Maria's house. She watched the digital display on her Fitbit change to 5:10 a.m. and looked up expectantly at the front door. Nothing. Toying with the idea of knocking, she slowly made her way up the driveway when Maria came out.

"Good morning," she said.

"Good morning!" Mallory replied, glancing at her watch. Still 5:10 a.m. She smiled at her punctual friend.

They stretched, then began jogging west down the street, both silent for a few minutes rather than the usual early-run small talk. Mallory's mind drifted to the program she was writing at work. They had a new contract with a multi-national corporation which would take them over a year to complete. She loved these kinds of projects because she could really sink her teeth into them. They challenged her problem-solving skills. Her current task involved repairing code that had malfunctioned after a co-worker had added a new module. She shook her head and refocused. There would be time to fix it when she got to work.

Maria glanced at her. "Work?" It wasn't really a question. Maria was confirming that she knew where her friend's thoughts were.

"Yeah," Mallory said, glanced at her Fitbit and smiled. Her heart rate was within range. "Sorry."

Maria waved a hand dismissively. "Must be nice."

"Hm?"

"You know. Worrying about something other than homework, soccer practice, and what to make for dinner."

Mallory stiffened and saw that her heart rate jumped a bit. "I worry about that stuff, too."

Maria glanced over at her friend and crinkled her brow. "I'm sorry, I didn't mean . . ."

"No, no," Mallory said with a little laugh. "*I'm* sorry. To be honest, I don't give meal planning enough thought. Most nights I don't even make it home in time, and if I do, I throw a Minute Meal from the freezer into the microwave and call it done. Jonathon usually handles the cooking."

They continued to jog, picking up the pace. When they began their cool down routine twenty minutes later, Mallory said, "You know, I think it's great that you stay at home with your three kids. I mean, there's part of me that would love to do that."

"Why don't you?" Maria asked.

*Why don't I?* Mallory thought, but she said, "I love my work."

It was a simple answer, one that had a lot of truth to it. But it was also incomplete. So much so that the answer left her feeling as if she'd just lied to her friend.

Mallory shrugged.

Maria gave her a little smile. "Well, if you like what you're doing, that's what's important. Same time tomorrow?"

"Yes," Mallory said, feeling relieved that the conversation about work and family had come to a close.

She jogged back to her house and checked her watch. 6:05 a.m. The Fitbit gave a little surge.

*How had that happened?*

She was five minutes late. Well, not late exactly, but five minutes off schedule. She needed to be in the car at 6:30 a.m. sharp if she wanted to be sitting at her desk at eight.

Mallory took the stairs two at a time and jumped into the shower. As she let the water run over her head, her mind flashed back to a rainy day when she was eight years old.

She remembered rushing around the small, single-story house looking for her necklace and blue hair ribbons to match her dress. She wanted to look her best for Becky's birthday party. She knew she had to hurry because Moe, her father, was waiting in the blue Buick with the engine running.

She quickly twisted her hair into twin braids, then attached the ribbons to the ends. *Nice*, she thought as she looked at her reflection. Her dress was free of wrinkles and stains. She'd pressed it earlier that morning.

With her heart racing, she picked up the box with the pretty yellow bow and ran to the car. When she got in, she looked at the gift and dried it the best she could with her sweater.

She put on her seatbelt and looked up expectantly at her father. "Ready!"

Her father's intense blue eyes peered at her from the rearview mirror. Then he looked down and shut off the engine.

Mallory felt as if her heart would stop as she stared at his back. "What's wrong?" Her voice quivered.

His eyes slowly rose to meet hers in the mirror. "What do you think is wrong?" Each word was punctuated. Her heart sunk.

She desperately thought and searched for understanding. "I don't know."

"Don't you?" he asked with a shake of his head. "You're late. Five minutes late. That's unacceptable."

"But . . .," Mallory said. She frantically thought of the right words that would get him to turn the engine back on and drive to her friend's house. "Please, I really want to go."

"I know you do," he said. His voice was both calm and hard. "That's why I'm not going to take you."

She knew there was no point in any further pleas. When he'd made up his mind, hat was that.

Tears spilled from Mallory's eyes and washed down the drain of her shower. Her heart still ached thirty years later. She wiped her eyes and took a ragged breath, then released it.

It was only after her father had died that she'd learned what made him tick. At the memorial service his brother, Martin, described how her father had been in machismo heaven when he'd entered boot camp with his best friend, Peter.

"Moe was a man obsessed with killing Viet Cong," he said with a slight shake of his head. "Not so much Peter, though. He was a sensitive guy who had only joined up because his recruiter had a silver tongue."

Martin explained that her father had lost his best friend at the end of boot camp, right when they were ready to ship out. Peter had hung himself in the showers. Nobody ever found out why. He hadn't left a note. After that, Moe had become numb. According to Martin, "It was as if his heart had turned to stone. He never expressed any emotions again."

Moe returned from the Vietnam War a highly decorated captain, having received numerous medals for acts of bravery. Martin figured he was trying to get himself killed, but failed. Instead, he wound up a hero and a member of the walking dead at the same time.

When she heard this story, Mallory finally understood why her father had always ridden her so hard. Moe never seemed to care when she had burst into tears. Instead, it seemed to disgust him. She had learned to squelch her sorrow and do her best to put on a brave face.

Looking back, missing that one birthday party had a staggering toll on her in many ways. Becky never forgave her, not really, and the rest of the students treated her coldly for a long while after. It was just unacceptable to miss a popular girl's party after accepting the invitation.

Mallory sighed, stepped out of the shower, and managed to get behind the steering wheel at 6:29 a.m. Her shoulders relaxed in relief.

*Not late.*

She unwrapped a peanut butter protein bar and took a bite. It wasn't her favorite kind of breakfast, but it was fast and would keep her stomach from rumbling all morning.

It was 10:45 a.m. when Mallory returned from her fifteen-minute break. One last cup of coffee and a handful of almonds. Sitting down in her chair, she swiveled into position. A silver frame off to the side caught her eye.

*Such a handsome boy.*

Dillon had turned six the previous month and promised to be taller than her.

*It's my father's genes.* She remembered how he had to bend down to pass through most doorways.

***

A few days prior, on a relaxed Saturday morning, Mallory found herself on the black leather couch, cuddling with Dillon. Jonathon had taken Chloe to practice, and Xane was off with friends at the mall, so they had the house to themselves. Dillon was having fun playing with his favorite toys: little green plastic dinosaurs.

"Who's this long neck?" she asked, pointing to one.

"That's Chip, the *Brontosaurus*," he answered, not missing a beat. He glanced up at her. "You know that, Mom!"

"And this one? The *Tyrannosaurus rex*?" The corner of her mouth quivered slightly.

"That's not a *T. rex*, Mom!" he said with a dramatic roll of his eyes. "That's a *Triceratops*!"

"Right," she said, as if it had been a huge revelation. "What's his name?"

"He's Bill."

She laughed. "Bill?"

"Bill."

"Bill the *Triceratops*."

"That's right."

Mallory fell silent as she watched Dillon march the different dinosaurs up and down his leg and across the cushions of the couch. Finally, he stopped and turned around to look up at her.

"Mom?" he asked. His voice was serious, so serious for a six-year-old.

"Yes?"

"Why don't people ever feel sorry for the dinosaurs?"

She frowned. "What do you mean?"

"It's just that millions and millions of dinosaurs died, right?"

"I think so."

"They did," he said matter-of-factly. "But you never see anyone getting sad about that. Do you?"

She shook her head. "No. I don't think so."

"But when Aunt Mildred died, and we all went to her funeral, there were so many people crying. You were sad for a long time after. Why is that?"

Mallory smiled and she gently ran a finger across the cool frame on her desk. She hadn't had any idea about what to say to her wise little boy, so the words that came out of her mouth surprised her.

She'd explained how people come and go and that was just the way of it. It wasn't good or bad, it just was.

"People stay in our hearts forever, sweetie," she said, giving him a squeeze. "They never truly leave us. When I figured that out, I wasn't as sad about my sister's passing."

"You weren't?" Dillon had asked.

She shook her head. "No. It took me some time, but I was grateful for the moments I'd had with Milly. See, in life, when something leaves, like the dinosaurs, something new always comes in to replace it. We just need to remember to appreciate the new thing as much as we appreciated the thing that left."

She wasn't sure if he'd understood. After all, he was just six. But she thought he had. He was such a smart cookie, always quietly observing everything and everyone around him.

The day sped by at a dizzying pace. Caught in a last-minute meeting, Mallory did her best not to glance at her watch every few minutes. She'd planned to leave at 6 p.m. sharp, but there was a problem with the module she was working on and the whole team was asked to stay behind to discuss it.

6:05 p.m. Well, she could still read Dillon a bedtime story. His bedtime was 8 p.m. sharp. There would be time if she could just leave now. She'd purchased *The Little Red Lighthouse and the Great Gray Bridge* last week, but hadn't been able to read it to him yet.

She silently willed the group of programmers to quit their incessant jabbering.

Mallory exhaled sharply, then checked herself, giving a small smile to Larry when he glanced her way. She couldn't leave, but the discussion wasn't pertinent to her section of the program. She tried not to look bored, but knew she wasn't succeeding. Finally, when the team leader excused everyone, she nearly bolted for the door, giving the team a hurried wave.

*6:20 p.m.? Are you kidding?*

*Well, maybe I can at least start the story.*

She weaved in and out of traffic, knowing that it would only shave minutes off her time. She glanced at her GPS and groaned. There was an accident up ahead and no way around it. Google was predicting a fifteen-minute delay.

Mallory banged her steering wheel and let out a high-pitched squeal as she saw the brake lights come into view. Glancing around, she was grateful her windows were up. No need to cause a scene. No need to share her frustration with others.

When she finally pulled into her driveway, it was 8:05 p.m. Five minutes after Dillon's bedtime.

Late.

Again.

*How does this keep happening?*

With a heavy sigh, Mallory opened the front door. The house was quiet. She glanced up the stairs and knew Dillon would be trying to fall asleep. If she walked into his room now, it would be a long time before he settled down again.

She heard the clanking of pots and pans in the kitchen and poked her head through the door.

"Hello," she said.

Jonathon turned around and gave her a smile. "Hey, honey! How was work?"

"Fine," she said. She walked over to him and gave him a quick peck on the cheek. "What about you?"

"Nothing exciting."

"Home at four?"

He shook his head. "No, it was more like 4:30 today."

*Must be nice.*

"Want some Cabernet?" he asked.

She frowned. "You know I don't drink during the week."

"Yeah, it just looked like you might need a glass."

She plopped on a bar stool by the counter. "I'm good."

*No, I'm not. OK, but there's no need to vent to Jonathon.*

Jonathon cocked his head to the side. "What's going on in there?"

She forced her lips into a small smile. "Nothing. Really. How are the kids?" She sorely wanted to change the subject. "Are they all upstairs? It's so quiet."

Jon shook his head. "Xane's at rehearsals for the college concert next week. He's getting pretty good at the trombone."

"Good. That will help him with college applications."

Jonathon studied the white-tiled counter in front of him. "You know he doesn't really like it, right?"

She shrugged. "Sometimes you have to do things you don't like to get ahead."

She frowned as she realized that she sounded just like her father.

Jonathon stiffened slightly. "Chloe," he continued, "is still at cheer practice."

"Competition's in two weeks." Mallory stood up and got a glass of water. "It's a big one, right?"

"Yeah, semifinals. She's feeling the pressure."

Mallory nodded in approval. "Good."

He chewed his bottom lip with his teeth. Then he looked up at her. "I'm not so sure," he said.

She studied his brown eyes carefully before she asked, "What do you mean?"

"I mean, I think it's too much pressure, Mal. I don't think she likes it as much as she did when she started."

Mallory swallowed the urge to repeat the same phrase she'd just uttered. Why was Jonathon suddenly so preoccupied with the idea that the children should enjoy all their activities? After all, did she always enjoy every moment at work? No. No one did.

Glancing at her watch, Mallory saw that it was nearly 8:30 p.m. Dillon was bound to be asleep, yet she was dying to check in on him. "I'll be down a little later, and you can catch me up on anything else."

Jonathon nodded and turned back to the sink. Mallory watched him for a moment, then turned and walked to the stairs. At the top landing, she pulled the book she'd purchased out of her bag. She ran a hand over the smooth cover, then opened it, enjoying the subtle cracking of the binding and the smell of the new pages.

She crept into Dillon's room and gently sat on the edge of his bed. She watched as his chest rose and fell.

Mallory opened the book and, in a whisper, started reading about the little lighthouse on the Hudson River. So fat and so proud. She smiled. It was a pleasant memory from her childhood. Her mother had read that book to her so often that the binding had completely ripped. But she hadn't cared. She loved hearing the story over and over. She knew Dillon would love it, too, and couldn't wait to share it with him.

Mallory reached out to touch one of Dillon's wayward curls, but she checked the impulse. She didn't want to risk waking him. Every study she ever read said that wouldn't be good for him. As she continued to watch the rhythm of his breathing, Mallory's eyes began to droop. She put the book on the nightstand and folded herself carefully next to him, keeping an invisible barrier between them.

*Just a quick catnap.* She knew it was a lie, but didn't care.

It was well after midnight when her eyes popped open with a start. *Damn, not again.*

Mallory rolled out of Dillon's bed and groggily made her way to her room. Jonathon was fast asleep, so she quickly undressed, crawled into her side of the bed, and closed her eyes. Before she allowed herself to drift off, she checked her Fitbit to confirm the alarm was set.

Damn, waking up to climb back into bed wasn't the way to improve her sleep score, now was it?

\*\*\*

A few days later, Mallory was happily engrossed in sifting through code when the phone on her desk rang. Puzzled, she just stared at it for a moment. Who would be calling her midmorning?

"Hello?" she said tentatively into the receiver.

"Your cell went straight to voicemail." Jonathan's voice shook as he let out a ragged sigh.

A shiver coursed up Mallory's spine. "Is everything OK?" Her voice came out as a squeak. She knew the answer. No. Everything wasn't OK.

"It's Chloe," he said.

He went on to explain how she had suddenly fainted in geometry class. The school nurse had their daughter in her office. She'd called Mallory first, but hadn't been able to get through. Fortunately, she'd reached Jonathon. "I'm taking her to St. Jude's to get checked out."

"I'm sure she's fine."

"Yeah."

"Do you need me?" Mallory asked.

"No," he said quickly. Then he paused. "I mean unless you want to come. It's up to you."

"I have a lot of work to get through. We don't both need to be there," she said, staring at her computer screen. The lines of code seemed to waiver in front of her. "Just please check in with me when you get there, OK?"

"You got it."

Mallory hung up, then pulled out her cell and checked the battery. It was fully charged, but she'd lost the signal since the phone had been in her purse under the desk. She put it up higher and got a couple bars.

After a few minutes of trying to think through the pea soup that had formed in her mind, she realized she would be useless at work. Mallory went to Mr. Tillon and asked for a personal day. When she explained the situation, he immediately granted it.

The traffic was light, so Mallory floored the accelerator. Her cell rang and she hit the button on the steering wheel to answer.

"We just arrived," Jonathon said, his voice carrying through the speakers of the car.

"I'm on my way," she said.

"Really? What about work?"

"Couldn't concentrate."

"Yeah."

They were silent for a while.

"How's she doing?" Mallory asked.

"She seems OK. We're waiting to get seen. I'm filling out forms. Here, why don't you talk to her?"

She could hear a shuffling noise, then, "Mom?"

Her little girl's voice sounded so weak. Mallory felt her throat catch. She coughed to relieve the strain. "How are you feeling?"

"I'm fine. Really," Chloe gushed out. "You don't need to worry. It's all so silly. I'm sorry."

"Sorry? Sorry for what?"

"For bothering you and Dad."

"Don't be stupid," Mallory said, then checked herself. "I don't mean stupid. You know what I mean."

"Yeah."

"Any idea why you fainted?"

"I don't know. I was sitting at my desk one minute and the next I was looking up into the faces of my teacher and half the class. It was crazy. But I'm fine, really. I tried to tell Dad that we didn't need to go to the hospital, but he wouldn't hear of it."

"Of course, you should see a doctor. I agree with him."

"You do?" Chloe's voice sounded surprised. "I thought for sure you'd say it was overkill."

Mallory frowned. "You know your health is important to me."

She could almost hear her daughter's shrug over the phone. "I guess

I thought you'd think I was wussing out. You know, 'You've got to be tough to make it.' Right?"

"Yeah," Mallory said slowly. Her head was spinning. "That's true, but it doesn't apply here."

"Why doesn't it apply?"

She shook her head. "Look, I never want you to take unreasonable risks."

"But you're always saying to push yourself," Chloe said. "You know, be committed. Don't go halfway."

"Uh huh," Mallory said as she merged into the left lane. "All of that's true. But this is different."

"Oh."

She could tell that her daughter didn't understand and, truthfully, Mallory wasn't sure she understood either. She looked at her GPS and followed its instructions. "OK, I've got to go. I'll be there in about thirty minutes. Hang tight. We'll continue our conversation then. Just know, you're doing the right thing. You're in the right place."

"OK, Mom. See you soon."

Mallory hung up and made it to the hospital parking lot in good time. She paused in the parking spot and looked over at the tall, gray building. Somewhere in there was her little girl, frightened and confused. She grimaced and turned the ignition off.

As she walked along the sidewalk, she dialed her husband.

"We're on the third floor. Pediatrics," he said in a low voice.

"Got it. I'm walking in now."

"That was fast," Jonathon said. He paused then added, "I'm glad you're here."

"Me, too."

She hung up and smiled at the tenderness in his voice.

*It's been a while*, she thought as she made her way to the elevator.

Mallory checked in at the reception desk and was directed to a room down the corridor to the right. She stood at the entrance for a moment, taking in the scene. Two of the four beds were filled. The other two were perfectly made, ready for new occupants.

*How depressing.*

Chloe was positioned close to the window, propped up with a few pillows. Jonathon was leaning in toward her, perched on the edge of a chair next to the bed. They were engaged in a lively discussion about something, both grinning.

Mallory moved closer, slowly, wanting to eavesdrop. She couldn't remember a time when she'd seen both of them so relaxed and carefree. They always seemed so serious. And quiet. But now they were actually enjoying their time together.

"Oh, Daddy. You're too funny."

"I fell right down on my you-know-what."

Chloe giggled. "Serves you right for chasing the puppy across a frozen pond. What did you think would happen?"

"What choice did I have? He was a tiny ball of black fur. I didn't want him to be mistaken for the hockey puck."

Chloe giggled louder, then looked up, saw her mother, and froze. "H-hi, Mom!" she said, quickly schooling her features.

Mallory smiled at her, walked over, and gave her a peck on her cheek. It was then that Mallory noticed her daughter was hooked up to a monitor and IV.

She grimaced. "How are you feeling?"

"Fine," Chloe said with a bright smile.

Mallory noticed how pale her daughter was. And her eyes were sunken. She looked exhausted. Mallory nodded and looked at Jonathon.

She opened her mouth to say something, but a doctor came in and introduced herself as Dr. Glaston. She wore the traditional white coat and had a stethoscope around her neck. Her salt and pepper hair was pulled into a tight bun at the nape of her neck. The doctor looked over the chart at the foot of Chloe's bed.

"So I hear you fainted in class," she said.

"Yes, ma'am."

"Call me Joyce."

Chloe looked up at Mallory, who nodded an approval. "It's OK," she whispered. Normally, her children were expected to address adults with formality, but in this case she didn't care.

*Why did I ever care?*

As Chloe described the fainting episode, Dr. Glaston nodded.

"It was so embarrassing," Chloe said, glancing at her mother. "I'm sorry."

Mallory furrowed her brows slightly. She looked from her daughter to the doctor and back again. "That's nothing to apologize for," she said gently.

Dr. Glaston checked the IV, took Chloe's pulse and made some notes on the clipboard.

"What do you think's wrong, Doc?" Jonathon asked.

Mallory found herself holding her breath as she waited for Dr. Glaston to respond.

"I won't know until we run some preliminary tests, but if I had to guess, I'd say your daughter is severely dehydrated. Have you been doing a lot of physical activity lately?"

"Yeah," Chloe said slowly. "But no more than usual. I mean, I'm getting ready for a cheerleading competition."

"Oh, I know all about that," Dr. Glaston said. "My daughter is part of the squad at Saxon High."

"It's pretty intense," Jonathon said.

"You're telling me!" the doctor said. "It's not like it was when I was a kid. The stunts they do today are insane."

Jonathon stroked Chloe's head. "You've been at it for hours every afternoon for the entire week. No breaks."

"I've got to," Chloe said. "We're learning a new high-flying basket move."

"Are you the flyer?" Dr. Glaston asked.

"No, I'm a base."

The doctor whistled low. "That requires a lot of strength and stamina."

"But it's not hot out," Chloe said. "I mean, don't you get dehydrated when you're out in the sun all day?"

Dr. Glaston shook her head and smiled. "Sadly, too many people forget to drink water and replace electrolytes. Most Americans walk around all day in a mild state of dehydration. When you keep depriving your body, it can cry uncle."

"So I'm here because I didn't drink enough water?" Chloe asked.

Jonathon smiled. "Let's hope that's the problem. That's easy enough to fix."

Dr. Glaston made a few more marks on her pad, then clipped it back to the foot of the bed. "As I said, we'll know more soon. I'd like to keep her here overnight."

Both Jonathon and Mallory nodded, and the doctor left.

"Can I get you some coffee?" Jonathon asked.

"Sure, Dad," Chloe quipped.

Mallory and Jonathon laughed.

"Not exactly what the doctor ordered," Jonathon said. He turned to Mallory. "And you?"

"I'm not sure I can stomach hospital coffee right now," Mallory said, pinching the bridge of her nose gently. "It's basically colored water."

Jonathon tilted his head. "I think there's a Starbucks across the street."

She grinned at him as a burst of affection filled her. "That's sweet. But unnecessary."

"I'd like to get a little fresh air," he said. "A cappuccino with honey?"

She nodded, and Jonathon left.

Looking over at her daughter, Mallory noticed that she was struggling to keep her eyes open.

"Cupcake, why don't you get some rest. I'll be here."

"You haven't called me that in ages, Mom," Chloe murmured.

Mallory smiled. "Sorry. I guess you're too old for that now."

"No. I like it. I miss it," Chloe said as her eyelids fell. It didn't take long before she began to snore lightly.

Mallory sighed and walked over to the window. From on high, she could see the coffee shop and noticed a crosswalk from the hospital directly over to it. As she continued to peer down, waiting to see Jonathon cross the road, her mind drifted back to a field hockey meet. She'd been about Chloe's age.

*** 

After she had missed three goals, the coach had mercifully put her on the bench for the rest of the game. She hadn't minded. She rather enjoyed cheering for her team from the sidelines. She hadn't bothered to look up at the stands because she knew her father wouldn't be pleased.

After the game, Mallory walked to the bleachers along with her teammates. The other parents greeted their daughters with a hair tousle or a "Better luck next time."

However, that wasn't her fate. Her father stomped toward her with a stormy expression.

She had wanted to run in the opposite direction, but she'd known there was no point. Instead, she planted her feet and waited for the inevitable.

"What do I always tell you?" he barked.

A few of the parents glanced his way. Suzanne, their star forward, shot her a sympathetic look. Her father's outburst wasn't new to any of them.

"That I need to do better," she whispered in response. She hoped that if she lowered her voice, her father would do the same.

It never worked. "Be committed! Don't go halfway!" he yelled even louder. "What the hell was *that*?"

*** 

Jonathon stepped into view, interrupting her trip down memory lane. Mallory was thankful for her husband yet again. She smiled as she watched him almost skip across the street. She realized he enjoyed the mission of bringing her a cup of coffee. It was a simple thing that would bring her a measure of comfort. And that made Jonathon happy.

When Jonathon disappeared into the squat building, Mallory turned back to her daughter. There she lay, in an exhausted slumber. Why had Chloe pushed herself so hard?

*Because I told her to*, came the ready answer.

How many times had she told her daughter to drive herself to her limits? Victories were the only true measures of success, after all. Enjoying the experience was trivial in comparison.

*Do I really believe that?*

"Again!" came a haunting voice through her mind.

Mallory shook her head to chase away the sound. However, it rang through her like a dull bell. "Again!"

\*\*\*

Her father stood over her as she hit the field hockey puck into the net for the hundredth time. "Again!"

Her hands had bled, but she hadn't stopped. She hadn't even asked for a break because she knew it wouldn't be granted. Besides, it would just weaken her position. Practice through the pain. That's what was expected. That's what she would do.

She'd scored one goal in the next game, after which her father had merely grunted. No ruffling of her hair, no compliment, but also no anger. Just a guttural sound of acknowledgment for a satisfactory job that had been expected of her.

She'd quit soon after and joined the hiking group instead.

\*\*\*

The next morning, Dr. Glaston confirmed that Chloe had been dehydrated. "She'll need to rest for a few days, but then she'll be back to cheering before you know it."

After they returned home and settled Chloe into bed, both parents headed down to the living room. Neither had slept well the night before. Mallory had insisted on sleeping on a cot the orderlies wheeled in for her next to Chloe's bed, while Jonathon had gone home to take care of Xane and Dillon.

"Pour me a glass of red?" Mallory asked.

Jonathon cocked an eyebrow. "Really? It's a weekday."

She grinned. "Shut up."

"OK." He walked off and came back with two glasses of red wine. He handed her one and sat next to her on the couch.

She took a sip, then another. "I think maybe I pushed Chloe too hard," she murmured.

When Jonathon didn't say anything, she looked up. "Aren't you going to disagree or something?"

He shook his head slowly. "No."

She hit him in the arm.

"Ow, that hurt," he said. The corner of his mouth twitched slightly. "No, it didn't."

"No," he said with a smile. "It didn't."

They were silent for a few more minutes. "Why didn't you say something?" she asked.

"You can be a bit intimidating, you know," he said.

She looked back at her wine and took another sip. "I don't want to be."

"I know."

"You do?"

"Sure," he said. "It's not you."

"Then who is it?"

He shrugged. "That's not for me to say."

She frowned. "I seem to hear my father's words coming out of my mouth a lot these days."

He nodded. "Yeah, I noticed."

She let out a rattling sigh. "So now what? What do I do?"

"Just talk to Chloe. Let her know it's OK for her to do what she wants. She'll either decide to stick with cheering or she won't. Maybe she'll want to compete harder. You just don't know. But it's got to be her choice, you know?"

Mallory nodded. "You're right. I'll sit down with her. And honestly, I don't care, as long as she's happy. That's all that matters." She laughed and felt her whole body relax.

*Now that sounds like me.*

She put down her wine glass and leaned back against the cushions, feeling younger than she had in a long time. "How strange to say those words, but it's true."

Jonathon grinned at her. "I love you, Mal."

She leaned in toward him. "We have a little time. You know, before the boys come home."

Jonathon's eyes widened slightly, then sparkled. "We do."

She took him by the hand and led him upstairs.

\*\*\*

The next morning, Mallory jogged to Maria's to find her standing out on the sidewalk with a concerned expression on her face.

"You're late," she said.

Mallory glanced at her watch. It was 5:13. "I suppose I am. I apologize."

"With anyone else I wouldn't call three minutes late. But with you, I was worried."

Mallory laughed and began stretching.

A little while into their jog, Mallory turned to Maria. "I'm thinking about quitting my job."

Maria immediately stopped running and her eyes widened incredulously. "What?"

"I can't stand being away from my kids all day, every day," Mallory responded. Then she pulled Maria along. "Come on, I don't want to stop."

Maria nodded and continued to run. After a few minutes, she turned to her friend. "Look, it's just that you love your work, right?"

"Yeah, but I love my family, too."

"Couldn't you do both?"

Mallory stopped.

Maria laughed and said, "I guess jogging and serious conversation don't exactly mesh."

Mallory laughed and resumed running. "That's another thing. I never seem to have time for friends. I mean, this time in the morning is nice, but why don't we ever go out for a cup of coffee anymore?"

"We should," Maria said. "I really liked that."

"Agreed."

They ran in silence for a while, then Maria said, "Talk to your boss. Tell him what you want. Maybe there's a solution."

When she got to work, Mallory headed straight to Mr. Tillon's office. His door was ajar, and she watched him for a minute, feeling her stomach flutter. His silver-dusted head bent over some paperwork. She noticed he wore a playful tie with penguins on it.

Mallory waited a few more moments for him to notice her presence, but when he didn't, she knocked lightly on the door.

He looked up at her and gave her a wide smile. "Oh, Mallory! Good morning. Come on in."

She took a seat across from him and pointed to his tie. "I like it."

He looked down to see what she was referring to, then said, "Oh, my tie. Yes, Greg bought that for me last Christmas. He's crazy about anything from the Arctic."

Mallory grinned. "Then he'll probably tell you that penguins don't live in the Arctic."

"Hm?" he said.

"I only know this because Dillon is super into these things. Penguins actually only live in the Southern Hemisphere. The Antarctic. It's the polar bears that live in the Arctic."

"Huh, I didn't know that. So the two never meet?"

"Guess not."

His eyes crinkled. "I'm glad you told me. Saved me from looking like an idiot in front of my eight-year-old!"

She laughed. "No problem."

"So, I'm sure you didn't come in here this morning to chat about the poles of our planet," he said.

"Yes and no," she said. When she saw confusion cross his features, she shifted her position. "I wanted to talk to you about my kids."

He nodded in understanding. "I was so happy to hear that Chloe will make a full recovery. How is she doing?"

"Good! She's back in school today."

"Glad to hear it."

Mallory paused for a moment, then let out a long sigh. "It's just that I am missing my kids growing up. I love my work, don't get me wrong. I just need to be in my kids' lives more."

He grimaced. "The commute's rough, isn't it?"

"Yes. It kills three hours a day. I never seem to make it home in time to see my youngest. I leave before he gets up and return when he's in bed."

Mr. Tillon leaned back in his chair and stroked his chin. "I've been toying with a new idea. Hear me out."

She nodded and remained silent.

"What if you could work from home?"

"Really? I didn't think that was possible."

"It wasn't. But I've been talking to IT about implementing a remote program. As you know, a lot of companies have moved in this direction. We'd have to start slowly, maybe two or three days a week, but we could build it to a point where you'd only need to come in a few times a month. How does that sound?"

"Amazing!" she breathed. "When can we start?"

"Soon," he said. "Can you hold on a little longer?"

"Sure," she said. "Of course."

When Mallory got back to her desk, she picked up her phone and dialed Jonathon. He cheered loudly upon hearing the good news.

# DAN

STORY 4 IN THE "DISCOVERING KINDNESS" SERIES

## Kevin J. Smith
### with Laura Sherman

Daniel Johnson rested an elbow on the large conference table and leaned into his client, inhaling her floral perfume. She had carefully swept back her platinum blonde hair in a conservative bun, just as he'd suggested. She wore a business suit that he'd picked out last week. Daniel smiled. He liked clients who could follow instructions. It made his job a lot easier.

"Give a small nod, Agnes. Don't say anything," he whispered into her ear. "Now nod again. Don't smile. In fact, frown a bit. That's it."

Daniel pulled away and straightened the 24-karat gold cufflink on his right sleeve before looking up at the opposing attorney. He gauged the girl to be fresh out of law school. She had long brown hair and perfectly trimmed bangs. Her Gucci glasses sat a little skewed on her nose. Were they real or were they for effect, meant to impress him? Maybe to impress the client? Either way, it wasn't working.

He sat back in his chair and continued to study the young girl until she fidgeted slightly under his scrutiny. No one could outwait him. This was his boardroom, his kingdom.

Giving her a small smile, Daniel said, "We're going to be asking for the two vacation homes and the Lamborghini, as well as half of the pet care business." He paused a moment and waited for the girl across from him to relax. Then he continued, "And, of course, half of the twenty-five million that your client tucked away on the Isle of Man."

The man next to the girl gasped loudly. As Daniel's eyes settled on Mr. Calderman, he noticed that the man was turning a bright shade of purple clear up to the top of his balding head. No, on second thought, the color was more a fresh eggplant.

Daniel gave the man a mocking smile. "Oh, you didn't think we'd find out about that, did you?"

The man sputtered beautifully in response.

Mrs. Calderman's mouth fell open. "Is it really twenty-five?" she said in her Jersey accent. "I thought it was more like ten."

Daniel stiffened and frowned at her. He'd instructed her to stay quiet, and here she was giving away information. Not much, mind you, but still, she wasn't following his instructions.

Mrs. Calderman quickly saw her error and lowered her gaze. "I'm sorry," she murmured.

Daniel gave it a beat, then gently squeezed her arm. "No harm done."

Turning back to the opposing lawyer, he noticed she was sheet white. He reached out and picked up the heavy Baccarat water pitcher and slowly poured a glass of cool spring water for her. All eyes were trained on him and the flow of water until he handed her the glass. Never let it be said that he wasn't a gentleman. He'd won. No need to let the girl faint.

"I think this is a good place to end for today," Daniel said, breaking the stone-cold silence in the room. He opened his planner and turned to his client. "Wednesday, April 10th at 2 p.m. work for you?"

Mrs. Calderman nodded, keeping her lips sealed. It was a test, and she passed with flying colors. Daniel smiled at her. Her previous lapse was now completely forgiven.

He turned to the two across from him. "And you?"

Both nodded mutely.

"Splendid," Daniel said as he stood. "We'll see you in two days."

Mr. Calderman and his attorney stood simultaneously. Agnes looked at Daniel, who nodded almost imperceptibly, indicating that she could indeed stand, too. When the two left, she exhaled loudly.

"Thank you, Daniel. You're my hero!"

He smiled graciously at her. "It's my pleasure. May I walk you out?"

Not waiting for a response, Daniel gently grasped Agnes's arm and guided her to the large bank of elevators. They waited in silence as the numbers on the display climbed to fifteen. Behind him, he heard Helen's high heels on the white tile floor. Her gait was unmistakable. The clicking stopped a few feet away. His personal secretary for the last ten years knew to wait until the client had entered the elevator and the doors closed before speaking.

*Ding.*

After the doors slid open, he deposited his client into the elevator and said, "See you on Wednesday at 1:30 p.m. sharp. I'd like to go over a few things with you before the meeting."

Mrs. Calderman nodded, and he maintained eye contact, smiling until the doors shut completely.

As soon as the two doors touched, he turned back to look at Helen. She held herself at attention, her long gray hair pulled back in a tight chignon that rested on the nape of her neck. She peered up at him through horn-rimmed glasses and waited for him to speak.

"Messages?" he said, holding out his hand to her.

"Yes, sir," she said, handing him a half-dozen pink slips. Unlike so many around him, she didn't flinch at his abruptness, nor did she attempt to engage him in trivial chitchat. It was one of the reasons why he paid her more than double any other personal secretary on this floor.

Daniel quickly sorted through the stack of slips as he strode back to his corner office. The first two he needed to handle this morning, the following three he returned to Helen with instructions. Then his eyes fell on the sixth message.

He stopped suddenly and frowned. Helen stopped her forward motion as well.

*Ben Miller? Really?*

"Helen," he barked. "How many times do I have to tell you that you're my *filter*. That means you *filter* my messages. Your job is to keep time wasters off my plate."

He was aware that his voice had risen a few decibels, but shrugged it off. It was good to let those around him know when they'd screwed up. It was an effective way to make sure they wouldn't do it again.

He could feel the other personnel wince. That was good, too. There was nothing wrong with starting the day with a little fear and respect.

Helen didn't blink and simply took back the pink paper. "Yes, sir."

Daniel glared at her a few moments longer before giving her a quick nod. Then he walked into his office, closed the door, and placed the two messages on the desk. He stood in front of the floor-to-ceiling glass window and looked down at the traffic of the Big Apple below.

He remembered the day he'd landed in the City of Angels, fresh out of high school, ready to venture out to college and be on his own for the first time. When the plane had descended into the brownish-gray air, Daniel had wondered if he'd ever be able to breathe properly again.

He'd met Ben Miller that first day after dumping his two suitcases on his new bed. His first roommate. Whoever had paired them seemed to have some third-eye insight, as the two had become inseparable. When they entered law school together four years later, they shared a small, two-bedroom flat. Amazingly enough, he hadn't grown bored of Ben; they remained the best of friends.

It was only after they graduated, both in the top ten of their class, that Ben announced he was starting an immigration practice.

"I want to give back to the people," he'd said.

Daniel closed his eyes and felt himself being transported unwillingly to the old pizza joint in the basement of the student center. It was the last time he and Ben had spoken. And it was the last time Daniel had eaten pizza; he couldn't stomach it after that encounter.

\*\*\*

"What do you mean, 'Give back to the people?' " he'd said sharply. "Since when was that our goal?"

Daniel felt completely betrayed by his only friend. How many times had he spilled his heart and soul out to Ben about his dreams to rule the world through law? It was his sole purpose in choosing this profession. Power. There was nothing more alluring than that. Of course, with power came money, but power was the ultimate goal.

He'd always imagined traveling that road with Ben. But his friend chose to take the least powerful route possible. Immigration law? Helping the dregs of society. Why?

When Ben didn't respond, Daniel banged his fist on the table of the Red Barron so hard it hurt for weeks. "When did you become a bleeding-heart sap?"

Ben's response was to simply stare hard at him in silence. He looked like a puppy doused by cold water. After a minute, Ben stood up and walked out. Later that night, Daniel returned to their apartment to discover that Ben had packed up all his belongings and moved out.

*Good riddance*, he remembered thinking that night. It was really a blessing in disguise. Now he was free to pursue his goals and conquer the world on his own, without the encumbrance of a wishy-washy do-gooder.

Daniel realized that his hands had clenched into fists by his side and his entire body was tense as he stared out his window. He briefly wondered what Ben was up to and why he'd called, but then shoved that thought away. He sat in his chair and picked up the phone to return the first call.

\*\*\*

The orange glow of the setting sun filtered through the office windows when Daniel dismissed Helen for the day. He leaned back in his chair and propped his feet on the desk. He surveyed the plush decor of his office with pleasure.

It had been a good day. First, he bested Mr. Calderon's naïve attorney. Then some big wigs from Markim Pharmaceuticals had booked an appointment. And, finally, he had crushed his phone interview with Susie Luke from *The New York Times Magazine*. She was putting together a feature on the most successful lawyers in the city and had let it slip that he would be on the cover. Daniel mentally scanned his closet at home, trying to decide which of his Armani suits he would wear to the photo shoot.

The sky turned to purple, and the lights in the building across the street winked out one by one. Daniel stretched. He wanted to celebrate. But with whom? The office was empty. Everyone had gone home to their families.

He picked up the receiver and paused for a moment before punching the digits of his son's landline. It rang eight times, and just as he thought it would go to voicemail, he heard a tentative, "Hello?"

"Junior," Daniel said cheerfully.

"Dad. What do you want?" As always, his son's voice was cold.

"Hey, I wanted to take you out for dinner. I had a really good day and want to celebrate."

"It's eight o'clock. I've had my dinner."

"Come on. Sky's the limit. You can pick the place."

"You're not listening. I've eaten."

"Come on. You can bring your wife, if you want."

He heard a click, then the dial tone. He briefly considered calling back, but shrugged off the impulse. *Who needs him?*

Daniel approached his building an hour later, and the doorman rushed to open the doors with a bow and a smile. Daniel gave the man a curt nod. He then glanced over at the security guard and returned the man's nod with another curt one of his own. He appreciated the unbroken stone silence of the lobby. No one engaged in conversations about the weather or pets. It was a well-oiled machine.

Daniel stepped into the bronze elevators and barely gave the uniformed attendant a glance. The man slipped his key card into the slot, and within moments Daniel arrived at his penthouse suite on the thirtieth floor. He turned his key in the lock and opened the door.

The suite was fragrance-free, and the décor was white and black. His interior designer had said it was Art Deco, but Daniel didn't care. It had cost him a small fortune and was exactly how he wanted it. His housekeeper, Sylvia, kept the apartment white-glove clean every day. She had one client. Him.

Daniel opened his refrigerator and pulled out a prepared meal for one. Sylvia happened to be a good cook, which was convenient. He put it in the oven according to the handwritten instructions and waited, musing.

Today *had* been a good day. He really should celebrate. And if it couldn't be with Daniel Jr., then there was only one other person who would do.

Daniel pulled out his phone and typed out a quick message to Belinda, inviting her over in an hour. He was pleased when she immediately responded that she would be there. She wasn't always available, but she had made it clear that he was top on her list. He'd considered making her exclusive, but then eventually more would be expected. No, this was much better. No future commitment on either side.

Daniel ate and cleaned up after. He looked around the apartment again, making sure nothing was out of place. When his Howard Miller Langston grandfather clock chimed ten, he smiled. The brass and midnight-blue dial, showing the phases of the moon, twinkled playfully against the cherry wood. He loved that clock. It was the most expensive one he could find.

As the last chime echoed through the apartment, a knock sounded at the door. Daniel smiled. He liked Belinda's punctuality. She knew how to please him on many levels.

He walked the twenty paces to the front door and opened it to a stunning woman in a dark red dress, which sculpted her form perfectly. She was curvy, but firm, with flowing blond hair that teased her waist.

"Hello, Belinda," he said. "Right on time. Won't you come in?"

She smiled, bent her head in assent, and softly kissed him on the cheek as she passed through the doorway. She smelled faintly of gardenias from the soap he'd given her for her last birthday.

Belinda went directly to the chess set in the corner of the large open room. She sat down in front of the white pieces of the wooden carved Jacques chess set. It was their ritual, the surest way into his heart. Beauty was one thing, but intelligence was the most potent aphrodisiac.

Daniel had taught her the game when they'd first met, and he was pleased when she'd picked it up. He was certain that she'd read a few books on openings and the middle game. In addition, she'd probably hired a local master to teach her a few strategies.

She allowed him to take the center of the board, capturing the long diagonal instead. When she castled queenside, she thew her pieces at his king in a relentless attack. Daniel successfully defended his position, then turned the tables and quickly cornered her king.

She studied the board. "Looks like you got me. It's mate in two."

"You played very well," he said graciously. He meant it. She had. And she had really tried to win, which pleased him tremendously. "Care to go over the game?"

He phrased it as a question, but they both knew the post-game analysis was part of the dance.

"Of course," she said demurely. "Maybe you can teach me how to play the Nimzo-Larson Attack a little better."

After they discussed the game for twenty minutes, Daniel stood up and went to her side of the table. She looked up at him, and when he reached out his hand, she accepted it and allowed him to pull her up.

He gave her a long kiss before he pulled back and whispered, "You're intoxicating." Then he gently put his arm around her shoulders and guided her back to his bedroom.

***

Sitting in the dining room the next day, Daniel could feel the weight of the two hundred years of history of the hallowed club—his private club. He'd been on the board of directors for only a year, yet had the clout of a seasoned member.

The maître d' had seated him and the three executives of Markim Pharmaceuticals at his usual table. The location of the table was perfect. Not too close to the kitchen or bathrooms, and just a little off from the center of the room.

The staff was always attentive. A Hispanic busgirl delivered a napkin that had been missing from the table when they'd sat down. Her olive skin stood out in the room filled with white waiters and patrons. Daniel thanked her, more to impress his future clients than to acknowledge the girl for her service. She murmured a response that he barely heard and didn't care about.

Two men and a woman from Markim were there to convince him to take their case. He'd already done the research and was more than ready to defend them. The retainer would be handsome; this company had the deepest pockets he'd ever seen.

Still, he enjoyed the game of cat and mouse. He'd let them dangle for a while and offer him the sun, moon, and stars before he graciously offered to win their case for them.

As if on cue, the president of the club walked over to greet them. Nick Granger, a forty-seven-year-old man in a three-piece suit and gold tie, shook Daniel's hand.

"Good to see you again, Mr. Johnson," he said.

"And you," Daniel said. Then he introduced him to his guests, who looked suitably impressed to be meeting the president.

After a few pleasantries, Nick excused himself, and the waiter came and took everyone's orders. When he left, Daniel cleared his throat.

"Why don't you tell me what your biggest problem with the suit is," Daniel suggested. "I've done quite a bit of research on Diovebrim 43, and the drug seems to have a slew of side effects. More than most. The death rate of users in the latest trial is one of the most problematic issues."

The three looked at each other nervously before the woman spoke. "Do we have attorney-client privilege?"

Daniel paused for a moment, more to be dramatic and prolong the chase a little longer. There was nothing in the rule book that said that he couldn't keep his clients on edge as long as possible. It made them more cooperative as the process continued.

"Yes, you have it," he said finally. "I'll need my usual retainer, though." He pulled out his phone and sent his first invoice, enough for two new Jaguars for his antique car collection and a diamond bracelet for Belinda.

The woman paid it without hesitation. Then she gave him a wobbly smile. "Thank you."

"You are welcome. Now, what is the key concern?"

The three launched into the details of the case, each scrambling to talk over the other. Daniel put his hand up, and they all fell silent.

"One at a time, please," he said.

He turned to Jerry Blythe, an elderly man, who had been Markim's senior vice president of marketing for the last twenty years.

Jerry explained that the biggest problem they were facing concerned the top witnesses for the prosecution. There were dozens, if not hundreds, of women and children who had suffered alarming side effects.

"The worst is probably the children who are now paralyzed with impaired brain function," he said.

"Can they link it to the drug with certainty?" Daniel asked.

The man nodded. "Absolutely. There is no doubt that Diovebrim 43 was the culprit."

Daniel paused a moment and rotated his knife in place on the table a few times. He didn't have many compunctions, but harming a child, let alone hundreds of them, didn't sit well.

His own son had cut ties with him years ago, but still, he couldn't imagine the horror of something happening to Daniel Jr. It would be like having his right arm severed. He took a deep breath and settled his feelings. Cold, calm, and unemotional. That's what they expected of him. That's what he'd deliver.

He stilled his fidgeting fingers and looked up at the man. "Anything else I should know?" Daniel asked quietly.

"A few women and men in their early twenties committed suicide," Jerry said without blinking an eye. "That's harder to link to us. I mean, they were probably depressed before they ever took our medication."

Daniel nodded and did his best to quell the turmoil in his gut. Odd, he'd never had physical reactions to his client's crimes before. He thought he'd seen it all, but these three were literally turning his stomach. He tried to take a deep breath, but found it difficult.

Suddenly, his breaths were harder and harder to catch, as if he'd just run a race. And his left arm felt as if someone had injected fire into his veins. Daniel realized he couldn't stop his body from sliding to the left. He felt the tug of the white linen as it followed him to the floor.

The crash of the plates and the cries of the patrons echoed as if far away from him, down a long tunnel. He could sense the chaos churning all around him, as well as inside his mind, yet he couldn't do anything but listen and dread the next moment.

Then Daniel heard a loud voice say, "Call 911!" The voice had a distinct Spanish accent. It was calm and authoritative, while maintaining a sense of femininity.

Soon, that same voice came closer to his ear. "Mr. Johnson," it said in a near whisper. The voice was so soothing. "My name is Adriana. Can you tell me if you're allergic to aspirin?" He could feel strong hands loosening his tie and unbuttoning the top buttons on his shirt.

"What?" he tried to say, but no words came out. It felt as if there was a lead weight sitting on his chest, putting intense pressure on his lungs. He managed to open his eyes and look directly into those of the busgirl.

*Adriana.* Was that what she said her name was?

There was something reassuring about those brown eyes. Did they have little flecks of gold in them? She gave him a smile and said, "You're having a heart attack. We've called 911. The paramedics will be here soon. Now, do you have any allergies to aspirin?"

He didn't dare look away or close his eyes. Adriana's eyes were his one and only lifeline. Speaking was too much of a chore, but he could slowly shake his head back and forth.

"No? Good," she said.

Nick knelt down and handed her a first aid kit. Daniel could see that the club president's hands were shaking. "There should be aspirin in there," he said.

She opened the kit, pulled out a white packet, and ripped it open. She put a small tablet into his mouth and said, "Chew it. We need that in your blood system."

"Shouldn't you give him CPR or something?" a voice said. It sounded irritated and maybe a little bored. Daniel looked over. It was Jerry. The three clients were still seated at the table, frowning. None of them had gotten up to help him.

He turned his gaze back to Adriana, who kept her eyes locked on Daniel. He could tell that she was suppressing annoyance. "No," she said, continuing to keep her voice calm. "He's conscious. That wouldn't be a good idea."

Nick turned back to the room and said, "Adriana was a nurse in Mexico City. She's the most qualified to help Mr. Johnson." Then he turned back to Daniel. "Help will be here shortly. The station is right around the—"

Just then four paramedics came racing in. Adriana stood up and backed away. He could hear her telling them about his condition. Her voice sounded so far away. As he listened to her, it sounded as if it was getting further and further away.

*Don't leave me*, he thought as he passed out.

\*\*\*

The sound of muffled sirens stirred Daniel momentarily as he felt the ambulance shift from side to side. He opened his eyes, but immediately passed out again.

Then, he felt himself jarred awake as the gurney extended to hit the ground at the emergency department.

Hospitals.

He hated them.

He'd defended enough doctors and administrators to know how much negligence abounded in these buildings. He wondered briefly if he'd be stuck in some corridor, forgotten until it was too late.

"Put him over there," a strident voice said. "Bed number three."

He closed his eyes and opened them again. Obviously, time had passed because he now had an IV inserted into his left arm. He could hear a lot of commotion around him. He turned his head and watched as a gaggle of people of varying ages surrounded a bed nearby. He couldn't make out words, but it sounded like Italian mixed with English. And there was a lot of gesturing. A few of the women were crying.

"All but one of you will have to leave," a buxom nurse shouted over the din, her hands on her hips. "I have no idea how you all managed to get this far, but this is the *emergency* department. We can't have this many people here!"

The nurse managed to usher out half the people, then came back to escort more out. Finally, only two remained, and she shook her head and said, "Just keep out of the way."

It was then that Daniel could see the stocky, middle-aged man in the next hospital bed. The two women who remained looked to be his wife and daughter. Or maybe one was his sister. It was hard to tell. Each was holding one of his hands and crying softly.

"*Il mio amore,*" the man said softly to a small woman in a flowered dress. "I'll be OK. I promise."

She nodded and whispered something to him. Daniel strained to hear, but it was useless. There was too much noise all around.

Just then a petite nurse blocked his view. She looked as if she was still in high school.

She gave him a bright smile. "You're awake. That's good," she said. "I'm Sarah and will be tending to you while you're in the ER."

His eyelids fluttered closed. "How . . . ?" was all he could muster.

"You're stable," he heard her say. "It's a good thing that nurse at the club gave you an aspirin. You can thank her next time you see her."

Daniel tried to nod, but conked out again. When he opened his eyes, Sarah was gone and he was in a different space. This must be the CCU, he thought as he turned his head. A tall man in blue scrubs rushed over to him and looked directly in his eyes.

"You're in the Coronary Care Unit. I'm Nurse Terry, and I'm going to take your blood pressure." He wrapped Daniel's left arm in the cuff and continued, "Dr. Berns will be in shortly to talk to you."

Daniel nodded and considered asking more about his condition, but knew they would need to do a series of tests before coming to any conclusions. Instead, he watched the staff move around, checking readouts and making notes in his chart.

He really wanted to ask the question burning in his mind: How close had he come to dying?

He didn't, though. He knew it would be a waste of breath to ask it. No one could or would answer that. However, deep down, he knew he'd come closer that day than on any other, and the very thought sent chills up his spine.

A young man in a suit approached the bed, snapping Daniel's attention to him.

"I'm Mr. Soren," he said, "and I just need to fill in a few blanks.

We were able to get a lot of your personal information from your wallet. However, there was no emergency contact person there, and your phone is locked. Is there anyone we should call?"

Daniel looked away and shook his head. No one. He was glad that the hospital staff hadn't been able to break into his contacts while he was unconscious. The last thing he wanted was for Belinda to show up. Caring for ill people wasn't her thing.

One person popped into his mind, but he knew he couldn't give Mr. Soren that name.

*Daniel Jr.*

His son would never come. Not after the scene he'd created at his wedding. His only son's wedding. His only *child's* wedding. Of course, there might be another in a few years. After all, who stayed married to the same person for any length of time? He sighed. If anyone would, it would be Daniel Jr.

***

"I can't believe you no-showed my wedding," his son had said that fateful day after Daniel had arrived an hour late to the reception.

Daniel felt his chest constrict. This time it wasn't from a heart attack, but from emotion. So unfamiliar to him.

He tried to push the unwanted memory away, but it bubbled back to the surface, impossible to ignore.

Why hadn't he just apologized?

Instead, he'd railed at the boy. "I was with a client!"

Daniel's voice had filled the cavernous room packed with guests who seemed to have nothing better to do than to stop and stare at him. The chatter had died suddenly. He could still hear the echoes of the DJ's selection of alternative rock music playing in the background. He had lowered his voice, silently willing the guests to go back to their conversations and mind their own businesses.

"I was with a client," he repeated more quietly when he saw how hurt his son looked. Unshed tears threatened to spill.

"You're *always* with a client," the boy whispered.

His bride, Sharlene, came up to him and pulled on his arm, "Come on, Liam, he's not worth it. Come dance with me. It's your favorite song."

*Liam.*

*Liam.*

Again, Daniel's chest constricted. His only son had changed his name the minute he'd turned eighteen. How many ways could the boy disrespect him?

If Daniel had just left, he'd probably still have a relationship with his son. But he couldn't just leave. He couldn't just walk away. No, he had to push it. He had to win the argument.

So he'd said, "Who do you think paid for this reception at the prestigious Weylin?" Daniel panned slowly around the room, counting. "Forty thousand dollars just for the reception."

Sharlene's sharp intake of breath caused him to turn his attention to her. "And your lovely bride's five-thousand-dollar gown," he said snidely. "She just had to have the latest from France, right?"

He watched Sharlene wobble and pale slightly, but didn't stop going on and on about all the things he'd paid for over the last year alone. It was as if he were presenting a closing argument to the two hundred guests who all just stood there with their mouths agape.

He was sure that somewhere in the crowd was his mousy ex-wife, Daniel Jr.'s mom. Correction: *Liam's* mother. She was probably cowering in a corner, afraid to say anything.

That woman had allowed him to run roughshod over her in the divorce proceedings, never asking for more than he was willing to give. Which was nothing. She didn't deserve anything. Not in writing, at least. He'd been more than generous with all of Daniel Jr.'s expenses, paying any bill she sent him. Any reasonable bill.

Daniel continued to rant for a few more minutes, then stopped. The sorrow in his son's eyes had turned to anger.

"Get. Out. Father," he bit out. Although his voice hadn't risen, the intensity of his bitterness was obvious. "Leave. And don't bother to call me later to apologize."

Daniel froze at the conviction he heard in the boy's voice. No one had ever talked to him in that way, let alone his son. He opened his mouth to say something, but found he was speechless for the first time in a long while.

He knew he had gone too far.

Suddenly, it was clear to him that his entire rant made no sense. He'd been the one to insist on the venue. The fact was, the newlyweds had stressed many times that such extravagance wasn't necessary. And Sharlene had only mentioned the kind of dress she would like to have when she was flipping through the various bridal magazines. He'd taken it upon himself to get her "only the best." She'd been shocked when he'd gifted it to her.

\*\*\*

"Mr. Johnson?" Mr. Soren's quiet voice pierced through the cloud of the memory. "I need someone, anyone, to put down on the form. Who would you like to put down?"

"Helen Yagerman," Daniel finally said and gave the young man the phone number for his personal secretary. "Can you call her for me and explain the situation?"

"Of course. I'll do that right now," he said.

Nurse Terry came over and checked the IV. Daniel's energy waned again, and he allowed himself to drift off to sleep.

In a dream, Daniel found himself back in the club, sitting alone at his table. He looked out at the other people chatting at neighboring tables. Every race was represented, and Daniel was the only Caucasian present. Instead of feeling uncomfortable, he felt at home.

His attention was drawn to the waitress's eyes. Beautiful brown eyes with gold flecks. The rest of her image was fuzzy, but he imagined dark, long hair and olive skin. However, he was focused on those eyes. He'd never forget those eyes.

As he continued to look at her, he felt a peace wash over him. She was there for him. He was content to just hold her gaze. He didn't feel the urge to order anything. He wasn't hungry. He just wanted to stay there for a while longer and be with her.

\*\*\*

Daniel's eyes flickered open and he wondered if he was still ensconced in the dream, because there, in front of him, sitting on a chair only five feet away, was a woman with those same brown eyes with gold flecks.

Maybe he was in a layered dream, the kind where you keep "waking up" only to discover that you're in another dream. Who knows what drugs they'd given him in the last few hours? Some were probably pretty potent.

"Hello?" his vision said with the Spanish accent he remembered.

"Hello," he replied with a scratchy voice.

She stood up and walked over to him. "I'm Adriana."

"I know."

She smiled. "How could you know that?"

He found his lips naturally mirrored her smile. Normally, he only smiled if it helped further his goals in some way. Smiling had always felt a little as if he were molding his lips to manipulate the situation. This was different. It felt good. Natural. Relaxing.

"I . . .," he said. "I remember."

"You've got a good memory, Dan. It's Dan, isn't it?"

He paused, then nodded. "Yes." No one called him that. His name was *Daniel*. He'd always been Daniel. Even as a child, his parents had called him by his full name. The shortened nickname had always seemed so immature to him, but from her lips he liked the sound. It was perfect. He was Dan.

"I have to have a good memory," he said.

"Why's that?"

He hesitated. Everything was perfect. Why ruin it with reality? His eyes dropped to the blanket. "Dunno."

In the silence that followed, he realized that he wanted to be completely honest with her. Nothing else would do.

His eyes flicked back up to hers and he said, "The fact is, I'm a lawyer. I have to remember details."

She nodded solemnly. "Ah. I see." The gold flecks still sparkled, and he knew she wasn't bothered.

"It's just that some people don't like men of my profession," he said, feeling the need to explain.

"I don't judge people that way."

He nodded. "I can see that."

They fell silent for a while, then she said, "I'm on my way home from work. I wanted to check in on you to make sure you were OK."

"Thank you," Daniel said in a rush. "Thank you for saving my life." The words sounded so trite and hollow to his ears. He sighed, and his gaze dropped again.

"You are welcome, Dan," she said. Her voice was creamy and made him feel nourished and cared for. His eyes lifted to her, and he saw she was smiling.

*Perfect teeth. Just lovely.*

"I'm glad to see that you are recovering." She stood up. "I really should be going."

"Will you come back?" He wished he didn't sound so much like a stray puppy dog longing for her affection and presence.

She nodded. "As soon as I can." Then she bent down and kissed his brow. She smelled like spicy vanilla. Something deep within him stirred as he held his breath. If only he could capture this moment in time and hold on to it forever.

"When?" he whispered.

She giggled, and tiny, rippling waves of pleasure ran through him. He broke into a grin.

"Soon," she said.

He wanted to say something else to keep her there for another minute, but over her shoulder he saw the shape of his personal secretary standing in the doorway. "Helen!" he said, shifting his attention.

Adriana turned briefly to look at the woman, then back to him. "I'm glad you have company. Goodbye, Dan."

"Goodbye," he said with a wave.

Adriana smiled at Helen on her way out.

"Thanks for coming," Daniel said to Helen.

Helen frowned slightly. "Yes, sir. How are you feeling?"

"Fine, fine," he said. Then he coughed and straightened a bit. "Does everyone in the office know?" He dreaded the feeding frenzy that would most likely attend his absence.

Her eyes widened a bit. "Of course not. I would never betray your confidence."

"Thank you."

She frowned again, but didn't say anything.

Daniel tilted his head to the right and asked, "What's wrong?"

Helen's mouth opened and closed silently. Then she sputtered, "Y-you're acting so strange."

He crinkled his brow. "How so?"

"For one thing, you've just thanked me twice in the last minute. I can't remember a single time you've ever thanked . . ." she trailed off and blushed. "I'm sorry. That was rude."

"No," he said with a grimace. How many times had he just barked orders at her? "You're right."

"It's OK," she said awkwardly.

"No," he said. "It's not. And here's another first. I'm sorry."

Helen plopped down in the chair that Adriana had occupied just a few minutes before. "I've heard of this happening."

"What?"

"People changing when they think they're dying."

He frowned. "Maybe," he said noncommittally. "Well, in case I revert back to my old self in a day, let me say that I appreciate you and all you've done for me."

Helen stared blankly, then nodded. From her expression, Daniel thought that she might consider him to be rather unbalanced. It would take some time for her to adjust.

"You'll need to break the news to the rest of the partners," he said. He detailed which partners and associates should get which clients. "Make sure they know it's only temporary, but I need to take some time off."

They talked for another twenty minutes, and then Nurse Terry came in and shooed Helen away.

"You need rest," he said.

"That's all I've been doing," he muttered. But even as the words escaped his lips, he felt drained of energy. He looked up at Terry. "Sorry, you're right."

He left, and Daniel slipped into a deep slumber.

\*\*\*

The next day, the medical team transferred Dan to the telemetry floor. He was pleased. That meant he was one step closer to going home.

He realized he had mixed feelings about that. His immaculate and sterile home suddenly wasn't the refuge it once had been.

Though he felt his strength returning, Dan felt restless. Not so much from being cooped up, but from his budding desire to flex a few new muscles. He looked at the messages Helen had brought him earlier, but his attention kept wandering.

He was relieved that Helen had successfully turned over all his current clients to others, because Dan found he had no drive to continue with them. Each case was different, but they all had one thing in common—they were all about money. With his new lease on life came the desire to do things differently. Rather than go for the big bucks, he now wanted to take a stab at helping others. He wanted to actually make a difference.

Dan turned his attention back to the message in his hand.

*Ben Miller.*

Good old Ben. Over the years, Ben had never given up on him and attempted to reach out to him regularly. And each time, Helen had passed on the note, despite the fact that he growled at her every time. Perhaps she knew her boss better than he knew himself. She was such a trusted assistant. She probably deserved another raise.

Then it occurred to him. Could it be that Helen had stuck around so long because she actually cared about him and wanted to help him? That thought made him feel a sudden warmth, and he smiled.

He was lost in thought when he heard a greeting from the door.

Dan's pulse quickened at the sound. He looked hopefully at the door. When he saw it was indeed Adriana, he grinned. "Hello! I'm glad you found me."

She returned his smile. "I know my way around a hospital. I expected you to be in telemetry today."

"That's right, you're a nurse," he said. Then he indicated the chair next to the bed. "Please come in. Have a seat."

She thanked him and sat down. "How are you feeling, Dan?"

"Great! I'm ready to leave."

She stood back up, looked at his chart, and nodded. "Looks good for tomorrow. They'll want to observe you for another day, I think."

He nodded. "That's what one of the nurses said when they transferred me. Hey, can I ask you something?"

"Sure," she said.

"Why are you working at the club instead of as a nurse? You obviously know your stuff."

She sighed. "I'd like to. Believe me. It's just not that easy."

"Are you a registered nurse?"

She nodded. "Yes, I completed my four-year program and am licensed in Mexico. I was a practicing RN there for five years."

Dan closed his eyes and tried to remember the requirements. "Did you take your English proficiency test?"

She nodded. "And I took the NCLEX exam here in New York. Passed with flying colors. I just can't seem to get the TN visa I need."

"What if you became a permanent resident?"

"I need to find an employer willing to go through the process and wait a year. So far, no luck."

"You know, I know someone who specializes in immigration law. Maybe he could help!"

When she broke out in a huge smile, he felt as if the sun had filled his room with its warm glow. "That would be amazing! I've been here for months and can't afford to hire anyone. Lawyers are expensive."

He laughed. "Yes, we are. But Ben's not. And he's an old friend." *If he'll still take my call.*

"I am very grateful for your help," she said.

As Dan felt her hand touch his, he looked down at it and realized that some people helped others for a very different kind of pay. Her gratitude was a very real sort of payment, one that he'd never valued before. Before today, the only thing he'd ever enjoyed about his job was cashing a client's check.

When he thought of all the people he'd helped in the past, his smile faded. The fact was that when he'd assisted his clients, it ended up hurting others. He'd used his abilities to help large chemical companies minimize their payouts and spouses bilk their husbands or wives of their money. And then there was a whole group of people who just hired him to stall lawsuits.

Dan wracked his brain to think of one morally decent client he'd had and couldn't come up with a single person. He looked up and realized Adriana was his first real client.

"I'll do everything in my power to help you," he said.

\*\*\*

The next day, Adriana was by Dan's side as he was preparing to leave the hospital. "Where are you going to go?" she asked.

"Home," he said, feeling the creep of dread climb up his spine. "You know, my apartment."

"Who will look after you?" she asked with a frown. "You live alone, no?"

He nodded as he put some things into a bag. "It's fine."

"No, it's not," she said. "You should have someone there to check on you."

"That would be nice. But I don't have anyone."

"You do now."

His hands stopped moving, and he turned to look at her. He searched her face and felt a twinge of hope. Was she really offering what he thought she was? "You mean . . ." he couldn't bring himself to voice the words in case he'd misread her.

She laughed. "Yes, I'm offering my nursing services. If you'd like them."

"Oh, would I," he breathed.

"Do you have a guest room?"

He nodded. "All made up."

"Perfect. I'll get you settled in, then I'll run home to feed my cat."

"You have a cat?" he asked.

"Yeah. An orange tabby I rescued from the shelter."

He nodded, then said more to himself than her, "Kind of like me."

\*\*\*

A week later, Dan invited Ben to join him for lunch at the club. Dan also brought Adriana, who was a bit reluctant.

"I'm not sure the members will be pleased to see me sitting at a table as a guest," she said on the cab ride over.

"Why's that?" he asked.

When she didn't immediately respond, he looked over at her. She raised an eyebrow at him.

"What?" he asked. "I don't get it."

She let out an exaggerated sigh. "No, I guess you wouldn't. Not when you're a white male."

"You think the club members are racist?"

"Yeah," she said.

"No," he said. "I've never seen that."

"You wouldn't have," she said. "They're used to seeing me with my gray and blue busgirl uniform. I don't know that they'll take kindly to my pretending to be a guest."

"You're not pretending. You *are* a guest," Dan said, furrowing his brows. "You're *my* guest. This won't be a problem."

When the cab stopped, Dan got out and went around to the other side to open the door for Adriana. He took in her bright yellow dress and admired the fresh flower in her hair. Who could be offended by her?

As they walked toward the front door, Dan spotted Ben sitting on the bench outside the entrance. His old friend immediately stood up and walked forward to greet him. Dan reached out a tentative hand, but Ben pushed past it to hug him.

"How have you been, old friend?" Ben asked.

"Good. And you?"

"Couldn't be better!" Ben pulled back a little and patted Dan on the arm. "It's just so good to see you."

Dan smiled and introduced Adriana, caught him up on her situation, then said, "Let's go inside."

He led the way through his club and stopped in front of the maître d' station. Dan looked fondly at the short, portly man who was studying his large reservation book. "Gerald, I'm afraid I forgot to call ahead for a reservation. Do you have a table for us?"

Gerald immediately looked up, his face lit by a large smile. "It's so good to see you up and about, Mr. Johnson. Of course, we can find you a table. And who are your guests today?"

Dan stepped to the side, turned back, and indicated the two hidden behind him. "Well, you know Adriana, and this is my friend Ben Miller."

Dan watched Gerald carefully, wanting to show Adriana how mistaken she'd been. He fully expected to prove her wrong. However, when the man's smile faltered, Dan knew he was the one that was wrong.

"I'm sorry, Mr. Johnson," Gerald said, looking down at his book. "Every table has been reserved."

"That's ridiculous!" said Dan. "I know for a fact that you always keep at least two tables free for just such an occasion. What's going on?"

Gerald leaned in close so that the others couldn't hear. "Please. It just isn't done."

Dan growled, "*What* isn't done?"

Gerald looked apologetically at Adriana. "Inviting the help to eat in the dining room."

"Look here. I'm a member of the Board," Dan gritted through his teeth. "This lovely woman saved my life. Here. In front of everyone. So now I'm treating her to lunch. Here. In front of everyone. Is that understood?"

"Of course, of course," said Gerald, holding his hands in front of him as if to defend himself against Dan's words. Then he coughed and said, "I'm afraid that *the gentleman* here will need a jacket, though. As you know, Mr. Johnson, we have a strict dress code."

Ben's face flushed red, which made Dan feel acutely embarrassed. He turned back to his friend. "I'm sorry. I should have warned you. That's on me," he whispered.

"Don't worry," Gerald said. "I have one he can borrow." He went to the coat check room and brought back a worn navy-blue blazer and handed it to Ben. "I think this should do the trick."

Ben hesitated, then donned the jacket, which was two sizes too big. He rolled up the sleeves and smiled thinly at Gerald. "Better?"

Dan shook his head and turned to Gerald. "Is this really necessary? What does it matter what he wears?" The irony hit him as he heard his words. How many times had he dressed a client or demanded a girl-friend wear certain clothes? The fact was that before now he'd always enjoyed the dress code.

"Yes, sir. I'm afraid it is."

"Fine. Now please take us to my table," he said stiffly.

Gerald tensed and said, "I'm sorry, but that table is reserved. However, we do have a very nice table for you. Please, follow me."

Dan clenched his teeth and nodded curtly. He followed the man to a small table in a dark corner of the restaurant. Only half the room was filled with patrons, and his usual table was unoccupied. He made a mental note to pay a visit to Nick after the meal.

As they sat down, Adriana gave him a told-you-so look that made him grin. She was probably the only person who could get away with such sass. He found it charming, and it worked to lighten the mood.

The server treated Adriana and Ben with respect, which was a relief. At least the whole world hadn't completely shifted to disappoint him.

Dan let Ben and Adriana talk throughout the meal, and in the end, they worked out a good plan. It would take some time, but Ben had a few ideas for things they could do to fast-track her application.

While Dan was waiting for the waiter to return with his credit card receipt, he turned to Ben and said, "What you do, it's amazing. Really incredible. You actually help people, don't you?"

Ben beamed. "I like to think I do. It's a wonderful feeling."

Dan nodded. "Need some help? I would like to try my hand at immigration law. Really do some good for others."

"Wow!" Ben exclaimed. "That would be wonderful." Then he paused for a moment. "There's not a lot of money in it, you know."

Dan shrugged. "I don't need it."

The minute the words escaped his lips, he was startled by them. Did he really mean that?

"You OK?" Ben asked, cocking his head to the side.

"Yeah, I'm fine. I'm good," Dan said with a laugh. "You know, I think I really am!"

He felt better than he had in a long time. He looked over at Adriana, who was smiling at him. She didn't say a word, but he knew she was proud of him. And oddly enough, that meant the world to him.

***

The next day, Adriana brought Dan his coat midmorning and said, "I'd like to treat you to lunch as a thank you for yesterday."

"You don't have to do that," he said.

"I know. I just want to show you something."

As he drove, she directed him to Brooklyn. He was surprised when she had him stop under a bridge. He looked around nervously and said,

"You're sure this is safe?"

She nodded. "It's fine."

"But where's the restaurant?"

She pointed to a taco truck and said, "Over there. Best tacos in the world. I promise."

Dan was dubious, but followed her to the brightly colored truck. To one side appeared to be an art gallery. A dozen people were standing around admiring the sketches and watercolor paintings while eating tacos.

"What if I want a burrito?" he asked no one in particular.

"Then you'd be out of luck," a man from behind the window said. He had a riot of curly brown hair and an easy smile. His attention shifted to Adriana, and he cheered. "Adriana! It's been too long. And who is your friend?"

"Felipe, this is Dan. Dan, this is the Taco Man," she said with a grin.

"Taco Man, eh?" Dan said. "Well, then I guess I'll order a beef taco."

"He'll have three *chicken* ones," Adriana said, giving him an admonishing look. "No beef for you."

"Ah, so you're a practicing RN again?" Felipe said.

"No, but Dan here is helping me figure that out."

Felipe nodded and quickly made Dan three chicken tacos. While he waited, Dan looked at the artwork.

"Good, aren't they?" Felipe called out.

Dan nodded. "You do these?"

"No, I'm afraid the only art I create are tacos," Felipe said with a chuckle. He handed Dan three tacos.

Dan took a bite and exclaimed in pleasure, "You weren't kidding! These are incredible."

"Thank you," Felipe said. "The painter is a young Frenchman, who will be along later this afternoon."

"So everything is working out with Gabriel?" Adriana asked.

"Yeah, he's doing great. His mom got a new sponsor and they're applying for permanent residency. It's slow going, but you know how it is."

"I do, but you know Dan here is an immigration attorney," Adriana said.

"You are?" Felipe exclaimed.

Dan nodded and grinned. "I guess I am."

If that sounded odd to Felipe, he didn't let on.

Dan continued, "Give me a few days and we'll come back and meet this boy. Have him bring his mother. I'll see what we can do."

"*Gracias*," Felipe said. "*Gracias*."

"And I'll take this watercolor called *Cherry Blossoms from the Brooklyn Botanic Garden*. How much is it?"

"Oh, good choice," Felipe said. "You pay what you want to pay."

"Come again?" Dan asked, looking to Adriana for help in understanding.

She shrugged. "It's the way the Taco Man does business. You pay three dollars a taco, which is the going rate, but everything else is up to you. Advice, art, tonics, whatever you need. You pay what's in your heart, what you can afford."

"Uh," Dan said, looking at the painting and at Felipe. "I can afford a lot."

Felipe laughed. "Pay what's in your heart. Anything you give the boy will be appreciated."

Dan reached into his pocket and pulled out his billfold. Opening it, he saw a hundred-dollar bill and pulled it out. "This good?" He really wasn't sure.

Felipe whistled low. "That's very generous. Gabriel will be thrilled!"

Dan grinned in relief. "Good!" he said as he pulled the painting down. Then he turned to Adriana and handed it to her. "For you. As a thank you for all you've done for me."

Adriana looked at him with wide eyes. "It's gorgeous!" she said. "Thank you!"

At that moment, he felt as if all the cells in his body were alive. How could he have missed the small pleasures of life? Tacos under a bridge in Brooklyn, helping people who needed it, giving a simple gift to someone he loved and watching her eyes light up. That's where life lived.

*Someone he loved.* That had a nice ring to it.

\*\*\*

Dan sat under a weeping willow tree in Guilford, Connecticut, sipping a lemonade Adriana had made. She'd said it was an old family recipe dating back at least a hundred years. It had a touch of cayenne pepper and maple syrup. He found the concoction energizing.

It hadn't been a difficult decision to sell his ostentatious penthouse in Manhattan and purchase this roomy home on a small farm with rolling hills. One of his new clients had set him up with a home office that allowed him to avoid the big city most of the time. He still had to meet clients when a courtroom visit was required, but Ben handled most of the leg work. In addition, Helen made the commute whenever needed. She was his eyes and ears at the new office, and was studying to become a legal assistant at nights.

Dan closed his eyes as the summer breeze swelled to a mild wind. There was nothing like the feeling of fresh air on his face.

When he opened his eyes, he saw a brown sedan approach. He stood and brushed his hands against his pants. Dan was nervous and excited as he walked to the driveway to greet his son. He stopped at the edge and watched the car as Adriana came out of the house to stand beside him.

Liam stepped out of the Honda and hurried around to the passenger side to open the door for his wife.

"Did he learn that from you?" Adriana murmured as she slipped under his arm. "I love it when you open my door for me."

"I'd like to think he got something from me," Dan said. "Something good, that is."

He held his breath as the young man and his wife walked toward him. They stood there staring at each other for a few moments. Finally, Adriana said, "Hello, Liam. My name is Adriana. It's a pleasure to meet you."

They continued the introductions and engaged in polite pleasantries for a few moments until Adriana said, "Come, Sharlene, let me give you a tour of our new home."

Sharlene glanced at her husband, who nodded briefly.

"Why don't you two go on out to the tree," Adriana said to Dan. "Sharlene and I will bring out some refreshments soon."

Dan guided his son to his favorite spot and indicated where Liam should sit before he took his own seat. They remained silent until Adriana brought out more lemonade and cinnamon cookies, another family recipe.

Once Adriana left, Liam said, "You look happy."

"I am, Liam. I am." He shifted uncomfortably in his chair and exhaled. "Look, I owe you an apology."

"Just one?" Liam said with a tilt of his head.

Dan burst out laughing, feeling some of the tension leave him. "More like dozens. I know."

Liam nodded. "Well, it means a lot to me that you are calling me by my name now."

"Yeah, it took some time, but I realized that you have every right to change your name."

"You never asked what my middle name was," Liam said with a grin.

Dan felt a surge of adrenaline. "Really? You kept it?"

"Sure. I just didn't like being a 'junior.' That's all."

They fell silent again. Then Dan said, "I owe your mom an apology, too." Quickly he added, "I know, I know. More like a hundred."

Liam nodded. "Yeah, you do."

"I don't know where to start."

"Pick up the phone."

"She might not accept my call."

"Then try again. And again. Until she does."

Dan let out a ragged sigh. "I guess no one said it would be easy."

"Nope."

He refilled Liam's glass and sat back in his chair. "Either way, I'm going to give her everything she asked for in the original divorce settlement. Everything she wanted."

Liam lifted an eyebrow. "Really?"

"Really. I have to make it right."

"That's great, Dad," Liam said, looking him in the eye. "Really it is."

Dan smiled. "Dad. I like that. Hey, do you think you two can come out and visit on Sunday? Adriana's going to make a pot roast that will blow your socks off."

"Sure," Liam said with a nod. "We'll be there."

# JOE

STORY 5 IN THE "DISCOVERING KINDNESS" SERIES

## Kevin J. Smith
with Laura Sherman

Joe could feel his heartbeat pulse through his entire body. The rush of blood in his head was deafening. The bricks dug into his back as he pressed his body against the building, and the padlocked door across the narrow alley swam before his eyes. He held his breath so they couldn't hear him.

*Please don't let them find me.*

He knew he had to keep moving, so he peeled himself off the wall and cautiously stuck his head out of the alley. Steam rose off the puddles beneath the streetlamps. The boulevard was deserted. Still, he knew they were there. Somewhere. All around. He could *feel* them. It wasn't safe. He had to reach his destination. Then it would be all over.

Joe felt the adrenaline rush through his system as he sprinted down the street. Fortunately, he could run fast—that was his saving grace.

Abruptly, the cityscape turned into what seemed like a thick rain forest and he found himself slipping on moss while jumping over ferns and ducking the thick vines that hung into his path. Most likely there were snakes weaving in and out of the branches overhead, but that wasn't his biggest fear. No, his pursuers were the real threat.

Within moments, he was out of the brush and back onto pavement. His office building loomed high above. Without hesitation, Joe pushed his way through the revolving doors. Security was gone and the lobby was like a ghost town.

Joe ran past the elevators, opting instead for the stairs. His heart pounding all the way, he raced up to the roof. At the top he bent over, sucking in air. He straightened, shook his head to get the sweat out of his eyes, and brushed away the hair plastered to his forehead.

The roof was crawling with them. The shapes and shadows of indistinguishable bodies moved slowly toward him. They never spoke, but he knew they wished him harm. He just knew they were out to kill him. He looked down and knew his fate before he jumped.

Joe's eyes popped open as he jolted up in his bed, sweating and panting. He looked over at his clock. It was two minutes before the alarm was set to go off. He fell back against his pillow and groaned, drained of energy. He felt like he'd run a marathon.

If only he could escape the dream for one night.

Joe jumped when his phone alarm went off a minute later. He rolled out of bed, took a shower, and got dressed. He tiptoed to the front door and held his breath as he opened the two deadbolts to look into the corridor. No one was there. He exhaled and quickly retrieved his newspaper, then locked the door again.

Joe poured some bran flakes and milk into a bowl and sat at the tiny kitchen table squeezed into the corner of his flat. He pored over the front page of the Friday edition of *The New York Times*. Relations with

China had taken a turn for the worse, while tensions in the Middle East continued to escalate. Iran shot down another jet from Ukraine, while five civilians were caught in a crossfire in Lebanon.

His hand trembled as he opened the newspaper to the US section. Congress was voting to add a trillion dollars to the deficit, and the Dow Jones was down fifty points.

Turning to the local news, Joe read that crime in New York was up, and there were a total of ten rapes within Manhattan last night alone.

His cereal felt like cardboard in his mouth.

Joe only ate it because he knew he needed to keep his body fed, but his taste buds were lifeless. He glanced over at his front door. He felt some measure of safety within the confines of his home, but had read on a blog somewhere that the ideal number of deadbolts for the city was, in fact, three.

Two was obviously better than one, but three would give you the requisite time to phone the police before an intruder would be able to force his way through the door. After all, deadbolts couldn't actually keep anyone out for any real length of time.

Joe glanced at his watch. Time to go. He liked to be early and avoid the crush of people.

He walked across the four-lane boulevard, carefully keeping his head down to avoid eye contact with the other pedestrians. The gray sidewalk was littered with trash and discarded gum. He passed three homeless men who looked too vacant to even ask him for a quarter.

"Watch where you're going!" Joe heard someone behind him shout. He didn't dare turn around to find out who the angry voice was yelling at. It was probably him.

A few car horns blared, and Joe continued until he was in front of his office building. He always had a moment of trepidation as he pushed on the revolving door, probably due to the fact that each night he fell to his death from the rooftop.

It was 7:30 am, so there was no line for security. He put his possessions in the plastic bin and walked through the metal detector.

"Hiya, Joe!" the balding man on the other side of the machine said cheerfully.

"Hello," Joe dutifully replied.

It was important to remain polite to security. After all, they were the first line of defense against any criminal element who might try to disrupt the office.

He glanced at the elevators and noticed a few people waiting, so he headed for the stairs. Five flights. It was good exercise, he reasoned. His footsteps echoed through the empty stairwell.

Reaching the fifth floor, he opened the door to a large room of cubicles. The lights were on, but he couldn't hear a sound. He smiled. He'd be alone for at least thirty minutes.

Joe found solace in his work as an accountant. He could devote his time to precise tasks and have very little interaction with others. He had only one supervisor, and whenever the man stopped by, he rarely stayed long.

As his co-workers started to arrive, indistinct voices filled the air, bouncing off the gray fabric walls and ceiling. The muffled noise filtered into his space, and he frowned at the disruption of his peace.

Loud, raucous laughter pierced the air. It must be that tall guy three cubicles over.

"Started my weekend early, don't you know," the voice said. "Pub crawled with the boys until two. Think I'm still drunk."

"Shh," a female voice said. "Someone will hear."

"Who cares," the man said.

Joe put on his noise-canceling headphones and connected the Bluetooth to his music player. The classic music succeeded in bringing back a sense of tranquility.

*If only they'd give me a door.*

He felt a vibration flow through the desk and knew someone had bumped into his wall. He turned around abruptly and looked into the eyes of a middle-aged man with blond hair that reached his shoulders. Larry worked in the neighboring cubicle. Joe removed his headphones.

"Hello, Joe," Larry said.

Joe nodded. "Hello, Larry," he replied tentatively. Then he waited, wondering if he would be required to engage in idle chitchat.

After a moment, Larry straightened and said, "Have a good weekend."

Feeling relief that the conversation would come to a quick close, Joe said, "You, too."

He put his headphones back on and turned to his work. The morning went by quickly. Mr. Jenkins came by just before lunch, and Joe turned in his chair to face him.

"Hello, Mr. Jenkins," he said, rubbing the sweat from his hands on his pant leg. He stood, showing the respect the elderly man deserved for the position he held at the company.

Mr. Jenkins smiled at him. "And how are you today, Joe?"

"I'm fine," Joe replied with a nod.

After an awkward silence, Mr. Jenkins cleared his throat. "Do you think you'll be able to finish the Tressiac file today?"

Joe felt the sharp pins of fear prick his skin. "No, sir. I can try my best, but I'd need a few more hours. I thought it was only due next Wednesday."

Mr. Jenkins nodded. "Yeah, that changed. We need it today."

Joe nodded, working hard to suppress a frown. That meant he'd have to stay late. He came early each day, and by Friday he was ready for the complete solitude of his apartment. However, he was afraid that refusing a direct order could lead to his termination. The thought of having to interview for another job made him break out in a cold sweat. No, it was better to just stay late.

"Of course, Mr. Jenkins. I'll get it done before I leave."

Mr. Jenkins relaxed a little. "Good, good. Thank you."

When he left, Joe sagged into his chair. He worked through lunch and skipped his break. As long as he didn't have to walk home after dark, it would be OK.

By the time he finished and was on the street, the light was dimming over the city. Joe rushed past the other pedestrians who were obstacles in his way back to his apartment.

The only time he stopped was when the light at the crosswalk turned red.

"Why can't you take your eyes off that damn cell phone?" he heard a woman's angry voice say to his right.

Joe cringed and quickly looked away, feigning interest toward the storefront to his left. He fought the urge to cover his ears with his hands as he waited for the man's furious reply. Nothing. Joe held his breath.

"Honey, you're missing the sky. The colors are just gorgeous," she continued, annoyed.

The light turned green, and Joe picked up his pace to get away from the angry couple. If he ever found someone he could be with, a girl-friend, he vowed he'd never ignore her.

Joe raced into his building, sighing in relief, happy to be out of the darkened world that was filled with criminals, if *The New York Times* was to be believed. No reason not to.

He approached the door to his apartment and noticed a colorful paper rubber-banded to the doorknob. His stomach gurgled as he un-locked the bolts and removed the menu for China Inn.

He loved Chinese food. When he was a kid, his grandmama had taken him to a place a few blocks from her house.

"Joey and I will have two wonton soups and four eggrolls. Then bring us some moo shu pork," his grandmama would always order.

He'd loved the bamboo decorations and colorful porcelain cats that waved eagerly from the shelves. At the end of each meal, they'd break open their fortune cookies and read them out loud. That was Joe's fa-vorite part of the meal. Then he'd eat both crisp cookies before they walked home.

As he looked at China Inn's long rectangular menu, he longed to call and order wonton soup, egg rolls, and moo shu pork. His mouth watered at the thought. However, that wasn't realistic. Calling strang-ers and asking them for something could end in disaster. Instead, he opened the pantry, pulled out a can of soup, and poured it into a pan.

Soup was fine. Soup was safe.

Joe flipped on the news and ate his food. All the channels were airing follow-up reports on a mass shooting that had taken place two days ago at an elementary school. It turned out that the high school kid who had just walked in the front doors with a semi-automatic and blasted everything and everyone had been abused at home and was on heavy anti-psychotic medication. Apparently, he'd used the last bullet to die by suicide. All the families and traumatized children were interviewed extensively. None of the experts had answers or solutions.

All of this bad news soured Joe's stomach. He shoved aside his unfinished bowl of soup and slunk off to bed, where he buried himself deep under his covers.

At least he had two locks on his door.

\*\*\*

The next morning, Joe woke with a start and patted down his entire body to see if anything had broken in the fall from his office roof. Once his breathing returned to normal, he fell back into his bed and sighed. It was Saturday.

He glanced at his clock and realized he'd slept in until nine. That was something. At least he felt a little more rested than usual.

Joe got up and opened the front door. No paper. He frowned. Some neighbor had probably stolen it. He glanced up and down the corridor. As he looked to the right, he spotted his landlord, Mr. Solomon, and froze.

Joe desperately wanted to ask him to put in another lock, but didn't want to rock the boat. He tried to think of polite ways to make the request, but every time he considered the wording, he knew it was risky and not quite right. There would be no way around the fact that Joe found the security wanting. He would basically be insulting the man.

Joe continued to watch Mr. Solomon. He was a short man who always wore a ball cap. Today's was black. Joe tried to summon the courage to approach the man, but couldn't get his legs to move. His desire to flee battled with his desperate need for a third lock. The result was that he remained rooted to his spot right outside his door.

Mr. Solomon seemed to be checking for something near the baseboard and was slowly making his way toward Joe's apartment. As the man approached, Joe's pulse quickened, and he could feel beads of sweat forming on his brow.

"Hello, Mr. Lynell." Mr. Solomon pulled the black cap off his head and ran his fingers through his thin brown hair. "How's your weekend shaping up?"

"I need another deadbolt," Joe blurted out. He blushed when he realized he hadn't actually answered the man's question. "It's good. The weekend, that is. Thank you. Thank you for asking. Can I get another lock?"

If Joe's rambling communication was confusing to Mr. Solomon, he didn't let on. "Sure. If you give me a minute, I'll be back. I think I have just what you need."

"Really?" Joe asked, breathing out in relief.

"Why not? If that's what you need, I'm happy to help." With that, he walked briskly down the corridor and disappeared around the bend.

Joe stepped back into his apartment and closed the door. Out of habit, he locked both bolts. He hesitated. Would the landlord be offended when he found that Joe had locked him out? Joe wasn't sure. So he unbolted the door and cracked it open an inch. He hesitated again. If he left it open, some random stranger, a criminal, might come in and kill him. With a determined nod, Joe quickly shut the door and locked one of the bolts, opting to be cautious but less rude. It would be best if Mr. Solomon only heard one lock open when he returned.

A few minutes later, Joe jumped when he heard a knock on the door. He cleared his throat. "Hello?" he asked, hoping it was indeed Mr. Solomon.

"Hello," came the cheerful reply.

Joe opened the door and said, "Thank you."

"You're welcome," Mr. Solomon said and began working on the door.

Joe didn't want to leave the landlord there by himself, so he leaned against the nearby wall and watched the man prepare the door for the lock.

"I'm going to the park with my granddaughter this afternoon," Mr. Solomon said as he continued to work. "She just loves the swings. And she's always making new friends whenever she goes. It's fun to watch."

The sound of the drill caused Mr. Solomon to stop talking for a few moments. Then he continued to tell Joe all about his granddaughter, who was only four and lived a few blocks away. It was clear that the man loved her dearly.

"There you go!" Mr. Solomon said as he finished.

"Thank you," Joe said. He felt lighter than he had in a long while. "And enjoy the time with your granddaughter."

"Betsy," he said. "I will." He tipped his cap good-bye and sauntered down the hallway.

Joe closed the door and leaned against it. Looking around his apartment, he was struck by the sun streaming through the kitchen window. He looked out and saw that it was a beautiful day. Mr. Solomon's plan of going to the park sounded appealing. He put on a light jacket and jogged down the stairs. A few blocks later his stomach growled, and Joe realized he'd completely forgotten to eat breakfast.

He glanced down the street and spotted a coffee shop. Normally, he'd never think to go in, but today felt different. The people on the street didn't seem unfriendly. In fact, a few people had actually smiled at him as they passed.

He walked into the crowded coffee shop and stood in line. The woman in front of him wore a large-rimmed, black hat. When she was done ordering, she looked back at him and smiled, then walked quickly out the door.

Joe cleared his throat and looked at the menu. It had been about a year since he'd stepped foot inside one of these shops. There were so many options and he didn't want to ask what they all meant, so he just ordered a black coffee and a blueberry scone that he saw in the display case.

The barista, who appeared to be in his early twenties, repeated back his order, then smiled. "Your order has been taken care of by the woman who just left."

Joe stared at him.

"What?" he asked. He realized that might sound a little rude, so he added, "I mean . . . I don't understand." It must be some kind of trick. He looked around to see if there were any cameras or if there might be a group of people laughing at him in the corner.

The barista said, "The lady in front of you paid for your order."

"But why?" Joe asked. "I don't get it."

The woman behind him tapped him on the shoulder, causing him to jump. He turned back, expecting her to yell at him for taking so long. Instead she smiled and said, "It's called 'paying it forward.' You do something nice for someone and hope they do something nice for someone else."

Joe nodded, but didn't understand. "So, I should pay for you, then?"

"No," she said with a little laugh. "That's not necessary. Just enjoy the gift. A gift from a stranger."

Joe nodded again. He took his coffee and scone and thanked the barista.

As he left, a portly man held open the door for him to exit. Joe thanked him and walked down the street. He took a bite of the scone and stopped in his tracks. It was the best scone he'd ever tasted!

He felt as if his taste buds were alive, savoring the sensation and flavors of the blueberries and pastry as they dissolved in his mouth. Joe also marveled at the sunlight slanting down, bringing out the vibrancy of the buildings, the cars, and clothing. The people on the street were dressed in such a variety of styles and looked lovely. He took a sip of his coffee and again had to stop.

It was delicious.

By the time he got to the park, Joe had demolished both his scone and the coffee. He found a spot on a bench and watched the kids playing on the swing set.

"Push me, push me!" a girl in pigtails cried out to her father.

How he'd loved the swings when he was a kid. He had felt like he was flying, free of the constraints of gravity.

"Higher, higher!" he'd cried when his grandmama pushed him. He seemed to touch the azure sky with his feet. "Higher!"

"You got it, Joey!"

She'd always laugh and give him another push. He loved those days in the park. It was a respite from the arguing at home. His parents dutifully waited to get a divorce until he left for college. They felt it was best for him to have stability at home.

Joe guessed they probably had no idea that he spent most nights buried under the covers with his hands over his ears, wishing he were anywhere else.

Each weekend, his grandmama would take him out someplace. She didn't have a lot of money, but she always made each outing special.

A single tear fell from his eye when he thought about her passing the previous spring. It had been so sudden. She was just sitting in her apartment, watching her favorite detective show, when someone broke in and robbed her. The police said that she had been bludgeoned with a lamp and left to die.

He was all alone now.

The afternoon passed, and the sun crept down toward the horizon. Joe stood up, realizing he needed to return home before dark. He hadn't seen Mr. Solomon and his granddaughter, but then again, the park was huge. As he stretched his muscles, he realized he'd been sitting in one place for hours.

Suddenly, out of nowhere, Joe felt a blinding pain from a strike to his left temple. He turned to see a soccer ball bouncing away.

He looked around to see who had attacked him. When he noticed a few boys standing shyly off to the side, he relaxed.

"I'm real sorry, mister," one said, his voice trembling.

The others looked scared, too, and Joe realized they hadn't meant to hurt him. He was touched that they were concerned about his welfare.

"It's OK," he said as he jogged over to the ball. He picked it up and gave them a small smile. "I'm OK."

He tossed the ball back to them, and they ran off. The one who'd apologized turned and waved to him. Joe smiled and returned the wave.

As the sun kissed the horizon, Joe reached for the door to his building. He paused and turned to look at the deep, rich colors in the sky. It seemed like a canvas with orange and red blending in the lower half of the sky. He moved off to the side and waited until the sun fully disappeared and the colors muted before he entered his building.

Joe took the stairs two at a time, enjoying the feeling of energy coursing through him. When he reached his door, he unlocked the three deadbolts and went inside. He made dinner and turned on the news.

It felt like someone had dumped cold, dirty dishwater over his head. The reports were all about children who had been found decapitated, a murderer who had escaped from a maximum security prison, and a new bioweapon that had accidentally spilled in Asia.

He pushed the tasteless food around his plate and, with a jolt, realized he'd forgotten to lock the door. He jumped up and locked all three dead bolts before going to bed. The dishes could wait another day.

***

The next morning, Joe collected his newspaper and eyed it warily. He made breakfast, but chose to read a book instead. As he ate, he thought about the previous day and how wonderful it had been to watch the kids play in the park. There had been so much laughter and joy.

He put on his jacket, jogged down the stairs, and headed back out to the park. If only he could recreate that feeling.

As Joe waited for the light to turn at one of the street corners, he stood behind two women. They were glued to their phones, talking to one another without looking up.

"Jerry's coming over tonight," the woman in front of him said. She had long, blond hair that was pulled back in a neat ponytail.

"Isn't he the computer geek?" her brunette friend muttered.

"Yup," the ponytail said. "I like them smart."

They fell silent as they clicked their phones and waited. Finally, the chirp of the pedestrian walk signal sounded.

As the woman with the ponytail stepped off the curb, Joe spotted a white pickup truck barreling through the intersection. The driver was looking at his cell phone and only looked up when it was too late to do anything. His eyes locked with Joe's, and Joe knew he had only a moment to act.

"No, wait!" Joe cried out. The brunette looked at Joe with wide eyes and stopped, but the blond woman was oblivious.

"Janice!" shrieked the brunette as Joe grasped the ponytail and yanked the woman backwards.

"Ow!" she cried, dropping her phone and flailing backward. Joe grabbed her arm with the other hand and pulled her back onto the curb just as the truck whizzed past.

It was all over so fast it didn't seem real. Joe released the woman and stared at her in wonder.

The brunette stood gawking at Joe as her friend with the pony-tail pulled herself together. The man in the truck had slammed on his brakes and ran over to them.

"Is everyone OK? I'm so sorry," he said.

"You saved my life," the blond woman said to Joe. "Thank you!" She felt her body from head to toe to see if she was indeed uninjured.

Joe shook himself. "You're welcome."

He picked up the woman's phone, dusted it off, and handed it to her. "You might want to put that away until you get where you're going," he said.

"Yeah," the woman said, putting it into her purse. "I will."

The man in the truck thanked Joe repeatedly before he drove off. Joe stood watching everyone disappear down the street. He leaned against the lamp post and replayed the scene in his mind over and over again. What if he hadn't pulled that woman out of harm's way? He shuddered violently and reminded himself that he had saved her. It occurred to him that if he hadn't decided to go to the park today, she may not be alive now.

It took a while before Joe could bring himself to move. Finally, he carefully looked both ways and walked across the street. Many people greeted him on his way to the park. He stopped counting after ten and returned each of their smiles. He realized they weren't criminals. They were all friendly people, out enjoying the beautiful day.

Looking around, he saw many nice people. No one seemed angry or upset.

He walked around the trail in the park a few times. He noticed Mr. Solomon pushing his granddaughter on the swing. Joe called out to him and waved. Mr. Solomon waved back, as did the little girl.

As Joe continued to walk, he saw a rectangular, black, plastic card fall from a man's back pocket. He picked it up. It was a credit card.

He read the name and called out loudly to the man in front of him. "Are you Ralph Gardner?"

The man stopped abruptly and turned around. He sported a big, bushy mustache and a confused look. "Yes," he said tentatively. "Can I help you?"

Joe suddenly realized that the man might think that he had stolen the card. After all, it was now in his hand. He pushed those thoughts away and cleared his throat.

"I'm sorry. I think you dropped this. It's yours, right?"

The man's face split into a wide grin as his whole body relaxed. "Thank you! I'm forever dropping it out of that pocket. It's too shallow, you know? I shouldn't put it in there." He then gave a little laugh. "Can I give you a reward?"

Joe shook his head. "No need." Then he added. "I guess I'm just paying it forward."

The man nodded. "Cool!"

Later that evening, Joe picked up the phone and dialed the number on the takeout menu. The woman on the other end of the line was cheerful and even offered to throw in an extra eggroll since he was a new customer.

Joe grinned. *For you, Grandmama.*

***

Monday morning, on his way out the door, Joe stepped over the newspaper lying on the floor. He walked into his office building a little before eight. Larry was just ahead of him in the revolving door. As they both emptied their pockets for security, Joe turned to Larry.

"Hi there!" he said.

Larry did a little double take. "You know, I've never seen you here at this time. I used to wonder if you lived at the office. You just always seem to be here!"

Joe laughed. "Yeah, I know. I used to always come in early."

"Well, it's nice to see you. How was your weekend?"

Joe followed him to the elevator banks and told him about his walks to the park and how he'd seen the most beautiful sunsets. He continued to chat as he got into the elevator and only noticed the crush of people when he was inside, backed against the rear wall.

Odd, but there was no feeling of dread. As he looked around, he recognized a few people from his floor and said hello to them.

When they reached the fifth floor, the people up front moved aside to let him out. Joe nodded in thanks and continued to tell Larry about his weekend.

When he got to the point where he saved the woman, Larry abruptly stopped in the middle of the corridor.

"You did *what*?" he asked. "That's incredible!"

"Yeah, it was," Joe said with a smile. "It was amazing, actually."

The two resumed walking, and when Larry reached his cubicle he said, "Hey, Joe."

"You can call me Joey."

"Yeah? That suits you. OK, Joey. You want to join a bunch of us for lunch today? We usually go to Rex's for sandwiches on Mondays. It's a thing."

Joe felt a burst of pleasure course through him. "Yeah, that sounds good."

"We'll meet up at the elevators at noon."

Joe grinned and sat down at his desk.

It was going to be another good day.

# JENNIFER

STORY #6 IN THE DISCOVERING KINDNESS SERIES

## Kevin J. Smith
with Laura Sherman

Jennifer opened the front passenger window of her mother's Chevy sedan. She closed her eyes, took a deep breath, and then opened them again to watch the neighborhood zip by. She relished the way her long, blond hair whipped her face along with the feeling of the wind on her cheeks.

"You don't have to do this, you know," her mother said.

Jennifer turned back toward her and noticed that her mother's hands were shaking on the wheel. Her lips were pulled back in a taut line as she kept her eyes steadily on the road.

"I do," Jennifer replied. "I promised."

Her mother gave Jennifer a quick glance, then settled her eyes back on the road. That look spoke volumes. It was almost as if the petite woman who loved and cared for her felt betrayed by Jennifer's acceptance of the job interview.

"I'll never understand why you told Sally you'd teach again so soon after the accident," she said.

Jennifer balanced her head on her hand, propped up by her elbow in an effort to stop the world from suddenly spinning in slow circles. She had to concentrate to keep the contents in her stomach from spilling out.

*Deep breaths.*

When she closed her eyes, she could see the white pickup truck coming at her from the right. There had been nothing she could do to avoid the drunk driver that evening.

*Think about something else.*

It was a nice thought, but impossible. She could no more ask the sun to stop its ascent into the sky than push these unwanted images from assailing her at random times of the day and night.

Jennifer shuddered as she felt the shards of glass slicing through her skin and heard the horrible sound of metal and bone crunching. The smell of burning oil and rubber made her gag, even though it was only a recollection.

How long would it take before these memories would stop punching her in the gut? The doctors kept telling her to give it time.

*How much time?*

No one could answer that.

Her eyes were still closed when she felt the car come to a stop and heard her mother turn off the engine. She needed a moment. Opening her eyes seemed too much of a trial.

"Just say the word, and I'll take you home," her mother whispered.

Jennifer shook her head, forced herself to sit up straight, and opened her eyes. "No, Mother. I'm not turning back now."

Besides, she was dying to get out of the car. She feared this morning's cheese omelet would resurface if she didn't get out of the vehicle.

Her mother sighed and opened her door. She walked around to the trunk, pulled out the wheelchair, and brought it to the passenger side. Jennifer was a pro at this now. She could swivel around and hop into the chair.

Jennifer looked up at the campus around her. It hadn't changed much since the previous February. Everstone Preparatory Academy was still as manicured and imposing as it'd ever been. She had missed this home away from home. Pushing her way up the winding walkway, she could feel her breathing return to normal.

"Come on," her mother said, indicating a bench to the right. "Let's talk for a moment."

Jennifer followed her over and waited for her to sit down. She breathed in the scent of the nearby honeysuckle and roses. When her mother settled into her seat, she looked at her daughter.

"I don't think this is a good idea," she said with a ragged sigh.

Jennifer tamped down her bubbling irritation. "I know, Mother. You've told me at least a hundred times since I got the call last night."

"It's just that the last time you ventured off . . . well, you know what happened . . ." Her voice trailed off, prompting Jennifer to consider the past and fill in the gaps.

It worked.

Again, Jennifer found herself ripped from the present back into another time that she preferred not to remember.

\*\*\*

A few months ago, Jennifer's physical therapist had encouraged her to get out into the world quickly and learn her way around. Although she'd emphasized taking it slowly, Jennifer hadn't listened to that part of the advice. Never one to be patient, she was determined to be independent as soon as possible. Besides, she'd been dying to get out after her long confinement. In college, she'd been on the diving team, so jumping into the deep end had always been her mode.

Her mother had been against her venturing into the city by herself, so Jennifer had left the house early in the day, before her mother had risen. She didn't want to risk being be talked out of her decision.

Jennifer managed to push herself toward an elevator at the Metro station. It had been slow going, navigating through the throngs of people. When she arrived, she discovered it was out of order. The disappointment nearly swallowed her whole, but she was determined not to let anything stand in her way. She located a second elevator and prayed it was working. She rejoiced when she saw the doors open. However, there were twenty people waiting to get into the small space.

It took twenty minutes before she could get on the elevator car, but the people accommodated her and gave her room. It was cramped and she could smell the sweat of the two men to the right, but she was there and on her way. By the time she wheeled herself out, her nerves were frayed. She was exhausted.

She considered going home. Her mother was probably still fast asleep and wouldn't have had a chance to read her note. She'd never have to know that Jennifer had failed.

Jennifer tried to reason with herself that she'd done enough for the day. After all, she'd managed to venture out from her home. That was something, right?

No. It wasn't enough.

She wanted to see the new rose blooms in the free botanical gardens. Of course, her mother would take her in a heartbeat, but that wasn't the point. She needed to go completely on her own. She thought of the sweet and spicy fragrances of the different varieties, and put her hands on the wheels and pushed forward.

The platform wasn't too crowded. The stop was toward the beginning of the line, so there wasn't a crush to get on the train. It wasn't easy, but she was able to navigate from the platform onto the car and put the brakes on her chair before the train lurched forward. Her heart hammered as she locked her eyes on the digital map display.

*Four more stops. Then I'm there.*

People poured into the car at the next stop, and by the third stop, bodies were pressed against each other. Men and women enveloped her space, and again she could smell their body odor as they pressed against her chair. Jennifer focused on breathing in and out, reminding herself that she only had one stop to go. As the train slowed, she prepared herself to roll off the train, but there were so many people in front of her. She asked them to let her pass, but nobody took notice. She spoke too softly. It was like those dreams she'd had as a child: when she'd tried to scream, but only a whimper came out.

By the time Jennifer made herself heard, the doors of the train car closed again. Frustration got the better of her, and she felt hot tears wet her face. She couldn't stifle her sobs no matter how hard she tried. The others on the train noticed her and her plight. When they reached the next stop, people moved out of the way. She thanked them and did her best to ignore the looks of pity in their eyes.

Safely on the platform, she watched the train pull away. It was only then that she realized it wasn't an easy matter to board the returning train. Fear gripped her as she realized that she would need to take two elevators to reach it.

*Would they be working?*

With trembling hands, she pulled out her phone and asked her mother to pick her up. The car ride home was miserable. She barely registered her mother's shrill criticism as she sank into her seat under the weight of defeat. By the time they made it home, she was trembling and sweating. It had taken her two hours to accomplish nothing. On top of that, she had to spend the next few months listening to her mother cluck her tongue at her as if Jennifer had somehow wronged her.

***

Jennifer shook her head to free herself from the images from the past. "That was months ago, Mother. I was still getting used to this contraption."

"The odds are stacked against you. This world isn't made for the handicapped."

Jennifer closed her eyes against the onslaught of dizziness. "Why do you insist on labeling me?" she muttered.

When she opened her eyes, she saw Sally approaching with a spring in her step that made Jennifer instantly jealous. What she'd give to walk again.

"Hey there!" Sally said as she tucked her long, auburn hair behind her right ear. "It's great to see you."

Jennifer instantly felt better. Her breaths stopped coming out in halting jerks. "Same here."

"Come on, let's go into my office. We can talk about the class," Sally said.

Jennifer's mother shook her head and looked pointedly at Sally. "I'm going to say it again. I think this is a mistake. Jennifer's not ready for this."

Jennifer put her hand up. "Mother, please."

"Don't worry, Mrs. Chary," Sally said with a cheerful smile. "I'll watch out for her."

When Jennifer's mom stood up and made to follow them, Sally turned to her and said, "I'll bring your daughter home in a few hours. There's no need for you to stick around."

"It's OK," Jennifer added as her mother prepared to object. "I'll be back in time for dinner."

With a long, drawn-out sigh, Jennifer's mother agreed and shuffled back to her car as if a large weight were attached to her ankles.

Jennifer watched her go, then turned and said, "She means well."

"I know."

They made their way across the campus. Children were filing out of the classrooms and making their way to various sporting fields and elective activities. Jennifer realized that in her five-year stint teaching at this prep school prior to the accident, she had never seen anyone, student or faculty, in a wheelchair. As she pushed herself forward, the movement around her seemed to slow. A few of her former students waved tentatively, and she smiled at them.

She passed a group of sixth graders as she rolled under the covered walkway. They watched her closely as she maneuvered around a pillar. Jennifer smiled at them, too, but they just continued to stare, as if she were an exhibit at the zoo. She blushed and looked away.

Sally put her hand on Jennifer's shoulder. "Some of them might need to get used to you. Don't worry about it."

Jennifer nodded and avoided looking at anyone else as she focused on negotiating the passageway. When they reached the entrance of the admin building, Sally held the door open. Jennifer pushed her way down the hall and into Sally's office. She parked in front of the desk and waited for Sally to sit down.

Sally folded her hands on the desk and leaned forward. "Thank you so much for coming in on such short notice. I can't tell you how much your students missed you. How much we all missed you. You were one of our best teachers."

"I've missed you, too. I loved working with the seventh graders. I loved working here. It's just . . ."

Sally waited a moment before saying, "What is it?"

"It's just that I think my mother might be right. I'm not sure I'm ready to come back."

Sally leaned back. "I had planned to give you more time. Really, I had. It's just I don't know what else to do. We're losing teachers left and right with this class."

"What's the biggest issue?"

"The kids just aren't engaging. They are good children, but they're acting up in class."

"All of them?"

Sally ran a hand through her hair. "Well, no. There's Nathan, who's having some trouble fitting in. He's not our typical student. The Spencer family decided to foster a child this year and asked us to place him here. He's on the verge of being expelled. It's probably appropriate to call him *at risk*."

Jennifer closed her eyes. "Does he know he's considered at risk?"

"You mean do we call him that to his face? No. Of course not."

"But I'll bet he knows," Jennifer said with a sigh. "Those kinds of labels don't help anyone."

Sally gave her a small smile. "See, you're already halfway there to understanding the problem and you haven't even stepped foot in the classroom. So you'll help us, won't you?"

Jennifer nodded. "Let's see how it goes, but yeah, that's my intention."

\*\*\*

Jennifer was happy to be in bed, reading a book. It had been a long day. She glanced up to see her father leaning against the doorjamb to her bedroom. "So, I heard you're going to have a trial day at school tomorrow."

Jennifer grinned. "Yes. I'm excited. But also a bit nervous."

He came into the room and sat on the edge of her bed. "What're you nervous about?"

"That I'm not up to it. Mom says I'm not ready yet."

He picked up her hand and gently held it. "And what do you think?"

She closed her eyes and thought. She squeezed his hand and opened her eyes. "I'm ready. I want to get back to teaching. I miss the kids."

"Good. You'll be incredible," he said as he stood up. "Give 'em hell, darling."

\*\*\*

The next morning, Jennifer arrived a full hour early to the classroom. Seventh grade. That was the sweet spot in her book. The kids weren't all overwhelmed by their hormones yet, but they were old enough to have strong opinions about many things. It was just a matter of helping them find their way, giving them direction and an outlet for their passions.

Jennifer shifted in her chair and picked up the Social Studies folder. She read over the lesson plans. The class had gotten through the segment on the foundations of the American government, but the test results were poor. Way below the expected average.

As she continued to study the folder, she noticed there were four different sets of handwriting.

*Four teachers in two months? That has to be part of the problem.*

When the first bell rang, Jennifer looked toward the door and waited for the students to come in. They didn't disappoint. They'd been trained to be punctual.

"Come in, come in," she called from behind the desk.

The children filed in, dressed in their polo shirts and khaki pants. She smiled at each one as they looked at her with curiosity. Then, trailing behind, came a boy who stared at the floor. He took a seat at the back corner and immediately slouched down.

*Must be Nathan.*

Jennifer called roll, then took a moment to introduce herself. While she was talking, she could have sworn Nathan pretended to cough and say the word, "cripple." A few of the other kids laughed nervously, while a boy with spikey red hair glowered at him. She looked at her seating chart and saw that it was George Spencer.

*That must be Nathan's foster brother.*

She decided it would be best to ignore the comment and launched into the next social studies lesson. She did her best to engage the students, but only a few were interested.

Jennifer completed the social studies lesson, then moved on to math. When she turned her back, she heard a girl shriek in pain. She turned around to see a girl with pigtails rubbing her arm.

"Melissa? Are you OK?" Jennifer asked.

"Yes, ma'am," she said.

Jennifer noticed that Nathan was smirking at the girl. "What happened?" she asked.

"Nothing," Melissa responded.

Jennifer could tell Melissa didn't want to talk about it, so she quickly got the students started on the algebra worksheets.

Later in the day, she did her best to get the children to share their thoughts on *Oliver Twist*, which they had been reading, but most looked bewildered. She called on Nathan, and he responded by grabbing his backpack and storming out the door just as the last bell rang. Jennifer sighed with relief while the students got up and shuffled to the door. They streamed past Sally, who entered with an expectant smile.

"How did it go?"

"There were definitely some challenges. I see what you're dealing with here."

Sally raised her eyebrows. "Well?"

Jennifer laughed. "Yes, I'll take the job."

"Wonderful! We can discuss details and strategies over a cappuccino."

Jennifer nodded. "With an extra shot of espresso."

"You got it. It's probably been a while since you've been to Georgio's."

"Yeah, I miss that little shop."

As Jennifer pushed her way down the path, she noticed Nathan sitting under a tree reading a book while other kids formed groups around the courtyard. This was their free time. Most were on their cell phones or gaming devices.

"Give me a minute," Jennifer said to Sally.

Sally nodded. "I'll pop into my office and get a cardigan."

Jennifer wheeled closer to Nathan and her eyes widened when she saw that he was reading a worn copy of *Lord of the Rings*. "That's one of my favorites!" she commented.

He didn't look up at her and continued to read.

"Is that your copy?" she asked.

He stiffened, then looked up at her. "I didn't steal it, if that's what you mean."

"No, no," she said. "That's not what I meant. It's just that it looks well-read."

He shrugged. "I like to read it. My dad gave it to me."

"Oh, Mr. Spencer?"

His look turned glacial. "No." Then his head dropped, and he went back to reading.

Jennifer winced at her error. She spotted Sally waiting for her at the end of the walkway. It looked as if she was avoiding looking directly at Jennifer, probably in an effort to give her and Nathan a little privacy.

"Look, I'm sorry," she said to his bowed head. She waited a moment. When he didn't look up or respond, she continued. "You know, my father gave me a copy of *Huckleberry Finn* when I was young. I still have it. The cover's missing because I read it so many times."

Nathan didn't look up, but he murmured. "That's a good book."

Jennifer smiled at his bent head. She debated engaging him in further conversation, but didn't want to ruin the moment. So she wheeled away with a quiet, "So long." Halfway to Sally, she turned back to see that he was watching her leave.

\*\*\*

Saturday morning, Jennifer woke up to the delicious smells of her mother's cooking. She was starved. The previous night she'd been so tired that she went straight to bed. She could identify bacon and eggs, and figured blueberry muffins were probably browning in the oven.

Jennifer got dressed and made her way to the kitchen. Her mother was wearing her favorite apron, a bright yellow one with peaches all over. Jennifer hesitated in the doorway. Though she was hungry, she wasn't ready for another confrontation with her mother.

Her mother took the pan of muffins from the oven and looked up. "Good morning," she said with a tight smile.

"Good morning," Jennifer replied, taking her place at the table. "Is Father gone already?"

"Yes, he had to go into the office earlier." She made Jennifer a plate and set it in front of her. "Enjoy!"

Jennifer dug in. This breakfast feast was just what she needed. Everything tasted so good. Maybe she'd be allowed to eat in peace.

Just then her mother sat down across from her. "You were so tired last night I didn't want to bother you, but tell me, how did it go at school yesterday?"

"Good," Jennifer lied after she swallowed. No need to share all the stresses of the job with her. Then she took another bite. "I'm definitely needed."

Her mother nodded. "I'm sure you are. You're a great teacher. It's just, how are you going to get back and forth each day?"

"I'll learn the bus route," Jennifer said. "A lot of people do it."

"You do realize that I won't always be around to pick you up. What if you get tired?"

Jennifer put down her fork. "Then I'll get tired. Everyone gets tired."

"But you're not like everyone else," her mother said. "I don't mean any disrespect by that, but it's true. You need to face facts. You're handicapped."

Jennifer pulled away from the table. The food no longer was appetizing. "It's sad that you see me that way, Mother."

"Don't be like that. You know that I'm just trying to help."

"What is it you want for me? To stay here inside the house all day, every day?"

"We can support you. Your father works so hard and we have savings. And I'm happy to take you out whenever you want. We have fun together, don't we?" Her mother's eyes looked pleading to Jennifer.

Jennifer nodded. "Yes, we do. And I love to spend time with you, but I need something else, too. I want to work. It's important to me."

Her mother let out a long sigh. "Well, if you think that's best."

"I do," she said. "Thank you for breakfast. I'm going out this morning."

"Out?"

She wheeled herself back to her room and collected her things before her mother could try to further discourage her.

Jennifer slowed as she reached the Metro station. Sweat beaded on her forehead as she forced her hands to move her wheelchair closer. Giving up on a goal wasn't something that ever sat well with her. At least this time she knew which one was the working elevator.

It was Saturday. No rush hour. She smiled as she got onto the train, and she realized it wasn't all that difficult. It would just take practice. When she got off, she made her way to the botanical gardens.

Although most of the roses had disappeared, there were many other flowers in bloom. Jennifer pulled out her sketch pad and enjoyed recording the details of the violas, pansies, mums, and asters. She also sketched the brightly colored autumn leaves. Next to each picture she wrote a three-line haiku describing her feelings and capturing the many sensations available to her.

*i miss the roses...*
*orange and yellow leaves crunch*
*beneath my wheels*

After a few hours, she realized she was happier than she'd been in a long while. Somehow capturing this special moment within her brief poems helped release some pent-up emotions and made her appreciate everything she had in the present.

The trip back on the Metro was a lot easier than the ride out. It wasn't long before Jennifer wheeled herself home and through the front door. She smiled at the smell of chocolate chip cookies wafting from the kitchen. It was just like when she was young and came back from soccer practice.

*What I wouldn't give to kick a ball.*

She shook her head. There was no use thinking that way. Today had opened the door to new possibilities, which stretched out beyond her childhood home.

Jennifer wheeled herself into the kitchen and stopped to watch her mother as she pulled out a pan from the oven. It was at that moment that she realized her mother only wanted to take care of her, to shield her from the harsh realities of the world.

She understood her mother's fears. She had them, too, but less so after today. Navigating the trip to the botanical gardens had given Jennifer a newfound confidence that she could succeed outside of her home.

She still had so much to give to the children, to contribute to the world. Being confined to a wheelchair wouldn't stop her.

"You're home," her mother said, turning around.

Jennifer smiled at how relieved she looked. "Yes, Mama."

"You haven't called me that in years," she whispered. "Come have some cookies."

"I'd love that. And I can tell you all about my day."

\*\*\*

Jennifer smiled as she rolled up to her classroom door. She was ready.

This morning, her mother had offered to drive her in, but Jennifer had insisted on taking the bus. She had made it to the school well before the first bell.

She settled into her position behind her large pine desk and waited for the children to arrive. Today would break records for being the best day ever. She would see to it.

As the children trickled in, she greeted them each by name. They looked surprised to see her back and a little taken aback that she'd learned their names. A few gave her a tentative smile, which she returned. Nathan rolled his eyes at her and took his seat in the back corner.

After she called roll, Jennifer paused and wheeled to the front of her desk. The children all watched her and remained quiet as she pulled forward.

"I wanted to let you all know that I will be your permanent teacher for the rest of the year. And today, we're going to do something a little different."

She spoke slowly, looking at each student in her class in turn. She was pleased that she was able to lock eyes with most of them, though Nathan seemed to be enthralled by something on the other side of the window. She suppressed a sigh and continued.

"I'll make a deal with you. If you work with me in the morning, if you trust me and give me your attention, we'll do a special project this afternoon."

There was a low murmur in the group, and the kids shot looks back and forth. She let it sink in a moment. Then one child raised her hand.

"Ma'am?" she said.

"You can call me Miss Jennifer. What's your question, Marion?"

Again, the kids looked back and forth. Then Marion said, "What sort of thing do you have in mind, Miss Jennifer?"

"We're going outside this afternoon."

There was a murmur, and three hands shot up.

Jennifer's eyes flitted over to Nathan, who looked away the moment their eyes met.

*He's interested.*

Jennifer smiled at the class. "I'm sure you have a ton of questions. Let's save them for after lunch. Surprises are nice, aren't they?"

The hands went down and a few of the kids nodded.

"I need your agreement, though. Do I have it?"

The kids all raised their hands to signify they agreed. All except Nathan. Jennifer hadn't expected him to be that easy. But at least he didn't disrupt the class again.

She spent the morning reviewing the previous lessons. Although the children weren't too eager to revisit the past chapters, Jennifer reminded them that the afternoon would be fun.

One by one, the students started to participate in the lessons and Jennifer was reminded of her former classes. It was always a challenge to get them rolling, but she'd never had a failed class. They had a lot of work ahead, but she now knew she could help them.

After lunch, the students came bouncing in, ready to learn about the afternoon's surprise. When they were all seated, Jennifer shared with them her love of haiku, explaining what the Japanese poetry was all about.

"It's really just about sharing a thought with the reader," she said. "Often you're comparing something from the present with a moment in time from the past."

George raised his hand. "But we did this in math class in third grade. It's all about counting syllables, right?"

"I don't get wrapped up in counting syllables," she said with a wave of her hand. "English-language haiku really is about communicating your idea in just a few words. Once you have it, try saying it in one breath. You'll find you can't do that if you have too many words."

She spent a while going over a few guidelines. The kids seemed interested. Even Nathan was surreptitiously listening, although doing a good job of pretending he wasn't.

Jennifer went over a few examples of great masters of the art.

"Here's one of my favorites from Katsushika Hokusai:

*i write, erase, rewrite*
*erase again, and then*
*a poppy blooms."*

She let the poem sink in then said, "What do you think?"

Nathan raised his hand and Jennifer felt her heart soar in her chest. She grinned. "Yes, Nathan?"

"That's how I feel when I write."

"Really? How?" Jennifer asked. She saw a few kids swivel in their chairs to look at him.

He shrugged. "I don't know."

"Come on. I'm interested," she said.

He stared at her for a moment, then said in a low voice. "Sometimes when I write, it just suddenly works. The ideas just pop out, you know? It's how I feel when I read and understand something, too."

George looked back at his brother. "That's kind of cool."

Nathan glanced at him and nodded. "I get what the poet's saying. It feels like a flower. It blooms."

Others murmured in agreement and turned back to Jennifer.

Jennifer suppressed the urge to clap her hands together. She knew she had to keep her cool. Instead, she kept her voice even and said nonchalantly, "I like it." Then she turned and addressed the whole class, "OK, so today we're going to go out into nature so you can find something that inspires you. You may bring along a journal and write notes. Some people draw a picture to go with their haiku. If you want to do that, you're welcome to."

"But won't you get into trouble for this?" George asked.

Jennifer shook her head. "Nope. And if I did, I wouldn't care."

The kids chattered excitedly as they followed Jennifer down the corridor and out into the courtyard. Jennifer instructed them to stay within sight, but gave them free rein. "I'll be here if you have questions."

Students scattered around the yard. A few clumped into groups and chattered quietly to one another. Jennifer let them be for a few minutes, then helped them find their own spots. Soon all the children were busily scribbling and drawing.

She noticed that Cassandra had taken out her cell phone and snapped a few pictures.

"It's OK to do a little research, too," Jennifer said. "I do that all the time. For instance, naming the specific flower or insect can help create a stronger image."

"I'm not sure how to do that," Cassandra said, handing her phone to Jennifer. On it was a picture of an ant.

Jennifer helped her look up the ant on a search engine based on the photo. "See here. This is a black garden ant."

"Cool."

"Now you can learn about it. If you like."

Cassandra clicked a few buttons and read. "It says here that they tunnel and loosen the soil. They are actually good for a garden!"

She continued to read, while Jennifer looked on. After five minutes she said, "Those guys are amazing. I like to watch them scurry down the path. They remind me of a time when my sister and I built a fort in our living room. We had all these tunnels and rooms. We had to strip all the beds in the house. Mom wasn't too happy, but she had to admit the fort was more like a castle."

Jennifer nodded. "You have the makings of an amazing haiku there."

"Really?" Cassandra said.

"Yeah. Absolutely. Just taking words that you told me, you could do something like:

*black garden ants . . .*
*crawling through living room forts*
*with my sister*

"Wow, I love your haiku!" Cassandra said.

"It's your haiku, you know," Jennifer replied. "I just made a few suggestions. There's a tradition in haiku where a mentor helps the author. The haiku always belongs to the creator not the mentor. I'm just here to help."

Cassandra thanked her again, then went off to a different area and explored the underside of a leaf. Jennifer smiled. This project was like a nature treasure hunt. It helped the students learn more about the world around them. At the same time they were learning to express their thoughts and feelings.

She spotted Nathan and wheeled over to him. He was sitting in the middle of the lawn with his head in his hands looking mutinously at the blades of grass.

Jennifer stopped a few feet away and said, "How's it going?"

He grunted, then looked up. "This is stupid."

She grimaced, then smoothed out her features. He was entitled to his feelings. "Tell me about it."

"Grass is grass. It doesn't symbolize anything. It doesn't have anything to do with me."

Jennifer nodded. "Fair enough. Is there a memory you want to share in your haiku?"

Nathan shrugged. "Don't know."

"OK."

Jennifer allowed the silence to linger. Looking around, she could see that the rest of the class was now fully absorbed in the project. The only sound was the occasional rustling as the wind swept through the autumn leaves.

"I miss my dad," he said after a moment. The statement startled Jennifer out of her musings.

"Can you tell me a little more about that?" she asked, her voice barely above a whisper.

"He left when I was ten. I don't know why."

Jennifer nodded. "That's rough."

"Yeah."

Silence fell again until he said, "We used to go to the park and share a sandwich on the grass. That's what I think of when I sit in this grass. I think of my father."

"Do you want to write a haiku about that?"

Nathan nodded. "But I don't know how."

"Tell me more about a moment in the park with your father," Jennifer said.

"We'd sit cross-legged on the grass while we ate. Our favorite was ham and cheese. The grass was soft and would sometimes stain my jeans, but I didn't care. Mom would complain about the dark green stains."

"You have a haiku in there. Do you have any ideas so far?"

Nathan nodded. "I think the image of the green stain works."

"Agreed!" Jennifer said. "You have a good eye for this."

"And I also think people can relate to ham and cheese sandwiches."

"Yup," Jennifer nodded.

They discussed the haiku back and forth, and in the end, Nathan came up with one he liked.

"How about:

*dark green stains*
*i share a ham and cheese*
*with my father*

After he spoke, their eyes met, and both seemed to know it was right. "Thank you," he said.

She nodded and watched him pull out his notebook and start writing. He didn't look up until she called all the students back in half an hour later.

Back in the classroom some of the students shared their haiku and drawings. They all asked if they could do that again.

"We can, but not every day. We can also explore other activities that you might enjoy," Jennifer said. "What sorts of things might you like to do?"

The students called out ideas, and she took notes. They mentioned soldering, cooking, chess, and many other very doable activities. Jennifer knew she'd have to run them by the headmaster, but she was certain they would be approved. The school had always been progressive and supportive of enrichment activities that complemented the standard curriculum.

***

After a few weeks, Jennifer was happily engaged in her new routines. Her class was rolling along, and the headmaster had given her permission to take up any activities she wished. The kids had almost caught up with their studies and seemed to have a new zeal for learning.

At home, she was getting along with her mother. Her confidence boosted by her success at school, Jennifer planned weekly outings with her parents. During these, she demonstrated her abilities so that her mother could see that she was capable of taking care of herself.

One Friday, her father came home earlier than usual. After dinner, Jennifer gave him a huge hug and sat with him by the fire. She regaled him with stories of her students and told him about the various lessons she had taught.

"I'm so proud of you," he said.

"Thank you, Papa."

He paused for a moment. "So, what's next for you?"

She looked into his warm brown eyes. "What do you mean?"

"Well, I'd imagine that you might like to have your own place again," he said. "Before the accident you had that little apartment not far from here."

She grinned at him. "Tired of having me around?"

"Never," he said quickly. "I just think it might be time to use those wings of yours to fly again."

She nodded. "I think I'm ready. I'm just not sure Mom is."

Her father waved his hands dismissively. "She will come around. I'll talk to her. She won't like it at first, but that shouldn't stop you."

Jennifer stared at the crackling fire for a few moments. "I actually started looking last night. I found a place three blocks from here. It sounds pretty perfect."

"I'm taking the day off tomorrow. Let's check it out together."

# BARRY

STORY #7 IN THE DISCOVERING KINDNESS SERIES

## Kevin J. Smith
### with Laura Sherman

Barry caressed the handrail as he descended the stairs. Oak. It had been one of the few home improvements he'd done over the last twenty-five years.

*Twenty-five years. Had it really been that long?*

He flicked on the light in the kitchen and pulled out the French press. Barry sighed with pleasure as he poured the organic Ethiopian blend he loved so dearly into the grinder. He might be broke and in foreclosure, but there were certain luxuries he refused to give up.

As the coffee steeped, he stood at the empty counter. The table and chairs were packed up in the moving van that was sitting in the driveway of their Houston home. The place was barren save the materials he kept out to make his coffee this one last time in this kitchen.

Barry picked up the bank's letter that was sitting on the marble-topped counter. Since it had arrived, it had been the center of his focus. Sandra had tried to place it in their filing cabinet, but he'd pulled it back out. It needed to be out in plain view. He refused to become complacent about it.

People had advised him not to worry so much about foreclosure. Mortgage companies had to send a letter warning you of impending doom, but the fact was the banks were overloaded by delinquent loans and couldn't follow up well. Jim, a colleague at his old job, confided that he and his family had been living free in their duplex for the last six months while the bank took its time dealing with their foreclosure.

"I figure we have another year or so," Jim had said.

Barry shook his head and put down the letter. He walked over to the kitchen window and studied the manicured lawn as he sipped his black coffee. Living with that kind of anvil poised over his head wasn't the life for him. No, he was supposed to be the provider. Of course, since he'd been "let go" two months ago from his job selling dental plans, he didn't feel very much like a provider. Resolutely, he quieted the anxiety that seemed to be always roiling in his stomach.

"Let go." Such a polite word for "fired."

As a result, Sandra was forced to pick up a second shift at the hospital. Barry had immediately hit the streets looking for employment, but companies willing to take a chance on a fifty-plus salesman were hard to find. Most were in the market for the "fresh" outlook of recent graduates. He did secure a part-time position at the local grocery store. That job hadn't done much except help pay the monthly minimum on his credit card bills.

Continuing to look out the kitchen window, he sighed as the world slowly brightened into day. He heard creaking up above and knew the sound of running water would soon fill the pipes.

Just like every other day.

Except today would be different.

Two hours later, Barry locked the front door for the last time and walked to the large moving truck. His wife, Sandra, and their youngest daughter, Cassandra, sat in their Honda Civic that had passed 100,000 miles a few months ago. He watched them. They were deep in discussion, and he wondered if Sandra was comforting Cassie again. She'd been in tears the night before.

"But you said you loved Houston," Cassie had said through hiccups. "Why can't we stay?"

He'd tried to explain, but her eight-year-old ears were obviously not listening. His little girl's whole world was here, and the idea of leaving was frightening.

Of course, he had to admit that his stomach was doing flips as he backed out of the driveway.

*Green Bay, Wisconsin.*

It was Sandra's hometown. Her father had used his connections to help her secure a position at a better salary than she'd been earning in Houston. With her level of experience and excellent references, the Green Bay hospital was eager to have her join their team.

"Dad?" Barry was startled out of his reverie. "What's Green Bay like?" his teenage daughter Michelle asked. She had opted to ride in the truck with him.

"It's been a while since I've been there, Mike," he replied. "You were just a twinkle in your mother's eye."

She rolled her eyes. "That nickname's still in play?"

He suppressed a grin. "Always."

He'd nicknamed her Mike before she'd become a teenager. He was grateful that she didn't insist he drop it. Too much was changing as it was.

"Do you think I'll like Wisconsin?"

Barry nodded. "I hope so."

"It gets cold."

"That will be a change for sure," he said with a sigh.

"I'm OK with that."

He turned to look at her. "Yeah?"

"Yeah," she said with a shrug. "I mean, I'm going to miss my friends and all, but I like the idea of seeing new places."

"And you'll make new friends easily. I know you will."

*And hopefully I will, too.*

\*\*\*

It took two days to arrive in Green Bay. They were exhausted, but happy to be there.

Barry and Sandra toured the duplex to ensure the movers had

placed all the furniture in the right rooms. The place was smaller than their home in Houston. Their king-sized bed took up nearly the entire bedroom, and the girls had to squeeze all their belongings into one room. Downstairs, the open floor plan couldn't make up for the fact that the kitchen was the size of a postage stamp.

"It's hard to imagine that this will feel like home," Barry said as he put his arm around Sandra.

"It will. Wait and see," Sandra said as she leaned into Barry.

"I call dibs," Mike's voice rang out.

"No fair!" Cassie shrieked. "I want that bed."

Sandra let out an exaggerated sigh and began to pull away from Barry. He pulled her back. "Let them sort it out. Do you really want to get in the middle of their argument?"

Sure enough, the cries from the other room diminished quickly.

Barry gave her a squeeze. "I'm sorry."

"For what?"

Barry looked around the cramped living room. "For this. I mean, the move."

She leaned into him. "It's fine."

"I feel like a failure."

The words had spilled out without his consent. Although they were true, he wouldn't have chosen to speak them. It landed too much of a burden on the recipient, his wife, who already had too much on her plate.

"You're not," she said.

What else could she say? She was his wife, his life partner. She was required to be supportive.

"I feel like one," he whispered. "I want to pamper you in luxury."

She laughed. It wasn't a sarcastic laugh of rejection of his high and mighty aspirations. Instead, it was a carefree and musical sound that made him smile and relax.

"I love you," she said. "I have no desire for pampering. I love being a nurse and I love helping the family. We're a team."

He gave her a long hug and bent his head to hover over her soft lips. "I love you with every fiber of my being," he murmured.

\*\*\*

The first three weeks went by quickly and, as Sandra had predicted, the small place became cozy and felt like home. Barry was relieved to get a job selling dental plans. He liked the office and his co-workers. He especially liked that it allowed him to bring home a decent paycheck. He hoped the extra money would allow Sandra to reduce her hours soon so they could go back to a more normal schedule.

Whatever normal was.

It was a small office, smaller than the one he'd worked at in Houston. Three salesmen and a secretary. The boss was rarely in, which puzzled him. In Texas, the manager was the first to arrive and the last to leave. Maybe this guy had figured out a better system.

Agnes, the pretty receptionist, had shoulder-length auburn hair. Her desk was the nerve center of the office, which was usually pretty empty. Very few customers walked through the door, as the sales force spent most of their days going from business to business selling the plans. By getting out every day, Barry quickly learned the layout and culture of Green Bay.

Still, it was cold calling, and he heard a wide variety of noes and very few yeses. Most people weren't rude, but many were standoffish. Barry was obviously an outsider, with his Texan clothing and accent. The rejections didn't bother him too much, though. He'd learned long ago to shrug off the noes and ask again and again. It was the only way to get customers.

Late May, Barry came back to the office a little earlier than usual to eat his sack lunch. Agnes was chatting with a young salesman in a way that made him feel a little awkward as he passed. It was almost as if he was interrupting a date.

He intended to hurry past her desk on his way to the break room when he heard the young girl say, "Yeah, I'll be surprised if this next paycheck doesn't bounce."

Barry turned back and asked, "What?" He momentarily forgot the rudeness of admitting that he'd just overheard their private conversation.

The two looked startled, and Agnes straightened a bit in her chair. "Uh, yeah," she said. She looked around, then continued in a low voice, "It's just that Mr. Caufield let it slip that the numbers have been down for the last four weeks. He's just not sure that he can continue to cover payroll. I mean, he wants to, but I'm not sure how he will."

"So, you're saying that the check I'll get on Friday might not clear?" Barry asked.

Agnes shrugged.

The young salesman cleared his throat, then said, "I have my resume out with three other companies."

Barry nodded, thanked them, then shuffled to the break room. He pulled his sandwich out from the refrigerator and began eating. It tasted like Styrofoam with turkey and mayo.

*I can't lose another job.*

\*\*\*

Two weeks later, Barry sat at the dining table with Sandra. The girls had eaten and excused themselves. He could hear the canned laughter of the TV show they were watching in the neighboring room.

"I need to look for a new job," he said, keeping his voice just above a whisper.

Sandra closed her eyes and slumped in her chair. "So..."

"Yeah, Agnes said her paycheck didn't go through."

She let out a frustrated sigh. "Is that even legal?"

"I'm not sure, but either way, there's nothing I can do about it."

They were silent for a moment. Then Sandra said, "So what will you do?"

"I'll start putting in applications today."

"Where?"

He shrugged. "Everywhere and anywhere."

"I just don't want to see you waste away at another grocery store. It's easy to apply, get in, and just get stuck forever."

"What do you suggest?"

She tilted her head. "What do you love to do?"

Barry leaned back and stared at the little figurines Sandra had placed in the china cabinet across the table from him. His mind drifted back decades. Growing up in Grand Rapids, Michigan, as the youngest of five kids, he and his siblings learned early on that any spending money they had would have to be earned. He'd done well, scrounging for coins behind the machines at the laundromat or under the jukebox at the local bar. He had to be quick before he was shooed away by the owner, but it usually paid off.

He turned to Sandra. "I was an eight-year-old skinny, little freckled-faced kid. The nuns at the Dominican convent would let me sell raffle tickets. I'd make a quarter per book selling door to door."

"What was the prize?"

"A brand-new Chevy. One ticket cost a quarter and five cost a dollar. Most people went for that."

She whistled low. "A buck for a chance at a car? I'd take those odds."

He grinned. "It wasn't a hard sell."

In the days when a candy bar cost a nickel and an ice cream was a dime, he was considered rich amongst his friends. He was never one to hold onto his wealth, though; his friends and siblings reaped the benefit of his ingenuity. He had to admit, he liked the feeling of the awe and admiration his buddies would send his way when he pulled out a crisp dollar bill to pay the tab at the soda fountain.

Selling things was something that came naturally to him. His father always said that he'd do well to fan the flames of passion for sales.

"If you can sell, you'll never starve," he used to say.

Barry sat up in his chair. "I think I'll head down to the Green Bay Chamber of Commerce event tomorrow. There'll be vendors from all over town. Someone's got to be hiring."

"What about that company you were telling me about last night? You know, the financial planning business?"

Barry snapped his fingers. "Yeah! E.L. Anderson. I love their philosophy. In a world full of greed, they really seem to care about their clients."

Sandra stood up to clear the plates. "I looked them up. They have a branch in the downtown area."

"Really?" he asked, his eyebrows raised. "That's amazing."

"Maybe they'll be at the meeting tomorrow."

\*\*\*

There were dozens of companies at the chamber of commerce meeting. Barry's eyes were immediately drawn to the green and white E.L. Anderson logo with its large weeping willow tree. When he approached the booth, a balding thin man with a pencil mustache greeted him.

"My name is Sheldon," he said, handing him his card. "Are you looking for financial planning help?"

Barry had to concentrate not to laugh. The last thing he needed was direction on investing his non-existent capital. "Not exactly. I was wondering if you might be hiring."

"Not at the moment, but you should come in for an interview."

Barry's shoulders sagged. "Sure. Sounds good."

"We do hire regularly," Sheldon said. "But we train our sales force, so we can't take on too many at a time."

Barry thanked him and walked on. He skipped the next booth. Lawn care. Not his thing. He perused the next few, then stopped at another financial planning firm. The squat man behind the table looked him up and down, and handed him a card.

The man smiled at Barry in a way that looked like he rarely used his facial muscles. "I'm Mr. Pagosa," he said.

Barry took the white business card. "Thank you. Are you hiring?"

The man's smile vanished. "Maybe. Do you have any experience?"

"No. But I'm a fast learner."

The man rolled his eyes, then said with a long exhale. "Fine. Come in tomorrow. Four pm. Sharp."

"Thanks!" Barry said. "I'll be there."

\*\*\*

The woman in the car behind Barry leaned on her horn for a full three seconds, making him tremble in a combination of discomfort and anger. He looked at his watch for the third time in the last minute.

*Come on...*

It was three minutes until the interview, and he was in the wrong lane on the wrong street. He'd left himself a good fifteen minutes, but didn't anticipate faulty directions and traffic. There was no getting around it, he was going to be late.

*Please, please let me in.*

The woman honked again and again. Barry tried to tune it out. He tried not to care as the horn sounded a fourth and fifth time. Finally, the driver to his left took pity on him and allowed him to shift lanes.

He spotted the office, parked in the garage, and got into the elevator. He was ten minutes late. Barry adjusted his tie and pulled down his jacket to create a nice line in the shoulders.

Maybe their clocks were running late, too. Should he admit he was late or simply pretend that he was on time and his wristwatch was off? Or maybe the boss just wouldn't care.

When the elevator doors opened, the large nautical-style clock on the wall proclaimed he was, in fact, seventeen minutes late.

The secretary looked at him, then looked at her watch and back at him. "Mr. Smith?" she asked with a frown.

He gulped. "Yes, ma'am."

She hit the intercom and announced his presence. Barry stared at the black phone, expecting to hear Mr. Pagosa's voice when the door to left opened and the man popped out.

The man scowled at him. "Well, come in."

"I'm sorry I'm late," Barry said softly.

Mr. Pagosa grunted as he indicated the chair in front of his desk. "Not a great start, I'll tell you."

"Yes, sir. I'm sorry, sir."

"Fine, fine," he said as he let out a large gust of air and sat down. He pulled out a legal-sized sheet of paper with a lot of printed questions. "Let's start with a basic questionnaire."

The first few questions were routine identification questions. Then Mr. Pagosa began asking about Barry's personal assets and bank account information.

"I'm sorry. Is this part of the interview?" Barry asked.

Mr. Pagosa furrowed his brows. "This is a financial analysis sheet. The first step for anyone who walks through that door. And if you want to work here, we'd expect you to purchase our products, right? That's really a first step. You've got to know what you're selling."

Barry leaned back in his chair. "I don't have any assets and our bank account is pretty dry. That's why I need employment."

"So, you have nothing to invest? How about life insurance. Do you have any?"

"Can't afford it. Not at the moment," Barry said.

Mr. Pagosa crumpled the legal sheet and tossed it into the garbage can next to his desk. "So, let me get this straight. You have no experience. You have no assets. Maybe you have a ton of connections in Green Bay?"

Barry shook his head slowly. "We just moved here."

Mr. Pagosa let out an exasperated laugh. "So, *why* should I hire you?"

Barry felt his mouth go dry. He didn't want to repeat that he was a fast learner. After all, that answer hadn't impressed Mr. Pagosa yesterday. "I-I really would like to work in financial planning." Well, that probably wasn't the best answer, but at least it was the truth. "And when I can, I would like to invest."

"Get real. I didn't ask you why you wanted me to hire you. I know you want a job, and I assume you want one in financial planning because you're here. But why would I waste thousands of dollars to train you? What on earth do you have to offer *me*?"

Barry felt cold sweat drip down the collar of his shirt. "I-I d-don't know," he stammered. He wanted to say that he'd make it worth the man's time and that he'd give it everything he had. He was good at sales and just knew he could help people improve their financial condition. However, it was clear that Mr. Pagosa would probably laugh at him if he voiced those thoughts, so he said nothing more.

"Well, I do. Not much. I'm not interested. No, thank you," Mr. Pagosa said, standing up. He glared at Barry and indicated that he should leave. "You can find your way out, I'm guessing."

Barry stood up and thanked him. For what, he wasn't sure, but it seemed right. It was the polite thing to do. When he crossed the threshold of the man's door, he heard Mr. Pagosa mutter, "Why would anyone in their right mind hire someone like that?"

Barry flinched as if he'd been doused with a bucket of cold water. He didn't turn around to look at him, nor did he look the secretary in the eye, but kept on walking to the elevators. When the doors shut, he sagged against the shiny brass wall and concentrated on not allowing tears to spill down his face.

By the time Barry got home and walked through his front door, he felt like a rag doll, ready for bed. Sandra came out of the kitchen with an apron on. Her nose was slightly dusted with flour. She handed him a glass of red wine and said, "I'm making white lasagna."

He groaned as the aroma suddenly hit him. "That's our congratulatory meal. I'm not sure I deserve it."

"It can be a commiseration meal just as easily," she said with a lop-sided grin. "Whatever works."

He took a long swig of wine and felt the warmth envelop him. "It was a tough day. I was just going to lie down."

"Nah," she said, pulling him into the kitchen. "You're too young to take a late afternoon nap. Come, keep me company. You can tell me all about it."

Barry allowed her to lead him to the small table in the corner of the kitchen. The wooden chair creaked under his weight as he relaxed into it. He took another sip, then proceeded to tell her all about the job interview.

"Sounds like he was prospecting for clients," Sandra said. "Not a good sign when someone's so desperate for clients they pretend to give job interviews."

He sat up. "By God, you're right! That isn't ethical."

She shrugged. "You can't fault him for trying. But it does strike me that he isn't in the business to help people. He's just trying to make a quota."

"He seemed pretty irritated that I didn't have any assets."

"It sounds like it just wasn't meant to be," Sandra said as she opened the oven and closed it again. "Another ten minutes."

"I can't wait!"

She laughed. "You always forget it needs to cool for another twenty after that." She pulled out some crackers and cheese and made a little plate for him. "I know how red wine goes to your head."

Barry munched on the crackers and let his mind wander. He took another sip, and the green and white logo of the weeping willow flitted across his mind. He sat up and pulled out his wallet. He slipped out the card that Sheldon had given him at the chamber of commerce meeting and looked at it.

"I should give E.L. Anderson a call. That guy was pretty nice."

Sandra smiled. "Sounds like a good plan."

***

Barry left thirty minutes early for his appointment. Just to be sure. But this time he didn't need the extra time. He arrived at the offices of E.L. Anderson ahead of schedule. As he sat in his car waiting, he replayed the last interview over and over in his mind. What if this one ends the same way?

*Why would anyone in their right mind hire you?*

He couldn't get that question out of his mind. He knew he needed to answer it. So he took stock. He was dressed for success. That was something. He glanced at his resume. It was good. Lots of prior sales experience and positive references. Plus, he had a college degree. That meant something with some people.

*The reason why someone would hire me*, he reasoned, *is that I'm damn good at sales.*

Barry glanced at his watch and turned off the engine. It was ten minutes before the appointment. It wouldn't hurt to be early. Not too early, mind you, but just enough to show eagerness without desperation.

When he walked into the office, he noticed the atmosphere was relaxed. The employees smiled at him as they moved about. The secretary was cheerful and directed Barry to the small waiting room while she called Sheldon. The furniture in the waiting room was comfortable, and the walls were painted a soothing blue. Barry picked up a magazine but couldn't focus on the words.

Precisely at 10 am, Sheldon came out of his office, gave him a smile and waved him on in. He wore a brightly colored bow tie, which somehow put Barry immediately at ease.

Barry handed Sheldon his resume and took in the large office. There were artifacts from all over the world; it was as though he'd stepped into a museum rather than a financial planning office. As his eyes swept the walls, he saw photos from various continents.

"I like to travel," Sheldon said simply.

"Where was that one taken?" Barry asked, pointing to a picture of a large mountain with a thin stream of water flowing down it.

"That's called Angel Falls. It's in Venezuela."

"Amazing."

"It is," Sheldon said as he sat down. He cleared his throat. "So, as I said when we met, I'm not hiring at the moment, but I did want to meet you."

"I appreciate that. When do you think you might be hiring?"

Sheldon tilted his head to the side and thought. "Probably in four to six months."

Barry let out an involuntary groan, then blushed. "Sorry, but that's a long time."

"Yes and no," Sheldon said with a small smile. "There are a few things you can do in the meantime. And if something opens up sooner, we can talk. But for now, let me look over your resume."

Sheldon took a moment to carefully read it. Then he looked up and said, "Am I right that you have no prior training in financial planning?"

"No, I mean yes, you're right," Barry said as he wiped his hands on his trousers. "I have a lot of sales experience, though. And I have a degree in business."

"I see that. That's good. Actually, it's a plus that you'd be starting out fresh with us. That way I don't have to untrain you of bad habits. That's kind of a hazard in this industry."

Barry smiled and felt as if a weight had been lifted. "Well, if you're looking for an inexperienced man, I'm your guy!"

Sheldon laughed. "Tell you what. We'll set an appointment for four months from now. I'll give you some homework to do, then we'll meet up. If you need help in the meantime, don't hesitate to call."

Barry shook his hand, thanked him, and left.

He felt a sense of hope. If he could make this work, he felt certain he could have great income within a couple of years.

Over the next few days, Barry went door to door to various businesses, filling out job applications. He settled on a clothing store in an upscale mall. The manager hired him on the spot. They'd just lost two of their employees and she was eager to fill the slot immediately.

"It's commission only," the manager said with a warm smile. "Is that going to be OK?"

"Absolutely. I prefer it that way," Barry said. Since the average suit went for over one thousand dollars, that could be a sizeable paycheck.

However, after the first two days, he realized that moving the high-priced items wasn't as easy as he'd thought it would be. He'd only sold a few pairs of shoes and a couple of ties. He avoided eye contract with the manager, fearing that she might fire him. That fear hung over his head all morning, until noon. Barry offered to hold down the fort while the rest of the staff went for lunch. This was usually a dead time, so they were grateful.

Shortly after the others left, he heard the tinkling bell of the door opening. He looked up in surprise as two men in white doctor's coats walked in. They asked Barry to put together some outfits for them while they ate lunch. He asked a series of questions and took a few measurements, then sent them on their way. He pulled together a few combinations of pants, shirts, ties, and jackets, not completely sure what they'd like.

When they returned, one of them said, "It's your lucky day! We'll take them all. We have to get back to the hospital immediately. Please ring these up for us."

Barry stared at them for a second, then sprang into action. He couldn't believe the final total. It came to just under thirteen thousand dollars. His hand trembled as he handed them the bill, half expecting them to walk out in a huff. However, both doctors simply pulled out their platinum credit cards as if they were paying for a couple of burgers.

He held his breath as the cards went through the authorization process. Still not truly believing what was happening, he expected to see *declined* flash on the screen, but it didn't. It was only when they left that he took a breath. When the manager came back with the other sales-men, Barry showed her the receipt.

She clapped her hands together. "Nice work!"

"Do I really get eight percent?"

"Definitely!"

Earning one thousand dollars in a day, in an hour, was a new experience for Barry. It gave him new confidence and, by the end of the day, he'd sold another few thousand dollars' worth of clothing.

When they were closing up, the manager leaned against the service counter. "You know, I have to admit, I wasn't sure you were going to work out."

Barry nodded. "I kind of figured you might be thinking that."

"I wondered whether you'd been avoiding me. Were you?" she asked with a tilt of her head.

"As much as one can in this small shop."

She laughed. "Well, I was wrong. You did fantastic today. And it wasn't just that sale. You were on fire all afternoon."

\*\*\*

"And then she said if I played my cards right, I could be up for man-agement," Barry told Sandra later that night in bed.

"Wow, that's great. So does that mean you're going to give up on financial planning? I mean, this shop sounds pretty lucrative."

"Yeah, no. I know it's good money, and we need it, but there's more of a future with E.L. Anderson. I can make six figures and help people along the way. Lots of people need help with money. You know?"

She slid in under his arm and pressed her cheek against his chest. "That's one of the things I love about you. You're always thinking of others."

"That's really what sales is about."

\*\*\*

Four months rolled by faster than Barry had anticipated. He had October 15 circled on his planner and set his phone to alert him as well. These precautions against forgetting the appointment with Sheldon were unnecessary, though, as he thought about little else.

He considered calling Sheldon to confirm the appointment, but de-cided against it. He couldn't bear a postponement or, even worse, the instant rejection that might come from checking in. What if Sheldon had changed his mind? No, it was better to just show up at the sched-uled time.

Barry walked in at 10 am on the dot. The same secretary that had greeted him before smiled at him and let him know that Sheldon was running a few minutes behind. Looking around the small office, he noticed a few new posters on the wall, but otherwise everything looked the same.

He had enjoyed his stint at the clothing store, but when all was said and done, it was really just a job, not a career. Sure, it was fun, and he was making very good money, but he couldn't see himself selling suits for the next two decades.

Financial planning was a true vocation, one that was respected, challenging, and could really make a difference for families. He'd studied all the references Sheldon had provided, plus a few more. He'd also finished some of the preliminary courses for the licenses he'd need to get, but hadn't taken any of the tests yet. He wanted to be sure he'd get the job first. Besides, he needed to be sponsored by Sheldon's company for some of them.

"Hello, Mr. Smith. Good to see you again," Sheldon said. "I'm sorry to keep you waiting. Please, come on in."

Barry followed him into his office and noticed a few new photographs on the desk.

"Is that Machu Picchu?" Barry asked.

"Why yes," Sheldon replied. "I went last month. Have you been to Peru?"

Barry shook his head. "No, but I'd love to travel more."

"There's nothing like it. So tell me, how were these last four months?"

Barry detailed all the preparation he'd done. "I'm really excited about this opportunity. I'm ready to put in the work and pass all the tests." He then held his breath and wondered what Sheldon would say. After all, he didn't even know if they were hiring yet.

"That's great, but I need to know. Why should I hire you?" Sheldon said.

"I'm a hard worker, and I really want this. I really want to sell these products."

"Why?"

"Because they are great!" Barry said, leaning forward. "People need them, and I need to sell them." He went on to tell Sheldon about his experience at the clothing store. "I love sales. It's in my blood."

Sheldon studied him for a moment, then took off his glasses, folded them, and put them in the middle of his desk. "Sell me these glasses," he said, leaning back in his chair.

Barry immediately relaxed. This was his wheelhouse. "How is your eyesight?" he began.

He noticed Sheldon's eyes widen slightly before he answered. Then Barry asked a series of questions designed to help Sheldon see that he really did need these glasses, down to the style and prescription strength. He never actually tried to sell Sheldon his glasses; instead, he enlightened him on the perks and advantages they offered, while handling Sheldon's personal concerns.

After ten minutes, Sheldon picked up his glasses. "Sold!" he said jovially. "You're the kind of salesman I want on my team. I can teach you the rest."

\*\*\*

E.L. Anderson paid Barry a salary for the first three months, which enabled him to learn the products and get all the required licenses. The textbook learning was good, but he discovered that the apprenticeships with Sheldon were far more valuable. Sheldon allowed him to sit in on a number of client interviews. Afterwards, he'd carefully go over the products with Barry and explain the reasoning behind the recommendations he'd made.

Barry learned so much through those exchanges. Sheldon always went above and beyond to help the person in front of him. One elderly woman came in after her husband had died. She was in mourning and had to contend with a son who was constantly intimidating her to get more money from her.

E.L. Anderson had a strong legal department, and Sheldon brought them in to help the woman freeze her accounts until she could consult with her other children about how to handle the situation. She was grateful for the help. With that trouble out of the way, she could then discuss long-term strategies for the family.

After the woman left, Barry said, "That was very generous. I wonder if she knows that cost the firm thousands."

"Probably not, but she needed help quickly. She's been a long-term client and deserves a little backup."

Barry felt a surge of pride in this company. Not many financial advisors would go that far out of their way to help a client. This was definitely the place for him.

Another client came in to discuss rolling over his retirement account. As Sheldon explained the details of the investments, the man shifted in his chair and bit his lip. It was clear that he was keeping something back.

Sheldon spotted this immediately and asked about it. The man said, "I'd like to be able to access our funds."

Sheldon nodded and turned to Barry. "Barry here is one of our new crackerjack advisors. What do you think?"

Barry looked over the file and said, "I think an annuity might work." When Sheldon nodded, Barry turned to the client and said, "You'd invest the bulk of your savings and it would pay out a monthly or biweekly check for you."

"How much?"

"Well, let's see," Barry said, pulling out his calculator. "Based on your investment, you'd get a check for $1,200 every month."

The man smiled. "Thank you! That's perfect. How many years would I receive that?"

"For the rest of your life," Barry said. "It's a great product."

Sheldon smiled at him and helped the client get signed up.

***

By the end of January, the training wheels came off and Sheldon let Barry know it was time for him to find new clients. Barry nodded, but felt like he was being asked to dig a ditch with a teaspoon when the rest of the sales force had a backhoe. It was tough coming into a new town without many contacts.

He wanted to echo his youngest daughter's catch phrase, "It's not fair!" However, in the end, this is what he'd signed up for. This is where he wanted to be.

When the first check arrived, it was a whopping $640 for the month. His fifty-hour work week wasn't reflected in that figure. When he showed it to Sandra, she said, "You know we can't live off of this, right?"

Although that was the last thing Barry wanted to hear, it was the truth, and he couldn't argue with it. After all, she was working day and night to make ends meet and his big contribution to the household was $640. Not good.

"It's a bit different from anything I've ever done," he confided in her. "It's not like selling a suit or shoes, where people decide on the spot and never need to think about it. When it comes to their money, people need time to make decisions."

Sandra nodded. "That makes sense. Give yourself some time. You'll figure it out. I know you're working hard."

Although he felt some relief at her words, that sensation was short-lived. The next day, Sheldon rapped on his open office door. "May I come in?"

"Sure," Barry said, feeling the hairs on the back of his neck stand on end.

Sheldon sat down and gave Barry a long look. "You need to improve your production if we're going to keep you on."

Barry gulped and nodded. He looked his boss right in the eye. "I know. February's check was really low."

"Yeah, it was."

"What sort of figure are you looking for me to make?"

"At least what we were paying you as a salary, but honestly, we expect a lot more. March has got to be much better."

Barry nodded. "I'll make it happen."

*Somehow.*

Later that evening, Barry sat down to a meal with his wife. The children were both out for the night at sleepovers, which meant they could talk freely about Barry's situation and brainstorm possible solutions.

"I just need more clients," Barry said with a sigh. "But I don't yet have any traction here. How do I get people to respond to me? They need to trust me to be their financial advisor."

"It's no use trying to change the way people think," Sandra said. "But you can control and determine your own attitude."

Barry tilted his head toward her. "That's easier said than done."

"You're generally a positive guy. I think you just need to commit to that and be the enthusiastic person that you are. People will respond to that."

He nodded. "I'll have to face a lot of noes. That's never fun."

"Remember what you've always told me: noes lead to yeses."

"True."

Sandra put her hand on top of his hand. "You've been getting out there more. Meeting people. That's a good first step."

"I need to double or triple that effort," Barry said, running a hand through his hair. "I need to network more. That will mean less time at home."

Sandra smiled. "Mike can watch Cassie on the nights you need to be away. We'll make it work. Don't worry."

***

Barry folded his hands in front of him in an effort to stop waving them around as he spoke to the client prospect in front of him. Mr. Doran had come to him as a referral from a local networking meeting. After giving the man a twenty-minute presentation on his white board about various products, he asked the man a series of questions about his needs.

Mr. Doran was turning fifty this year and wanted to start an IRA. He had a pension coming when he turned sixty-five and also needed a life insurance policy to cover the gap in case something happened to him.

"I want to make sure my wife is cared for," he confided in Barry.

In the end, Barry realized that Mr. Doran just needed a fifteen-year term life insurance policy. Overall, his commission would be rather small, but that's what this man needed; it would be unethical to give him anything else.

"So, we'll invest in a Roth IRA and purchase a term policy, which will run you $45 per month," Barry said with a smile.

"You know," Mr. Doran said. "I've sat down with a couple other financial advisors, and they all recommended that I get more expensive policies. But I didn't want to spend hundreds of dollars a month. They just weren't listening."

Barry nodded. "I know the product you're talking about. It's a good one, but that's not what you need. You have a pension and some savings. This is a better plan for you."

"I imagine the commission is probably better on the universal life insurance policies."

"It is. That's why some advisors will be pushing it on you."

Mr. Doran stood up, and Barry rose as well. "Thank you," Mr. Doran said. "I appreciate your help. It's nice to know I have someone in my corner."

"Anytime. My door's always open."

Barry saw Mr. Doran to the door and watched him walk into the elevator. When he turned back, he caught Sheldon's eye. Barry gave his boss a weak smile.

"I know, I know," he said. "Not a big sale."

"I was eavesdropping. You did the right thing. Honestly, I'm impressed. I know how hard you've been working. And it probably doesn't help that I'm putting pressure on you to up your numbers. You've got integrity, Barry. I want you to know that I've noticed that and appreciate it. Keep doing what you're doing, and you'll do fine."

"Thanks," Barry said, feeling his shoulders relax.

That month, Barry's paycheck was a little over double what it had been the previous month. It still wasn't what he needed to make, but Sheldon patted him on the back and encouraged him to keep going. He'd been given a one-month reprieve.

By the middle of April, Barry closed a few decent policies and had collected another half-dozen referrals. He was on track to beat what he'd made when he'd been on salary, which was the minimum requirement their headquarters expected. Things were shaping up nicely. He was busy, and his family continued to be supportive.

\*\*\*

It was a Friday afternoon, and Barry was set to leave at 5 pm. He was looking forward to spending the evening with his family. Mike and Cassie had requested he pick up the latest Avengers movie on Blu-ray while they ordered an extra-large supreme pizza from Mario's. Just as he was packing up his briefcase, his phone rang.

"Mr. Smith?" the voice asked. It sounded familiar, but he couldn't quite place it.

"Yes," Barry said with a smile. Even if the client couldn't see your smile, they could hear it in your voice. "May I help you?"

"This is Mr. Doran. We met about a month ago?"

"Of course," Barry said, closing his briefcase. He sat back down in his swivel chair. "How have you been?"

"Good, good. I was wondering if I could come in and see you tonight. I need your advice."

Barry closed his eyes and thought about family night. No movie. No pizza. He considered trying to push Mr. Doran off until the next day, but didn't feel good about that. No, Mr. Doran was his client, and if he felt he needed to talk tonight, that was important. His girls would understand.

"Sure," Barry said easily. "What time's good for you?"

"I can be there in an hour."

"Perfect."

When he hung up, Barry phoned his wife. She let him know that Saturday night would work just as well. "Take care of your client," she said.

Barry grabbed some takeout and had just cleaned up when Mr. Doran walked through the door with his wife.

Barry stood and greeted them. After a little chitchat, Mr. Doran explained that his aunt from West Texas had passed away a couple weeks prior. She had a life insurance policy, and since she didn't have any children, she had listed him as the beneficiary.

"It has been years since I've been out to see her. I wish I'd taken the time to visit more," Mr. Doran said, his voice catching in the back of his throat.

Mrs. Doran put a hand on her husband's shoulder. She looked at Barry and said, "We just received the check today. It's more than we've ever had. Five hundred thousand dollars. We just don't know what to do with it."

Barry's eyes widened slightly, then he sat back in his chair. His mind raced with various ideas. He asked them a few more questions, then explained the different options, illustrating how each product worked in detail on the large whiteboard behind him.

An hour later, after the couple had left, Barry leaned back in his chair and grinned. He spun slowly around in a circle, feeling beautifully alive.

"Not bad at all," Sheldon said, coming to the door.

Barry quickly turned to his boss and said, "I didn't know anyone else was here."

"I stuck around to see how it worked out. The way I figure it, you just earned a cool five thousand tonight. Nicely done! I've been rooting for you."

"That's what I calculated, too," Barry said with a nod. "You know, don't get me wrong, I really could use the money and love the commission, but that wasn't the best part."

"No?" Sheldon said with a grin.

"It felt so great that they came to *me*. They trusted *me*," he said, then paused for a moment as he considered how to put his feelings into words. "The fact is, *I'm* their financial advisor. And I was able to help them improve their quality of life. That's such an incredible feeling."

Sheldon nodded. "There's nothing like it in the world. And what's truly remarkable is that we get paid well for it, isn't it?"

*\*\*\**

Four years later, Barry stood up from his desk and went to the E.L. Anderson waiting room. It was time. Barry smiled as he watched a slender man in a brown suit and red tie drum his fingers on the armrest of a chair. A magazine lay open on his lap.

"Mr. Greenleaf?" Barry asked.

The man quickly closed the magazine and stood up. He wiped his hands on his pants, then walked over to Barry.

"That's me," he said. "It's good to meet you."

"Come on in," Barry said, suppressing a smile. After all, it hadn't been that long ago that he'd been sitting in that exact same seat, pretending to read a magazine as he waited for Sheldon to interview him.

The man sat in the chair across from his and handed Barry a resume. Barry took it and read it line for line, commenting on various aspects. Mr. Greenleaf had a little prior experience with life insurance, but didn't have his Series 7 license, which would enable him to sell securities.

"I'm eager to learn," Mr. Greenleaf said. "I really do love helping people plan for the future."

Barry nodded. "That's great. I think it really is a prerequisite for doing well in this industry."

Mr. Greenleaf looked around the office. Behind Barry were numerous awards and certificates. "Impressive," he said with a low whistle. "Do you have any words of wisdom you can share?"

"It really comes down to perseverance. I guess you can say that I just kept showing up day after day. In the beginning, I'll admit, it wasn't easy. But I worked hard and put in the time. And I always paid attention to my client's needs."

"I can do that," Mr. Greenleaf said with a smile.

"Another thing," Barry said. "I'm grateful. Every day."

"Grateful? What would you say you're grateful for?"

"You know," Barry said, leaning back in his chair. "I wouldn't say that's it's a matter for being grateful for one thing or another. I'm simply grateful."

Mr. Greenleaf paused for a moment, then nodded. "I get it."

Barry sat up and shook the man's hand. "Then you'll do great with us here at E.L. Anderson."

# CASSIUS

STORY #8 IN THE DISCOVERING KINDNESS SERIES

## Kevin J. Smith
with **Laura Sherman**

Cassius sat bent over *Life Upon These Shores,* an engrossing exploration into African American history. He was always interested in his roots, wanting to know more about his ancestors. He glanced at his watch. Only a few more minutes until he'd have to pack up and head back home for dinner. As if reading his mind, the librarian, Mrs. Shuemaker, walked over and smiled.

"Do you want to check that out?" she asked.

He looked up at the librarian. She looked as if she was fresh out of college. Pretty with flowing auburn hair. "No, ma'am, I was just rereading my favorite parts."

"See you tomorrow?" she asked.

"No. School starts tomorrow."

"Oh, that's right!" she said. "Wednesday is the big day. High school. Are you nervous?"

Cassius shrugged. "I don't know."

Mrs. Shuemaker smiled. "You'll do fine. Don't worry."

Cassius stood up and picked up the books around him to put them away. The librarian shook her head. "Leave them. I'll clean up."

Cassius thanked her and walked out the door. The street was crowded with people hurrying home. Cassius kept his stride slow and steady. His large frame made it hard to make quick progress, and he always opted to let others who were in a hurry pass.

"Sorry," a skinny guy with wire-rimmed glasses muttered as he elbowed past Cassius. When the man looked up, he did a little double take. "I-I m-mean, I apologize."

Was that fear in his eyes? Probably. Cassius was used to it.

People often gave him odd glances, likely trying to figure out if he was a boy or a man. At a little over six feet tall and two hundred pounds of pure muscle, he naturally earned a certain kind of fearful respect from complete strangers.

Cassius kept his facial features neutral. No point in responding as the man hurried away as fast as he could.

As Cassius approached his small, two-bedroom home, he stopped. He could hear the loud rap music blaring through the closed windows. The curtains were half open, revealing a boy groping an emaciated woman against a wall, while another boy was doing lines on the coffee table.

Gangbangers.

Cassius steeled himself and opened the front door. Wrappers from various fast food joints trailed from the front door to the living room off to the left. His sister, Doreen, was sitting up on one end of the green sofa, which had slowly turned brown over the years. A man covered with tattoos lay on the other end, his eyelids half open. His name was Skrap, and he had twin ink tears trickling from his left eye, signifying his two kills from the previous year.

Skrap's eyes lit on Cassius, and he stood up. Giving him a wide smile, Skrap revealed two silver front teeth. "Big Man! I've been waiting for you," he said.

Dread crept up Cassius's spine like a daddy longlegs. He cringed as his body shivered. He dared not look the man in the eye, but couldn't risk avoiding his gaze either. "H-hi," he said, just above a whisper.

If only he hadn't come home.

Until now, Skrap had ignored him, but today was different. It was clear the scrawny man wanted something from him.

Two other teens leaned on the far wall of the small room and stared menacingly at Cassius. One dangled a joint from his snarling lips. The other rolled his neck, then stretched his arms and cracked his knuckles. They were Skrap's lackeys. Neither had ink on their faces.

"So Big Man's going to start high school," Skrap said in a cheerful voice. He turned to the other two, who immediately nodded and grunted something indiscernible. He turned back to Cassius. "That's a big deal. You know why?"

Cassius shook his head. He knew enough to know that whatever he said wouldn't be the answer the gang leader had in mind. Besides, Skrap was the kind of guy who preferred to hear himself talk.

"It's an *opportunity*," Skrap said, looking pleased with himself. He paused, and Cassius realized that he expected him to respond.

"Yeah?" he whispered. He wished he could just walk away. There was nothing he could say that would help him out of this.

"Absolutely. You see, it's a chance to make some cash. Easy money."

Every fiber of Cassius's being begged him to run away. He knew there was no such thing as easy money. Especially when it came to gang activity.

Beads of sweat formed on his brow. "OK." It was all he could think to say.

"OK!" Skrap said as he gave Cassius a hearty slap on the back. "Good! I like that. Look, we'll talk more about this later, Big Man."

It was an out, and Cassius took it. He went back to his room and was relieved that none of the gang members were in there, taking advantage of the free bed. He opened his backpack and started studying, then realized it was impossible with the blaring music. The library was open until nine. Maybe they'd be gone by then.

Cassius made himself a sandwich and headed out.

Later that night, when the house was still and his sister was asleep in the other room, Cassius's mind couldn't stop whirling like a top. What was Skrap going to demand of him?

"You're a no-good kid," a voice from his past echoed through his mind.

His father had never thought much of him. Of course, he always had a bottle of vodka in his hand when he made comments about Cassius's character.

"You're a waste of space."

"You'll never amount to anything."

These were favorite refrains of the nervous little man who bullied Cassius up until the time he'd finally left. Cassius figured his father had left because his only son had so sorely disappointed him.

Well, it looked like his father's prediction would come true now that Skrap was going to enter his life. Cassius didn't know much about gang life, but he knew the situation well enough to understand that Skrap wasn't going to let up. Was he destined to become a worthless gang-banger?

Not if he could help it.

***

The next morning, Cassius woke to the smell of bacon cooking. He popped out of bed and saw his door was open a crack. He smiled. The smell was a far better alarm clock than anything else. He threw on a shirt and pants, and squeezed into the chair at the little table in the kitchen. He always seemed to dwarf the furniture in this house. A large plate of bacon sat in the center. He immediately picked up a piece and started munching.

Doreen glanced at him and smiled. "Sunny side up?"

"Yeah," he said, picking up another piece. "Thanks!"

She made six eggs and put four on his plate, along with three slices of toasted bread, then sat down across from him. They ate in silence for a few minutes.

Doreen put down her fork. "So what did you think of Skrap's proposal?"

His fork froze midair. He carefully put it back on his plate. So there was a price for this breakfast.

"What proposal? Your friend didn't make one."

Doreen winced. "You know. He wants you to sell drugs. At the school."

Cassius stared at her. "What? No way."

"What do you mean?" she asked. "But you said you would."

"I did *not!*"

"Yeah, you did. You said 'OK.' Remember? He took that as a *yes.* He thinks you're going to help him."

Cassius shook his head. "I was just letting him know I heard him. That's all. What else was I supposed to say? I never meant I'd sell drugs."

"Well, he didn't get that memo," Doreen said with a head shake.

"He's expecting me to talk to you and report back. Now what am I supposed to do?"

"Leave him?"

"I can't."

"Why not?"

"Where would I go?" she said, waving her hands in the air. "What would I do?"

"I don't know. You could go back to high school."

"I can't. I'm too old."

Cassius fell silent. Finally, he said, "If everything wasn't like this. You know, so messed up, what would you like to do?"

She looked up at him with her eyes shining. "That's easy. Go to Los Angeles. The weather's great and there are tons of filmmakers. I'd love to act or something, you know?"

He nodded and smiled. "Yeah, that's cool."

"Yeah." Doreen sighed. "But that's just a dream. The reality is that now I'm with Skrap. I've got to go where he goes and do what he says. Or else he'll stop paying the food bills. However, if we get booted from the house, I'll probably take my chances in LA."

Cassius's shoulders slumped. The house had been in foreclosure for months and they had no source of income. After their father left three years ago, their mother did whatever she could to pay the bills, but she couldn't keep up. In the end, she'd resorted to breaking and entering, and was arrested earlier that year. Her children were left to fend for themselves.

"When do you think we'll be asked to leave?" he asked.

"No idea. We get letters every month, but nothing's happened."

"I read in the papers that there are a lot of people in foreclosure. The financial institutions can't keep up."

"You read the papers?" she asked. "Geez, you're smart."

"I like to read. At the library."

Doreen fidgeted. She lifted a trembling hand to straighten a wayward curl. "S-so, what do I tell Skrap?"

Cassius felt his irritation rise. Doreen was his older sister. She was supposed to be his guardian. Why didn't she protect him? Instead, she allowed murdering drug dealers into the house. The foreclosed-upon house.

He stood up. "Tell him whatever you like. I'm going to school. Don't want to be late."

"But..."

Cassius ignored her. He went to his room, picked up his bag, and walked toward the door. He could hear Doreen following behind him, so he sped up.

"I don't know what to do," she called out after he crossed the threshold.

Cassius paused on the front sidewalk and thought about turning around, but didn't. He had nothing to say, so he continued on his way.

The walk to school was only twenty minutes. He was early, which was fine. He liked to avoid the rush. He sighed as he glanced at the other kids—he was still the biggest kid there. What had he expected? In middle school, he'd shot up to his current height and had stuck out like a redwood in a forest of shrubs. He had silently endured the snide comments and accepted being a social outcast. Cassius had hoped that he would blend in a bit more with the older kids in high school, but looking around, he realized that wasn't going to be the case.

Cassius got his schedule and headed to his first class. History. They'd put him in an advanced class with older kids, which was nice. He smiled as he sat down and faced the teacher.

Mr. Haskell was a thin white guy with a trim mustache. As he took roll, Cassius noticed that the man seemed nice enough, but the kids were all slouched in their chairs. Half of them were passing notes, while the others were doodling on their notebooks.

He noticed a few boys in black, red, and gold jerseys sitting by the window. What would it be like to be a part of a team like that, with cool shirts and friends to sit with in class? He turned away. That wasn't for him, that's for sure. He could never afford the uniform.

Mr. Haskell gave a little intro to the class and confirmed they'd be covering American History. Cassius sat up straight. He'd read so many books on the subject. As Mr. Haskell discussed colonial life in America, he called on Cassius repeatedly. Cassius readily answered all his questions.

He was relieved that most of the students didn't seem to notice or care. However, one kid in a football jersey glanced at him a few times. He had short, light brown hair, and while he wasn't as large as Cassius, he looked to be much bigger than his friends or the others in the class. Gauging the boy's response, Cassius decided that the glances seemed to be of respect, not disdain. He frowned as he tried to figure out why he was the recipient of such looks.

The bell rang and Cassius shuffled out into the hallway. Students swirled around him in both directions as he tried to get his bearings.

"Hey! Get out of the way, freak!" a lanky boy with dark hair that fell in his eyes snarled over his shoulder before he passed Cassius.

A few students who were close by heard the boy and sniggered. Cassius hunched his shoulders and pressed himself against the lockers. He closed his eyes and took a deep breath. When he opened them, he saw a plump boy fumbling with the lock on his locker.

"Yo! Weirdo! Can't you even open your locker?" A tall, heavy-set boy bumped into George McGumphrey and knocked his books to the floor. George dropped to his knees to gather up the papers that had scattered.

"I don't know why they let people like you into our school," a girl with curly hair chimed in. "I bet you don't even understand what's going on."

"Yeah, Dumbo," said the boy. They both laughed and moved along, leaving George to deal with the mess.

Cassius glanced at George before he scuttled off. He didn't want to be late for class. He looked back at George and almost lost his balance as a wave of dizziness swept over him.

Why hadn't he stopped to help the boy?

It was clear that no one else would. Everyone seemed involved in their own business. Some of the kids simply stepped over the crying boy and his scattered papers as if they were rubbish.

Cassius felt bile rise to the back of his throat. He'd had classes with George ever since middle school. That's when George's family had moved from Nebraska.

Even then, George had worked harder than anyone else. That was probably due to the fact that he had Down syndrome. Cassius figured this condition accounted for the fact that people were always so nervous around George.

Despite the prejudice the boy faced, he was a good guy, soft spoken and with a smile for everyone. But he'd had trouble making friends. Cassius understood what it felt like to be an outsider. After all, the other kids were usually afraid of him because of his size. Even people on the street gave Cassius a wide berth. Maybe it had something to do with him being African American, too. Who knew? Whatever the reason, he knew he'd never be popular.

Cassius shook off his guilt with the thought that he needed to be to class on time. It was the first day of school and he wanted to make a good impression. He found the computer lab and slid into a seat in the rear just before the second bell. He was excited to learn more about programming. If he could pick one subject to master, this would be it, because he could get a good job and never be poor again.

Looking around, he saw that the other students seemed a little more interested in this class than they had been in history. Cassius stayed after class to talk to the teacher about the upcoming lessons.

"I know most of this stuff," he said.

The teacher, a short, balding man, smiled at him. "Well, if that's the case, we'll place you in the web design class fifth period. Would you like that?"

"Yeah!" Cassius said. "That'd be great."

"Good. I'll need to give you the final test for this class to be sure you know the material."

"I'll be ready."

"Good," the teacher said. "No need to make you suffer through a subject you already know."

By the end of the day, Cassius was feeling better about the world. He was relieved that the other kids were leaving him alone. He passed a group of goths leaning against the locker. They avoided making eye contact with him. Cassius sighed. He guessed that he must look like an ogre to them since they were about half his size.

Some boys in jerseys were outside the front door. He recognized a few from his history class. He put his head down and passed them quickly, not wishing to attract attention. He didn't want them to heckle him about his size.

Dread filled him as he approached his house. He pictured Skrap lounging on the couch, sharpening his knife, and glowering at his sister while she knelt in front of him wringing her hands, trying to explain why her brother wouldn't join the gang. He'd already decided that if Doreen's friends were over, he'd leave and hang out in the library until closing, then find a way to sneak back into his room.

Fortunately, the house was empty. Cassius made himself pasta and meat sauce with garlic bread, cleaned up the kitchen, and headed to bed. Doreen would probably be out all night. He tried not to worry and hoped she wouldn't wind up in prison sharing a cell with their mother. At least she didn't appear to be doing drugs. Yet. The way she was going, though, he figured it was only a matter of time.

\*\*\*

By the end the week, Cassius knew his routine at the school. He liked his classes and teachers. He was heading out for the weekend when a burly man with a buzz cut stopped him in the hall.

"Cassius?" the man asked.

"Yeah," he said tentatively.

"Karl told me that you're an ace in his American History class. He thought you'd make a good addition to our team. I'm Coach Dillon, the football coach."

Cassius shook his head. "Not interested."

"Why not?" the coach said. "You're built for the game."

"I don't know anything about football."

"I'll teach you."

Cassius continued to shake his head. "Look, Mister, I'm sorry, but I just can't."

"You've got to give me a decent reason. I'm not going until I hear it," he said with a lopsided grin.

Cassius looked around. The hallway had cleared out. "I don't know."

"Yes, you do."

He grimaced. This wasn't the kind of conversation he wanted to have with anyone, but it seemed apparent this coach wasn't going to just let it go. "Look, I've seen the uniform the players wear. There's no way I can afford it. No way. Sorry."

The coach relaxed and waved his hands in front of him. "We pay for the uniform. There's no fee involved. We cover it all."

Cassius looked sharply at the guy. "Really? Are you serious?"

"Yeah, I'm serious."

"But..." he trailed off. "I don't know."

"What else concerns you? Spill!" Coach Dillon said, curling his fingers toward him in the universal *bring it* gesture.

Cassius couldn't help but grin at the man's jovial spirit. He obviously cared about his team and had an interest in Cassius. "Why do you want me? Because of my size?"

"Yes. In part. I'd like to see what you can do," the coach said. "I mean, I'm not going to lie. You're a big kid, especially for a freshman. I think you just might be bigger than any of our other players. That's going to give you an advantage. But size isn't everything. Karl tells me that you're smart as a whip. Apparently, you're the only student who speaks up in class, and he says you always get the right answer."

Cassius snorted. "That's just study. I read a lot. How's that going to help me in football?"

"Oh, trust me, it will. There's study in football. And a lot of practice. It's half mental and half physical, you know?"

Cassius shook his head. "No, I didn't know." He thought about it for a moment, then said, "I have a lot of classes, and some of them are advanced. I'll need to study a lot. I don't want anything to get in the way."

Coach Dillon put his hand on his heart. "Swear to God, I'd never let it interfere. You're here to study. I promise the practice and games won't stop that. Look, we have special tryouts next Tuesday. John, our tight end, got injured a few days ago and will be out for the rest of the season. We need to replace him. Why don't you come and see how it goes? Then decide."

Cassius nodded. "Sure, OK."

\*\*\*

Cassius was a pile of nerves by the time Tuesday rolled around. As he put his stuff into his locker and headed out to the field, he could hear the echo of his father's voice.

"Who do you think you're fooling? No one's ever going to want you."

He shook his head, but the voice continued. "You're no good, Cassius. You'll never amount to anything."

Even in his head, his father slurred his words as if drunk. It became harder and harder for Cassius to put one foot in front of the other and walk out onto the field. The only thing that kept him moving forward was the fact that he'd given the coach his word he'd show up. He refused to go back on that.

"Cassius," the large boy from history class called out. "You came! That's great."

"Yeah."

"I'm Karl," he continued, then introduced the others on the team. Cassius nodded each time, but couldn't focus on Karl's words. He knew he'd never retain the names. His nerves were too frayed.

He waited until Karl stopped talking before he spoke. "Look, I don't know about this."

Karl looked like he was about to protest, but the coach came over and tilted his head to the side. "You promised to give it a try."

"I know," Cassius said with a deep sigh.

There were dozens of other kids who had showed up for tryouts. Cassius joined them in a series of calisthenics and running exercises. About one third of the kids had no stamina and were immediately weeded out.

Next came the 40-yard dash. They were instructed to start in the standard three-point football stance. Cassius watched a few kids do it before he bent down and put his right hand down on the ground.

"Hold!" the coach said.

He approached Cassius and said quietly, "That's pretty good, but let's make a few adjustments. Here, stand back up."

Coach Dillion showed him how to put his feet about shoulder width apart and how it was important to have them pointing straight ahead. "Most kids starting out tend to turn them out. It slows them down a lot."

"OK, Coach," Cassius said. He liked learning new things and didn't mind the coach correcting him in front of the rest of the kids. The fact was that Coach Dillon wasn't taking the time to give anyone else a little one-on-one lesson. He smiled. No matter what, this coach saw something in him. Something popped and the voice in his head faded a bit.

Coach gave him a bit more instruction, then stepped back. "Keep your head up!" he yelled. "Go!"

Cassius felt the burn in his legs as he shot out of the position. He had such a sense of power as he sprinted toward the coach, who stood still with a timer in his hand.

When he turned around, the rest of the team was staring at him.

"You never did that before?" Karl called out.

Cassius shook his head. "No. Why? Did I get it wrong?"

"Wrong? Are you kidding me? That was incredible," he said. "Hey, Coach. What was his time?"

Coach Dillon said, "4.5 seconds."

"That's like major league time," a wiry kid said.

"Xane," Coach Dillon said with a shake of his head, "I keep telling you. I just have this stopwatch. The majors don't time by hand. They have fancy electronic devices. Trust me, you boys aren't beating out the pros."

The boys all chuckled, and Xane blushed. He seemed to recover from his embarrassment quickly, though, and joined in the laughter. "Yeah, OK, Coach. But still. You know, it's pretty good."

"It's bloody amazing is what it is," Coach Dillon said with a grin. "You have strength in your legs. Did they burn?"

Cassius nodded. "Yeah."

"That's normal. And they'll be sore tonight after we run you through the rest of the drills, but you have muscle to build from. That's really good. Most people trying out don't."

Cassius shrugged. "I lift weights at home. It's no big deal."

The players all gave each other high fives.

Coach Dillon nodded. "You're way ahead of any other new player. Weightlifting is always part of the routine. Ask the others. I demand it. Most kids are starting from nowhere." He turned back to the others trying out. "No offense."

They all mumbled variations of "None taken."

Cassius watched the other boys who were trying out do their 40-yard dashes and saw a few of them had good times, but no one came close to his. He felt an odd sensation. One that he'd never felt before. Pride. The muffled voice in his head faded even more.

"Now, we're going to try some of you out with a blocking sled and see how you do," Coach Dillon announced.

He instructed the group to start from the three-point stance and hit the sled as hard as they could. Cassius watched a few boys struggle to move the thing. When it was his turn, he slammed into it and succeeded in pushing it down the field about ten yards at a rather good pace.

Afterward, Karl came up to him. "You obliterated that thing. How'd you do that?"

"How'd I do what?" Cassius asked.

"Push it that far, that fast. How'd you do that?"

Cassius wasn't sure what to say. He just did what he was told. "I don't know," he said, feeling confused.

"Hey, that's OK. I'm just impressed. That thing shot down the field so fast. I can never make that much distance."

Cassius noticed the other team members gathering around him, and he blushed. "I guess I just pushed forward. Not too high and not too low. There seemed to be a sweet spot, you know?"

They all nodded. Cassius heard the coach's whistle. "Let's try you out with the ball, OK?"

Cassius was feeling more and more confident. His father's voice in his head was a mere whisper. In a flash, Cassius realized that he was the one who had given it strength. After all, his father was long gone. The drunken brute was nowhere around. With that, the voice extinguished like a flame on a candle that had lost its oxygen.

Cassius felt a newfound freedom. In addition, he'd discovered a new home. It was clear that this field was where he belonged, where his size made him an asset and not a freak. He turned to the coach. "What do you want me to do?"

"Catch the ball," the coach said. "Don't worry if you can't. I don't really expect it. Our coaching staff can teach you how later, but for now I just want to gauge your timing and see how you do. OK?"

Cassius nodded. "Where do I go?"

Coach Dillon motioned to Xane, who immediately sprinted forward. "Show him what to do?"

Xane nodded. "I'm the quarterback. Follow me."

Xane moved away from the pack to the center of the field where there was a pile of footballs. He picked one up and said, "Here's what I want you to do. Run down the field ten yards, then turn back. I'll throw the ball to you. Try to catch it. If you do, drop it and cut 90 degrees to the right and run in that direction. If you miss the ball, don't worry, just keep running laterally. As you run, I'll throw the next ball. The idea is for you to catch it while you're running. If you do, drop that ball and run in the opposite direction. I'll throw a third. See if you can catch it." When he stopped talking, he looked at Cassius and waited for a response.

Cassius nodded. "Got it."

"You do?" Xane asked, surprised. Then he laughed. "Usually the newbies ask me to repeat it at least three times."

"No, I got it." Just for good measure he repeated the play back to Xane, who nodded.

"Don't sweat it if you don't catch any. Most kids don't."

Cassius nodded. "OK."

"Whenever you're ready."

Cassius took off running. He caught the first ball with ease, dropped it, ran to the right and looked back in time to see Xane toss the ball just ahead of him. He caught it like the ball was an extension of his hands. He'd expected it to feel hard and rough, but it was light and soft. He juggled the third ball, but didn't let it fall to the ground. He managed to hug it to his chest awkwardly.

He jogged back to Xane, who was smiling. Coach Dillon made his way over to them. Cassius shook his head at them. "I can do better. I was thinking about how good the ball felt in my hands and lost concentration. I'm sorry. Can I try again?"

Coach Dillon said, "No need. That was brilliant. I mean it. Really amazing. You have the softest hands I've ever seen." He paused when Cassius scrunched up his brows. "Oh, that means that you catch well. It's a compliment."

"Oh!" Cassius said. "Thanks!"

"Don't mention it. Honestly, I don't think I've ever seen someone catch all three balls their first time out."

Cassius tilted his head to the right. "But I didn't catch the last one cleanly. Not sure if that counts."

The other teammates, who had come up behind them, laughed. They slapped Cassius on the back.

"Absolutely, it counts!" Coach Dillon said, joining in their laughter. "You caught it, didn't you?"

Karl jumped in. "Cassius, you're a triple threat. You can catch, run, and block like a starter. What do you think, Coach? Can he replace John?"

Coach Dillon nodded. "He's perfect for it." He turned back to Cassius. "You'll need to practice and learn the plays, but yeah, you're in. That is, if you'll join the team. Will you?"

The rest of the players started clamoring, begging him to join. Cassius felt good. Finally, he nodded and said, "I really liked this. Sure, I'll join the team."

The cheer that went up was deafening. Cassius looked back at the others who'd come to try out. They didn't look irritated with him or jealous. Instead, they looked to be in awe.

"What about them?" he asked the coach.

"There are some good players among them," he said. "I'm going to add them to our second string."

"I need to learn the terms and plays. How do I do that?" Cassius asked.

Karl stepped forward. "The playbook is a sacred thing. I'll go over it with you, but you'll need to memorize it. Never write it down. Understand?"

Cassius nodded. It made sense. It was like a chef's secret recipe. "Sure."

"And the terms you can look up on the internet. I'll email you a few links."

Cassius nodded. He could use the computer lab or the computers at the library. "Thanks!" he said.

Cassius couldn't stop feeling the texture of his new fleece team jacket as he walked home. He'd never owned anything like it. All his clothes were second hand from one of the local thrift stores or donated by the church down the street. This was brand new and his.

He was so eager to show it off to his sister that he completely forgot to check for her friends before he walked in the door. His smile faded when he saw Skrap leaning against the wall, waiting for him.

"Big Man!" he called out with that wide smile of his. "Like your new jacket." He reached out and touched the material on his sleeve. "Guess you made the team!"

Cassius nodded, his mind whirling with ideas of how to get out of this conversation. His nerves were so tight, they felt like harp strings being plucked, sending painful shivers through his system.

"Doreen says you're not interested in working with me. That makes me sad, Big Man. Real sad." His smile didn't dissipate as he spoke. "Fact is, I need you."

Blood pounded in Cassius' ears so hard that Skrap's words sounded tinny. He'd only fainted once in his life, and he didn't relish doing it again.

"I'm sorry," he whispered.

"No need to be sorry. Just change your mind. Look, it isn't that hard. All you need to do is bring packages to school in that little black bag of yours. It's simple. You just deliver the package and pick up the money and bring it to me. No sweat." As he spoke, Skrap fiddled with a switchblade in his right hand.

Cassius stood there silently, his eyes riveted on the knife in Skrap's hand. He wished he could disappear. There was no way out. Skrap wasn't going to take no for an answer.

"I'll have something for you tomorrow, OK?" Skrap said more as a statement than a question.

Cassius continued to stare at the floor. He didn't want to nod as Skrap would take that as agreement.

"Doreen," Skrap called out loudly. Irritation filled those two syllables.

Instantly, Doreen appeared by his side. "Yes?" she said meekly.

Skrap grabbed her by the arm, causing her to shriek in pain. "You two should have a talk. Explain it to him."

"O-OK," she said.

"Fine," Skrap gritted out. "I'm a patient man, Big Man, but I won't be for long. Get it?"

Cassius nodded, staring at the floor. He only lifted his eyes when he heard the door slam behind him.

"How could you?" Cassius said, his eyes filling with tears. "How can you do this to me?"

"I'm sorry," Doreen whispered. She winced as she rubbed her arm which had turned red where Skrap had grabbed her.

"No, you're not. You're not sorry. You're part of his gang."

It was her turn to study the floorboards. "I have no choice."

"Yeah, you do."

She was silent. "Look, would it be that hard to just carry the stuff for him?"

"Are you kidding me?" he bit out in anger. "Why is he so convinced that he needs me anyway?"

Doreen shook her head. "He's afraid of the cops. They're on the lookout for him around the school. He doesn't want to be taken in."

"You want me to be a drug dealer?"

She looked up at him. "It's not exactly dealing. He's the dealer. You're just a..." she trailed off.

He straightened his shoulders. "You can search all the words in the dictionary. There's no other word to describe it. I'd be a drug dealer, part of a gang whose leader is a two-time murderer and proud of it."

"So, your answer is no."

"That's right."

She stared at him and Cassius could see her lower lip tremble. "You can't come back here then. Skrap isn't the kind of man to take no for an answer. He'll hurt you. Maybe kill you."

Cassius shook his head. "I don't have any other place to go. You have to handle this. You're my big sister. You need to protect me."

He didn't give her a chance to sputter out a response. Instead, he stomped into his room and slammed the door.

\*\*\*

The next afternoon, Cassius went to football practice. If the team noticed his sullen attitude, they didn't say anything. They were all happy to see him.

After they did a number of sprints and warm-up exercises, the coach paired up teammates to practice offensive and defensive moves.

"Your job is to defend the quarterback," Coach told Cassius. "Don't let the linebacker through to the backfield. Got it?"

Cassius nodded.

When the whistle blew, the boy playing defense came rushing at him. Cassius did his best to block him, but before he knew it, Cassius found himself down on the ground. He shook his head. The kid was a lot smaller than him. How had he done that? Cassius's job was to protect the quarterback and he'd just failed. Miserably.

The whistle blew. Coach gave both players instructions, and they set up again. Again, Cassius was caught off balance and knocked to the ground very quickly. This pattern continued for several more reps. After the tenth time, Cassius opted to just lie on his back, looking up at the sky.

Coach called time out and walked over to him.

"You OK?" he asked.

Cassius looked up at him. He didn't want to get up and face the rest of the team. "Yeah."

"Look, it takes practice. It's all about balance and footwork. The rest of the team's been doing this for a while. I'll bring Allen in. You can watch him. Notice how he moves."

Cassius stood up and walked over to the sidelines. He watched the team practice for a while, then walked to the locker room. He'd had enough. It was clear to him he wasn't cut out for this. There was no way he could master the sport fast enough to fit in with the team.

His father had been right after all.

He was a failure.

Now, he'd have to return the jacket. The thought made him tear up. He folded up the jacket and left it on the bench in the locker room and left.

\*\*\*

Cassius approached his house slowly. It was early, and he doubted the gang would be there. Still, he tiptoed around the side to peek in the window. He saw that all the lights were off and the house was quiet. His shoulders relaxed in relief. He just wanted to go bury himself under the covers of his bed.

He turned around and nearly smacked into Skrap and his two lackeys. Cassius backed up quickly, feeling his heart pound in the back of his throat.

Skrap shook his head slowly back and forth in a deliberate manner. "I've tried to be nice, Big Man." He turned to look at the kid to his right. "I've been real nice. Real patient. Right Slim?"

Slim nodded vigorously. "Yeah," he grunted.

Slim's face was covered in acne, and Cassius could see he had a few scars on his left cheek.

"Right," Skrap continued. He looked at Cassius. His voice was low. "But sometimes patience doesn't exactly work. You know?"

"Yeah," Slim repeated.

Skrap gave him a look, and the boy closed his mouth. Then Skrap looked back at Cassius. "So I guess I need an answer now. Are you going to work for me or not?"

Cassius glanced at the twin tear tattoos, then looked directly into Skrap's brown eyes. "No," he said. He swallowed the urge to explain. Better to keep things simple. Explanations encouraged discussion, and that's the last thing he wanted.

Skrap continued to stare him down. He reached behind him and pulled out a switchblade. He flicked it open. "I'm sorry to hear that."

Cassius gasped and backed up. He realized he'd been stupid. Of course, Skrap had a weapon. Now what?

"Respect. That's all I want. I see I have your attention now. Have I earned your respect? Good."

Skrap took a step forward, and Cassius took a step back. He didn't have much room—he was a foot away from the chain-link fence.

"Look, I don't want any trouble," Cassius said. "I quit the team. I'm nobody."

"Yeah, you're nobody," an old, familiar voice echoed through his skull.

"I'm not nobody," he countered silently to himself.

"Yeah you are," the internal debate continued.

"I'm somebody," he thought with conviction.

The voice stopped.

Unfortunately, Skrap still stood in front of him, but the gang leader wavered. He seemed to understand that Cassius couldn't be swayed. In frustration, Skrap sliced the air in front of Cassius with his knife. Cassius reacted instantly by leaping backwards. The blade missed him by a hair.

Not wanting to give him another chance, Cassius lunged right, then left. Skrap was slow to respond, and Cassius ran past him and the other boys as if he were sprinting a 40-yard dash. As he ran down the street, he could hear Skrap chasing him. After a few moments, Cassius glanced behind him and saw Skrap stop and bend over, obviously winded.

Cassius slowed. Doreen had been right. There was no way he could ever go back home. At least Skrap was afraid to go to the school. That was something. He'd be safe going to classes, but he had no idea where he'd live.

He was truly alone now.

Cassius walked to the library. It was right next to the school, so he figured he'd be safe there. But then what? Cassius entered and hid in the bathroom. Just to be sure.

At closing time, he thought about approaching Mrs. Shuemaker. But what would he say? He couldn't see asking her if he could sleep on her couch. It was too much to ask. So he walked out into the night. He shivered and bit his lip. He could have used that fleece football jacket right about now. It was thick and warm, just what he needed.

Walking down the street, he weighed his options. No friends he could call on. Well, maybe he could have called one of the football team members, but he'd thrown that option out the window when he'd walked out in the middle of practice.

Cassius surveyed the street and noticed a number of cars parked along the curb. He tried the handles of a few. If he could find one open, he could curl up in the back seat and get a little protection from the wind. But all were locked. Sighing, he continued down the road. It had been a weird idea.

Absentmindedly, he continued to test the handles of the cars as he walked down a side street. He gasped when one opened. No way! Cassius grinned as he slipped into the back of the full-sized car. It was old, but the seats were soft and well maintained. It wasn't exactly comfortable, but it was better than a park bench, which was the only other option he could come up with.

As he fell asleep, he smiled. Yeah, it might not be the best situation, but at least he was free of Skrap and that gang.

***

The following day, Cassius walked through the front doors of his school a bit bleary-eyed. He'd awoken feeling cramped and stiff. As the sun made its appearance, he had no idea where to go, so he just walked around the neighborhood of the school and waited for the doors to open.

He went to the restroom and tidied up as best he could. Would anyone notice that he was wearing the same clothes as the day before?

Cassius heard his stomach growl all through the morning classes. He'd never looked forward to the free meal in the cafeteria as much as he did that day. He loaded his tray with meatloaf and french fries, and sat at the nearest empty table to devour his food.

He usually ignored everyone in the room, but today his attention was drawn to a plump kid sitting at a table nearby. It was George Mc-Gumphrey. Cassius ducked his head to avoid making eye contact. He still felt badly about what happened on the first day of school.

"Dummy," a scrawny, short kid jeered as he passed George's table.

George flinched, but to his credit, he didn't say anything. His silence seemed to open the door for others in the room to add their comments. The mild flurry of insults became a raucous maelstrom within moments. With every word, George shrunk lower and lower on the bench. Cassius knew that feeling—when you just want to disappear into the floor.

Without further thought, Cassius stood up, picked up his tray, and walked over to the cowering boy. He allowed his eyes to slowly pan over the other kids who'd been giving George so much trouble. It was one of the few times in his life that he was happy to be the size that he was.

The others averted their gazes, and all went back to quietly eating their lunches.

Cassius looked down at George. He cleared his throat and said in a voice that carried. "Hi, George. You might not remember me, but my name is Cassius. May I sit with you?"

The look that George gave him made Cassius smile. "Yes, yes, thank you. Yes!" he said.

Cassius sat down and made small talk. George appeared to quickly forget the nightmare that had just occurred. He opened up to Cassius about his schoolwork and challenges. Cassius realized he had a lot of interesting thoughts about a variety of subjects.

After a few minutes, another voice called out from behind Cassius. "May I sit here?"

Cassius turned around and looked up at Karl. He did a double take. "Sure," he said, indicating the seat next to him. Then he turned back to George. "Actually, this is his table. George, do you mind if Karl sits with us?"

George's face instantly lit up in a wreath of smiles as he nodded vigorously. "Of course, of course." His eyes fell to Karl's jacket. "You're the captain of the football team, aren't you?"

"Yes, I am," Karl said. He set down his tray and reached out his hand. "I'm Karl. And you're George?"

"Yeah!" George said. "That's right."

Cassius looked at Karl and felt a rush of emotion. He knew this was a show of support, and he couldn't be happier. He nodded a thank you.

Xane sat down next to Karl. "Hey there, George."

"Hi, Xane!" George replied.

Within minutes the rest of the team had swarmed the table, each player making a point of greeting George, who was ecstatic. Each time someone new sat down, George wiggled with excitement.

When he was young, Cassius had seen a movie about a happy family. He remembered a little boy running down the stairs on Christmas morning to see a huge, beautifully lit tree with dozens of wrapped presents underneath. The look on that boy's face paled in comparison to the light that shone from George's eyes. It was clear that the rest of the team could see the effect it had created and was enjoying it as much as Cassius.

When the bell rang, Karl stood up. "George, you are always welcome at our table." His voice carried through the room. "Will you join us tomorrow?"

George nodded. "Thank you!"

Karl nodded. He turned to Cassius. "Can we talk after last period?"

Cassius nodded. "Sure," he said.

"Great. Mind if Xane joins us?"

Cassius glanced over at the quarterback. "OK." The team had done so much for him today. It was the least he could do.

The rest of the day went by quickly. As Cassius went from class to class, various kids greeted him with a nod and smile. He wasn't invisible anymore. People had noticed what he'd done. That gave him a warm feeling inside.

Cassius met up with Karl at the end of the day. He and Xane were going over plays in the locker room.

"Thanks for coming," Xane said.

Cassius nodded. "No problem."

Karl and Xane exchanged glances. Finally, Karl said, "I noticed you left your jacket and stuff here. We really hope that doesn't mean what we think it does."

Cassius shrugged. "Look, I don't think I'm cut out for football."

Xane shook his head. "Uh-uh. Don't do that."

"What?" Cassius said.

"Don't put yourself down like that," Xane said. "It's not smart. My mom would ask if you enjoyed football. I mean, she'd say that's what's important. I know you haven't been playing long. But did you like it?"

Cassius nodded. "Yeah, I really loved the tryouts."

"The first practice is always the hardest. Maybe we should have gone a little easier on you?"

Cassius rolled his eyes. "Don't make me hit you." As the words spilled from his lips he cringed. "I didn't mean . . . I . . . ."

Xane laughed. "You're among friends. Don't worry so much."

Cassius looked at him long and hard. "OK."

Karl nodded. "Fact is, we really want you on the team."

Suddenly, Cassius realized he didn't have a place to go that night. The thought of spending another night in a car sapped his energy. He sat down hard on the bench, held his head in his hands and groaned in frustration. "I don't think I can," he said. How could he have enough stamina for football now?

"What? Why?" Karl asked.

Cassius heard the alarm in his voice. He let out a deep sigh and looked up at him. "I . . . ." his voice trailed off as he thought about how he could tell his new friend all about his troubles. It was too much. He shook his head. "Never mind. I'll figure it out."

Xane sat down next to him and nudged him with his shoulder. "What on earth do you have to lose by trusting us?"

Cassius looked at him. He liked Xane. His cool blue eyes held his gaze with a confidence Cassius admired. "It's pretty bad."

"You stole something?" Xane asked. "You're taking drugs? What is it? Whatever it is, I can help."

Cassius laughed. "No, nothing like that." He took a deep breath and told them the whole story. He wrapped it up by saying, "So now I'm homeless. See, there's no easy solution."

"You slept in a car?" Karl asked. "Dude, that's legendary!"

Cassius laughed. "It may sound that way, but it really isn't. I'm sore. And tired."

Xane stood up and yanked on Cassius's right arm to get him to stand up. "Come on. We're going to see Coach Dillon. He'll know what to do. And I'll talk to my mom. She's super smart. She'll have ideas."

Cassius wasn't sure how it happened, but somehow he found himself walking in the direction of the coach's office. It was a few minutes before practice, and Coach was sitting at his desk.

When Coach Dillon saw the three boys standing by the door, he immediately put down the papers he was holding. "Come on in. What can I do for you?"

They walked in, and Karl shut the door behind them. The three boys stood while Karl explained the situation to Coach Dillon. Cassius shuffled his feet and stared at the ground, wishing he could be anywhere else.

When Karl stopped talking, Coach Dillon said, "Cassius?"

He looked into the man's hazel eyes. "Yeah?"

"I'm sorry," he said simply.

Cassius could see the man's compassion. His shoulders relaxed a little, and he plopped down in the chair in front of the desk. "Yeah," he said.

"Do you have a place to go tonight?"

Cassius shook his head.

"Then you'll come home with me," Coach Dillon said. "We have a guest room."

Cassius's mouth dropped open. "Really?"

The coach nodded. "Of course. There's no way you're sleeping on the street ever again. You hear me? I want you to come to me if you ever need help with something. Got it?"

Cassius nodded. "Got it," he said, as a small smile formed. "Thank you."

Coach Dillon nodded. He picked up the phone. "Good. I'm calling the police to report this. Why don't you boys wait out in the hall. It won't be long. Then Xane and Karl, you two run the practice today. I need to take Cassius home. I'd imagine you need a shower and a hot meal. Am I right?"

Cassius stood up. "Yeah. And some sleep."

Coach nodded. "I'll be out in a minute."

The three left the office and closed the door. Cassius leaned against the wall and closed his eyes. He was suddenly exhausted. He started imagining what Coach Dillon's guest room might look like. He couldn't wait to lay down and go to sleep.

He opened his eyes and looked at Karl and Xane. "Thanks."

They both nodded. "Sure," Xane said. "It's what friends do."

\*\*\*

The next Saturday, Coach Dillon arranged with the police department to accompany them on a visit to Cassius's old house. All of Cassius's books and clothes were still inside, just as he'd left them. As they approached, the yellow police tape rustled in the wind, warning people not to cross.

Officers escorted Cassius and Coach Dillon into Cassius's old bedroom so he could pick up his belongings.

"Can we ask you a few questions?" the officer said.

"Sure," Cassius said, looking at Coach Dillon, who nodded his approval.

"We found some stolen goods as well as drugs tucked in the floorboards of the hallway. The Ghost Cobras had a few stashes around town. Did you know about them?"

Coach Dillon stepped forward. "I can assure you he didn't," he said with a touch of anger.

Cassius held out his hand. "No, it's OK." He turned to the officer. "I didn't know all that. I knew they were a gang, but didn't know which one. I tried my best to avoid them. Skrap is the leader. They did drugs all the time here. He wanted me to deal at the school."

The officer nodded. "Yeah, your coach here told us about that. You're not in any trouble, son. We know you weren't involved. We're just trying to sort through it all. Do you know where your sister is?"

Cassius shook his head and felt the pricks of tears in his eyes. "No, sir. I don't."

"Well, we just want to talk to her. We can help. If you hear from her, let me know." He handed Cassius a business card with his personal phone number. "Call me any time. We managed to locate Skrap and his gang."

Cassius and Coach Dillon exchanged a look and smile.

"You have Skrap and the rest in custody?" Coach Dillon asked.

"Yeah, and the DA says we have enough to put them all away for a long time," he said.

Cassius bent over and put his hands on his knees. The rush of relief was overpowering. "So it's over, then. I don't have to look over my shoulder anymore?"

"No one's left to come after you," the officer said.

He left Cassius to pack the bags Coach Dillon had brought. Cassius crammed all his belongings into two suitcases, and they left as soon as they could. He looked around. It would be his last time in this house where he had experienced so much pain. He closed the door and followed the coach to his car.

Later that evening, Coach Dillon gave Cassius a chance to unpack. As Cassius put his clothes in the large oak dresser, he noticed a small pink envelope. He picked it up, turned it over, and opened it. He immediately recognized his sister's scrawl.

> *Cassy,*
>
> *I'm sorry about everything. I love you. I never really say that, but I do. I love you. I should have found a way to protect you better. I'm glad you did what you did. Not too many people go up against Skrap and live to tell about it. You did.*
>
> *When Skrap was taken in, I could get out and run. I bought a bus ticket to Hollywood. I don't know what I'll do there, but I promise I won't get involved with another gang.*
>
> *Anyway, I hope you get this. If you do, think of me once in a while. Who knows, maybe you'll see me in a commercial or something one day.*
>
> *Your sister,*
> *Doreen*

Cassius smiled with relief. That sounded perfect. She was following her dreams and would be OK. He pulled the officer's card out of his pocket, then put it back. No, it was better to leave it. Give Doreen a chance to do something else with her life.

***

A few weeks later, Cassius found himself on the football field in the middle of his first game. The coach had him on the bench for the first quarter. He was grateful for the opportunity to watch the plays and let his nerves calm down.

He was on the field for a few plays in the second and third quarters and successfully blocked his man more than half the time. The players on the other team weren't as big as him, but they were far more experienced. At least he held his own. He'd learned to use the strength in his legs to stabilize himself and maintain his balance.

Late in the fourth quarter, he misjudged the opposition and allowed the fancy footwork of the beefy boy in front of him to get by and sack Xane.

Cassius groaned. "You OK?" he asked as he jogged back.

"Yeah," Xane said. "I can handle it. Don't worry." He signaled that he needed a time out and huddled with the players. "OK, we're down

17-14 and it's fourth down. I'm going to pass the ball to Cassius."

"You got this," Karl said.

"OK," Cassius said as his heart beat hard.

At the snap of the ball, Cassius crashed into the player in front of him, then went to the left and ran his pass route. A linebacker was in hot pursuit, and Cassius could see Xane throw the ball just before being hit.

It was all on Cassius. He held the fate of the team in his hands. If he failed to catch this ball, the other team would just run out the clock and win.

As the ball fell into Cassius's hands, he knew he had to pull it in tight because the defender was going to hit him hard. His job was to hold onto the ball. At any cost.

When the blow came, Cassius fell and rolled, but held on. He heard the whistle. He'd managed to get the yardage needed for a first down. The defender muttered a few choice words, and Cassius's teammates came to help him up. He was sore all over.

"Damn good," Karl said.

Coach Dillon called time out, and they huddled. "You OK to continue?" he asked Cassius.

"Sure," he said, feeling the rush of adrenaline.

They broke and lined up. The play called for Xane to hand the ball off to Karl, but the defense seemed to anticipate the play. Several tacklers were on Karl before Xane could even get him the ball. Xane kept the ball and looked to make something out of the broken play. Seeing that Cassius was open off to the side, he dumped a short pass over to him.

Cassius took off running, but quickly saw the same linebacker who had tackled him on the previous play. He was coming at him from the left side. There was no way around it. He wasn't going to outrun the guy.

Cassius did a quick mental calculation and turned to the left to run straight at the defender. The boy wasn't expecting this and was caught flat-footed. He toppled to the ground, and Cassius leapt over him and continued down the field to the end zone uncontested for a touchdown.

The whistle sounded, signaling the game was over. Cheers echoed through the stands and on the field as his teammates lifted Cassius into the air and hailed the hero. He was amazed they could lift and carry him.

When the cheers died down, some of the parents came down onto the field. A woman with long, brown hair jogged over to Xane and gave him a hug. "Nice job!" she said.

"Thanks, Mom," he replied. Then he pulled back and turned to Cassius. "Hey, Mom, this is Cassius."

She put out her hand to him. "Good to meet you. I'm Mallory."

Cassius shook her hand. "Nice to meet you, too."

"That was an amazing play you pulled out at the end. What do you call that?"

Cassius shrugged. "Desperation?" he said.

Xane laughed so hard he bent over. "Dude, I think that play's going in the book. It will probably be called the Cassius Play. Mark my words."

Mallory grinned at her son. "Yeah, whatever you want to call it, it was brilliant."

"Thanks!" Cassius said.

"Xane tells me that you're into your studies. A straight-A student."

Cassius nodded. "Yeah, I like learning. Especially computers."

She bit her lower lip, then said in a lowered voice, "And Xane told me about your situation."

"Oh," Cassius said tentatively. Cassius glanced over at Xane, who looked uncomfortable.

"I hope you don't mind," Xane said.

Cassius shook his head. "No, it's fine."

"Good," Mallory said. "Because I think I have a solution, if you're interested."

"Yeah?" Cassius said.

"You can come stay with us," she said. "We have a room in the basement. It's small, but cozy."

Cassius stared at her. "That's a lot to ask."

"You're not asking. I'm offering. Besides, I could use some help with things around the house on the weekends."

"I'd be all over that," Cassius said with a grin.

"Oh, by the way, I have an older computer I was going to donate. You want it?"

"Are you kidding me?" he shouted. "That would be incredible. Thanks!"

"Sure," Mallory said. "When you're ready, we can pick up your stuff and head home."

Cassius grinned.

*Home.* That sounded so beautiful.

# TIMOTHY

STORY #9 IN THE DISCOVERING KINDNESS SERIES

## Kevin J. Smith
with Laura Sherman

Timothy pulled into his garage and lifted the parking brake just as the small, digital clock hit 6:00 p.m. Home. No matter what was going on at work, he made it a point to be home for dinner. Otherwise, he'd miss his kids before they went off to do their homework and extracurricular activities.

He got out of his car, closed the door, and paused on his driveway to stretch his legs. He walked through the garage and opened the door into his home. The smell of pot roast made him groan with pleasure as his stomach rumbled. Sara always cooked it slowly so the meat fell apart easily without the need of a knife.

As he rounded the corner into the dining room, he smiled. It was a picture-perfect Rockwellian scene. His family was seated around the old, oval dinner table. It had been his dining table growing up, and now it served as the nightly gathering place for his family. Sara and Elizabeth were engaged in a lively mother-daughter conversation, their shoulder-length, blond hair swishing in concert with their chatter. His wife looked so young, almost as if she were Elizabeth's sister instead of her mom.

He glanced at his son, Charlie, whose curly brown head was bent over a book. Hopefully, his son wouldn't inherit his receding hairline.

The food on the table was untouched, except for a yeast roll that Charlie had pilfered.

"Hello," Timothy called out.

"You're home!" Sara exclaimed as she stood up to greet him.

He grinned as he gave his wife a huge hug. She made him feel like a conquering hero returned from a battle. Timothy was always up before the sun and the children in the morning. His wife insisted on getting up when he did to make his breakfast. He knew Sara would prefer to sleep in, but she wouldn't hear of him making his own eggs and toast.

"You provide for us all," she'd said. "The least I can do is make sure you're well-fed."

"Hi, Daddy," Elizabeth called out.

"Hey, Pumpkin," he said with a twinkle in his eye. He looked forward to the banter with his youngest child each day.

"How was work, Acorn Squash?" she said with a wide grin.

"Excellent, Patty Pan."

"That's great, Butternut."

He was about to toss out another squash endearment when he spotted Charlie rolling his eyes. The boy picked up the platter of steaming meat and potatoes.

Timothy frowned just as Sara clucked her tongue. "Charlie, wait until your father has a chance to sit down."

Charlie didn't look up, but dropped the platter back on the table with a clatter and picked up his book again. It was clear he was doing his best to tune out the rest of the family.

Timothy sat down and said pointedly to his son, "You can eat now. If you like."

Without looking up or saying a word, Charlie threw his book on the table and picked up the pot roast again as if nothing had happened.

Timothy shook his head and turned to Sara, who gave him a little smile and shrug. Her sunny face cheered him up immediately.

As he picked up the platter that Charlie had left near him, he turned back to his daughter. "Everything all set for the car wash in two weeks?"

Elizabeth nodded. "I think so. We found a location and have the volunteers. Mom's going to be there."

"I'm proud of you," Timothy said. "It's your first leadership role in the group."

She took a nervous gulp of her water. "Yeah. Tonight we have a big planning meeting."

Sara put a hand on her arm. "You'll do fine. You have a good troop."

Elizabeth affectionately rested her cheek on her mother's hand. "It's just so important that we do well. I really want to go to Savannah and see the Girl Scout First Headquarters this summer. What a trip that will be!"

Sara nodded. "Savannah is steeped in history. You'll love it!"

Timothy turned back to Charlie. "And tonight's Boy Scouts," he said. He did his best to keep his voice chipper, but felt a little dread at bringing up the topic. Charlie was so unenthusiastic about everything.

With each interaction with his teenage son, Timothy felt his resolve to be positive slip away more and more. It was hard to ignore the negative thoughts that pierced his good intentions. Charlie didn't exactly bring out the best in him.

He reminded himself that, no matter what, Charlie was his son. He was a good kid. It might be a challenge, but Timothy knew he was up for it.

"I haven't heard much about it lately," he continued when Charlie didn't respond. "Any camping trips on the horizon?"

Charlie shrugged. "I don't know."

Timothy felt his eyebrows knit together, then smoothed them out again. "What badges are you working on?"

Charlie took another bite, then stood up. "Done," he said.

"Charlie!" Sara said. "Don't be rude. Answer your father's question."

Charlie paused and turned slowly to his father. He looked him in the eye for the first time that night. "I'm thinking about quitting, Dad. Seriously, Boy Scouts is lame."

Blood rushed to Timothy's ears, and he stammered, "W-what? I thought you liked it?"

"No, Dad. *You* like it. I don't. I know, you were an Eagle Scout. One of the youngest in your day. That's great. Really, it is. It's just not my thing."

Timothy pursed his lips as he contemplated his words. Finally, he said, "Give it more time. It's a great program. You'll see. You only have another couple of months. Finish the year."

Charlie nodded and grunted. "I need to change into my uniform."

"Me, too!" Elizabeth said as she picked up her plate and silverware. "I want to get there early."

Timothy watched both kids leave and shook his head. "How could they both come from the same household?" he muttered to no one in particular.

*** 

A couple of hours later, Sara came home with the two kids. Timothy came in from the living room and leaned against the arch to the long corridor. Charlie was speed-walking to his room when Sara called out to him, "You have to tell him."

Charlie stopped and swiveled back to his father. "I quit Scouts tonight."

"What do you mean, you quit?" Timothy shouted. "I thought we went over this."

"You talked. I listened. Then I decided to quit."

Timothy felt his face burn. "Why you little . . ."

"Watch it, Dad. You might lose your title of Mr. Positive."

Without waiting for a response, Charlie raced up the stairs. It was only when Timothy heard the door slam that he snapped out of his stupor and looked over at Sara.

"Why?"

When Sara didn't offer an explanation, Elizabeth piped up, "He said he didn't like the other boys very much and the projects weren't fun. He didn't want to pretend anymore."

Silence fell over the three as Timothy just stared at the closed door at the top of the stairs. Then he turned back to his wife.

Sara looked as if she might try to say something, but Timothy didn't trust himself to respond positively. "I'm going out."

He stormed out the door and slammed it behind him, hoping the sound might jolt some sense into his wayward son.

He drove to his favorite watering hole, The Rusty Spike, just a few blocks away. It was Monday night, which meant that some of his friends would probably be there.

When he walked into the bar, he immediately felt better. Although no one called out his name or anything, The Rusty Spike was his home away from home; a place he could go to unwind and meet up with his buddies.

Timothy scanned the room for anyone he knew and smiled when Shay waved him over. It was relatively quiet, which suited him.

"I wondered if anyone was going to show up tonight. How's it going?" Shay asked, patting the stool next to him.

"Let me order a beer, and I'll tell you," Timothy responded, signaling the bartender with his index finger. Bill nodded and began pouring a pint of Guinness on tap for him.

"So?"

"Teenagers," Timothy said as he plopped himself heavily on the barstool and let out an exaggerated sigh. "I forget. How old is your Mo?"

"Seven."

"Nice. Would that I could turn back time and be blessed with a seven-year-old Charlie again."

Shay chuckled. "Why? What's going on?"

Bill brought over Timothy's beer, and he took a long swig, then wiped his mouth on his sleeve. "It's been a series of things, really. But tonight, my boy directly disobeyed me. He up and quit Boy Scouts after I explicitly told him not to."

"Maybe he didn't like it." Shay said with a shrug.

Timothy scowled. "So? The answer isn't to quit!" The words came out a little too forcefully, and the bartender looked over in surprise. "Sorry," he said to Bill with a blush. He took another gulp. "I just didn't expect complete defiance, you know?"

"Yeah, my pop wouldn't have put up with that in our household. If any of us stepped out of order, it was the belt."

Timothy nodded. "Same here. Except that we had to go out and pick out the stick from the backyard. It had to be green. Man, that switch really hurt." He took another gulp. "I've probably been a little lax with Charlie. He needs more discipline. Yeah, that's the solution. Thanks!"

Shay looked a little uncomfortable. "You gonna whip him?"

"God no," Timothy said.

Shay sighed in relief. "Good."

"No, I just need to find a way to teach him some measure of responsibility. Maybe some hands-on experience. That's all."

\*\*\*

The next day, Timothy convinced Sara to stay in bed. He wanted to get into the office before the rest of the crew to handle some paperwork. He grabbed a bagel and cream cheese, and ran out the door well before the sun came up.

He unlocked the office, turned on the lights, and booted up his computer. The one-room office was small, but was able to fit three desks comfortably. The other two were neat and orderly, waiting for the auto repair business's service consultants to arrive. His had a stack of papers in his inbox needing his attention. Timothy sat down and pulled out the first invoice.

"Don't delegate every single task to your employees," he could hear his father say. "You need to have your hands in every aspect of your business. Especially finances. Never completely trust anyone else with the money, or you'll wind up bankrupt."

He'd started working for his dad when he was twelve. It wasn't by choice, but then what did he know? He was just a kid. Timothy did what he was told. That was that. And he was told to show up in the afternoons and on Saturday mornings to learn the ropes of his father's business.

"You'll take over all of this one day, Timmy," he'd said. "No reason to wait to learn."

Timothy would have much preferred to watch Saturday morning cartoons with his neighborhood friends. They would gather at 9:00 a.m. sharp at Jeremy's house, bringing a big old box of Froot Loops and lots of Pop Tarts to share. The kids all stayed until noon. Sometimes, Timothy was able to join them for the last hour, but only if he got his work done in time. It was definitely an incentive to keep productive. And as the years rolled by, he realized how much he liked the work and the business.

Timothy smiled as he looked around the office. This was the original shop. His father's. Over the last decade, he'd managed to open another five in the neighboring towns. Everyone always needed a mechanic, and his father had taught him how to hire good people.

"Sit down and talk to everyone you hire. Don't let them give you a pile of B.S. Pick the mechanics who love to work on cars." His father never minced words. "They're the ones who will stick it out."

Timothy had sat in on many job interviews before he turned eighteen. His father was careful and took his time with every applicant. He'd get the person's goals to make sure they were there for the right reasons. He also wasn't afraid of hiring women for the garage.

"If they know cars, who cares about gender," he told Timothy.

His father had insisted that his son go to college and get a business degree. As a result, there was no aspect of the business that Timothy wasn't prepared to handle by the time he took over.

Timothy's pile of paperwork slowly diminished as the sun's rays filtered into the room. When his employees started filing in between six and seven, Timothy greeted each by name and asked about their families. By the time the shop doors officially opened at eight, the place was humming with activity.

His two service consultants were fielding calls from customers when Gladys Nightly walked in. Her large, straw hat and bright spring dress covered with large magnolias made him smile. She was ninety-three and one of his oldest customers. His father had adored her eccentric personality.

"Sharp as a whip. Don't let her age fool you," he'd warned Timothy.

By the time his dad had retired, Timothy had known each of his regular customers as if they were all a part of his extended family.

Timothy immediately rose when he saw Gladys walk over to him. "How are you today, Mrs. Nightly?" he asked.

"Oh, fine," she said, waving away the arm he offered to help her to his desk. "I can manage. Just need a little more time to get there. That's all."

Timothy pulled the chair out for her and said, "I see you brought your Malibu in today. What seems to be the problem?"

Gladys put a hand on the back of the chair and slowly eased into the seat. "Not sure. It's just making a strange noise."

When Gladys was securely in her chair, he went around to the other side of his desk. "Can you describe the sound?"

"Sounds like a cranky cat," she said with a smile that revealed a few missing teeth. "You know, a kind of rough purr that tells you he's had enough petting for the time being?"

Timothy chuckled. "Yeah, I know the sound. Does it happen when you start it up?"

"Yes."

"Sounds like it could be the battery."

"You may be a young whippersnapper, but you really know your cars."

Timothy grinned. It had been a long time since anyone had accused him of being young. He liked it. Working with cars always made him feel young. "Leave it here and we'll test it for you. Do you need a ride home?"

"I do. Thank you."

Timothy called over one of his young mechanics and asked him to drive Mrs. Nightly home. Before she left, she reached into her bag and pulled out a few wrapped Snickerdoodles. "I know how much you like them," she said, squeezing his arm.

"Oh-h-h," he replied with a drawn-out groan of pleasure. "I really do. Thank you, Mrs. Nightly."

She winked and followed the mechanic out to his car. Timothy waited until she turned to wave goodbye to him, then went back to his office to call a few new clients.

\*\*\*

On the way home, Timothy rolled down the windows, cranked up the eighties music, and sang along to the Bangles. It had been a great day. Not only had there been a record number of new customers, but he'd emptied his inbox, except for one of Mrs. Nightly's cookies that he was saving for the next day.

He whistled *Walk Like an Egyptian* as he walked through the door, bending both hands at the wrist, one up, the other down, and rocking out to the music in his head. Elizabeth greeted him in the hallway and giggled.

"What's that?" she asked.

Timothy immediately stopped and gave her a sheepish grin. "It's an old dance from my high school days. You weren't supposed to see that."

"I'm glad I did." She turned and ran into the kitchen.

As he entered the dining room, his wife came in with a glass baking dish filled with spaghetti casserole.

"Oh, that looks and smells wonderful," he said.

"Have a seat. Can I bring you anything?"

"A Coke would be great."

"You got it!"

She disappeared and came back soon after with a tall glass of Coke with a squeeze of lime over ice, just the way he liked it. As he sipped it, Elizabeth came out with a large salad, then sat down.

Sara called Charlie and took her seat. Elizabeth began scooping out the casserole, but stopped when her mother gave her a look.

"We'll wait for Charlie," Sara said.

They sat in silence for a few moments, then heard the sound of creaking stairs before Charlie entered. He shuffled his feet, sat down, and pulled the casserole toward him. He dumped a pile on his plate, then picked up his fork to begin eating.

Sara sighed, then said, "Would you please pass the dish to your sister?"

He put the full fork in his mouth and grunted, then passed the casserole to Elizabeth.

"Sure looks yummy!" Elizabeth said as she scooped up a portion and passed it to Timothy.

"You say that about everything Mom makes," Charlie muttered.

Timothy glared at his son. "Maybe that's because everything she makes *is* delicious."

Charlie shrugged and continued to shovel food into his mouth. Sara put the salad bowl next to him. When he didn't take the hint, she said, "You need to eat some greens, too."

He dumped a spoonful on his plate and ate it quickly. When he was done, he stood up to leave.

"No," Timothy growled. "The family meal isn't done."

Charlie rolled his eyes and fell back down into his chair, looking for all the world like a broken rag doll.

Timothy put down his fork and gave his son his complete attention. He took a moment to really look at his son.

He was his flesh and blood.

He was a good boy in need of guidance.

As he continued to look at Charlie, he allowed his heart to fill with love. "I was thinking," he began slowly. "You should start putting in some time at the office. I'd like to show you the ropes. And if you do well, I plan to hand over the keys to the business to you. When you're ready."

Timothy leaned back in his chair and smiled with satisfaction. This was the first time he'd shared that plan with Charlie. He remembered fondly the moment when his father had first told him that his automotive empire would belong to Timothy one day. He'd been flooded with an overwhelming feeling of awe and gratitude. It was such a huge gift, one that he felt unworthy of receiving for many years. He hoped that this gesture would make clear to Charlie that he had faith in his son, and that he knew this was just a rough patch.

"No thanks," Charlie said, staring at a spot on the table in front of him.

If Charlie had stood up and slapped him with a wet rag, it would have accomplished the same feeling. "What? What do you mean, *no thanks*?"

Sara gave her husband a little hand wave to get his attention, then shook her head slowly at him. Timothy frowned at her, then turned back to his son. "Tomorrow after school, I expect you to report to my office. It's Wednesday, you don't have anywhere else to be."

"Is that all?" Charlie said, standing up. "I have homework to do." He walked away without looking back.

When they heard the door slam upstairs, Sara said, "He'll come around. Give him a little time."

"I'd like to come to your office," Elizabeth said. "I'd like to see what you do."

Timothy turned to her and smiled. "Sure, we can arrange that. Soon."

"How about tomorrow?"

He shook his head. "I need to focus on your brother. Another time."

\*\*\*

Mid-afternoon the next day, Timothy glanced at his watch. Charlie should have been there. It was a good hour after his high school had let out. Maybe the bus was running late. When 4:30 p.m. rolled around, he knew his son was a no-show. Timothy packed up his stuff and headed back to the house early.

He wasn't in the mood to listen to the radio; he allowed his thoughts to fill in the void left by the silence. When he arrived home, he shot up the stairs and opened Charlie's door without knocking, causing his son to jump.

The boy was in the middle of a video game on his laptop. Timothy took two long strides over to him, reached out a hand, and slammed the computer shut.

"What did you do that for?" Charlie cried out as if he'd been injured. He glared at his father. "I was in the middle of something."

"I see that. I have a half a mind to take this thing from you."

Charlie closed his eyes and sighed. "I was just taking a break. I've been studying all afternoon."

Timothy looked around and saw open books scattered on the desk, along with a notebook that had fresh ink on the pages.

He studied his son's defeated posture for a few moments, then said in a quiet voice, "You were supposed to come by the shop today."

Charlie opened his eyes and groaned. "I forgot. That's on me. I had a lot of Art History work to do for tomorrow's class, and it slipped my mind. I'm sorry."

Timothy looked over at the textbook that was in front of his son. It was the college class Charlie had enrolled in a few weeks prior. The local branch of the university offered free classes to high school kids.

"It's great that you want to go to college, but why don't you enroll in a few business classes? It will help you when you take over the shops."

Charlie stiffened. "I'll think about it."

"You do that," Timothy said. He turned and walked out of the room and slammed the door.

***

It was Friday night and Timothy found himself looking forward to family night. He had picked up a movie he was sure everyone would like. It had action, adventure and romance—something for everyone.

Sara had made pizzas, another Friday night tradition. She made the dough from scratch and topped it high with meats and veggies.

"Elizabeth, please call your brother," Sara said absently as she cut the first pie.

After Elizabeth called up the stairs to her brother, she ran back to the table. "Can I dig in, Mama?" she asked as she scooped up a slice.

Sara sighed. "Sure. If we wait for Charlie, it's just gonna get cold."

They all sat and engaged in conversation about the day's events until almost all the pizza was gone.

"Charlie never came down," Sara said with a start.

Timothy glanced in the direction of the stairs. "I'll get him."

He stormed up the stairs two at a time. It was one thing to show up to dinner sullen and argumentative, but this was too much. Timothy banged on the door so hard that it seemed to buckle under the pressure of his fist.

"Charlie, you come out here this instance. What's the meaning of this?"

No answer.

He tried the handle. The door opened into an empty room. All the air seemed to suck out of Timothy's lungs as if he'd entered a vacuum. "Charlie?" he called out, opening the closet door. Odd, but the idea that he might be hiding in his closet seemed more plausible than any other explanation.

Timothy ran down the steps and burst into the dining room. "When was the last time you saw him?"

Sara's mouth dropped open. "Charlie?"

"Yeah."

"This morning. When he left for school."

"And his college class. When's that again?"

"That was yesterday," Elizabeth said. "Thursday."

Timothy glanced at his watch. It was 6:40 p.m. The sun would be setting in about half an hour. "Any idea where he went?"

Elizabeth shook her head. "No, Papa."

He nodded. She was always honest. Not a deceptive bone in her body. Not like his eldest.

Sara stood up and called Charlie's cell phone. "Direct to voicemail," she said with a tremor in her voice. "I'll start calling his friends."

"What's the point of giving the boy a phone if he doesn't even bother to turn it on?" Timothy shouted to no one in particular.

"Maybe it ran out of juice," Elizabeth offered.

He ignored her. "I'm going to go looking for him," he said as he pulled out his keys and jogged to the garage door. He yelled over his shoulder, "Call me if you hear anything!"

Tires squealed as he pulled out of his driveway in reverse. Unwanted images of Charlie lying by the side of the road plagued him as he wiped his forehead with his sleeve. His hands trembled on the wheel as his head pivoted right and left.

Timothy had no idea where the young kids hung out. Was Charlie at a rave? He'd read about those. Maybe the college kids had a party going on.

He turned right and headed to the college campus. It wasn't far. New images flashed before him. Kids smoking weed from a bong and drinking alcohol, passed out on the lawn outside a frat house.

Would they allow a minor to join a frat?

His son was tall, so maybe no one asked him his age. Was he going to undergo a grueling hazing? There were so many online articles about youth dying in the first year of college after being forced to undergo dangerous pledging trials.

New pictures replaced the others, and he could see his Charlie laid out in a coroner's office with a white sheet over his head. Would he be asked to identify the body?

Tears pricked the back of his eyes as he pulled into a parking spot. Timothy shook his head against the avalanche of unpleasant images. He jogged to the center of the campus and spun around in a full circle looking for signs of parties. There were none. Maybe it was too early.

Seeing various kids walking up and down the paths, he stopped a few and asked if they knew his son. They all shook their heads. Some gave him a suspicious look and continued on their way without a backward glance.

Timothy ran a hand through his hair and continued to search for Charlie to no avail. Finally, he picked up the phone and dialed home.

"Did you find him?" Sara asked, her voice sounding as frantic as he felt.

"No." The word came out more like a frustrated sigh. "He's not at the campus."

"I called all of his friends. No one has seen him. I also called the hospitals. He's not there either."

"I'm coming home," Timothy said as he turned and walked back to his car. "Hopefully, he'll show up soon."

When he arrived home, his heart beat a little faster. Maybe Charlie was there waiting for him.

Opening the door, he knew the answer when he saw Sara's pale face. Elizabeth was sobbing quietly next to her. He pulled her into his arms and rubbed her back the way he used to when she was a toddler.

"I'm sure he's OK," Timothy said. He felt he had to do something to maintain his status of Mr. Positive, the moniker his son had given him earlier that week. Even if he didn't believe his own words, somehow saying them made him feel better.

Just as he pulled away from his daughter, Charlie walked through the front door. He looked as if he'd been whistling up until he saw everyone's faces.

"What's up?" he asked, his eyes widening.

"*What's up*?" Timothy shouted. "Are you kidding me? Where the hell have you been?"

"Timothy!" Sara chided.

"Sorry," he muttered. They had an agreement not to swear in front of the kids, and he'd just broken that promise. He turned back to his son, took a deep breath, and said, "Do you have any idea how worried we've been?"

Charlie shook his head. "I lost track of time. Sorry."

The apology sounded less than sincere to Timothy's ears, which made him clench his hands into fists. "Where were you?" He enunciated each word with laser precision.

Charlie gave his father a steady glare. "I was at the beach. I was practicing drawing buildings for my *art class*."

"You expect me to believe that?" Timothy barked.

Charlie shrugged. "Believe what you like."

They stood silently staring at each other. Then Charlie pulled a sketch book from his backpack and flipped to the last few pages. He handed the book to his father and said, "See?"

Timothy took the book from his son and looked at the drawings. Timothy knew little about art, but remembered studying perspective as a kid. These were spot on. There was real technical skill in each pencil sketch. They looked professional.

Still angry, the last thing he wanted to do was validate his son's work. "OK, so you were at the beach. Why was your phone off?"

"Battery died," Charlie said. "I forgot to charge it last night."

Timothy grasped at the straw that was given him. "No sense of responsibility," he said. "Well, that changes right now. You're grounded until further notice. And you're coming to the shop with me tomorrow morning. We're leaving the house at a quarter 'til seven."

Charlie grabbed his sketch pad from his father and ran up the stairs. "If you're not out of bed by 6:30 a.m., I'll drag you out!"

\*\*\*

When Timothy came out of the kitchen the next morning, Charlie's head was slumped against the hallway wall with his eyes closed. Timothy couldn't help but smile at his defiant son. At least he was ready and on time.

The car ride wasn't pleasant. Charlie chose to stare mutinously out the passenger window the entire trip. When they arrived, his son dragged his body into the office like he was hefting a sack of potatoes.

Timothy pulled a chair over to his desk and set up for the morning's work. He did his best to remember the points his father had taught him when he was young. They made for a good starting point for Charlie's lessons. He went over case files to help orient the boy to the work.

Timothy quickly realized that his son had no clue about cars. His eyes glazed over as Timothy did his best to bring him up to speed.

"Do you want to see a few engines?" Timothy asked with a grin. That had always been his favorite part of his father's lessons. Looking under the hood and learning about the different parts of the car and how they worked always made his heart beat a little faster.

"Not really," came the response from the boy with drooping shoulders and eyelids.

Timothy wanted to scream at him to wake up and take an interest, but all his energy had been sapped. "Fine. I'll take you home," he bit out.

Charlie immediately stood up and walked to the door. Timothy had meant his words to be a punishment, but he could tell his son was relieved. He wasn't sure if it was his imagination, but there appeared to be an added spring to his step.

When they got home, his wife and daughter were having breakfast together. They looked up when the two men walked into the kitchen.

"Charlie is not to leave today. He's to remain in his room," Timothy stated. Then he turned around and walked to the front door.

Behind him he heard the heavy footsteps of his son climbing the stairs. He also heard his daughter calling out something to him, but he couldn't make out the words. His head was filled with the sound of rushing blood.

He slammed the front door and was halfway back to the office when his mind began to decipher Elizabeth's words.

"Can I come with you, Daddy?" she'd asked.

Timothy slumped against the steering wheel and sighed. She was always so eager to please.

\*\*\*

That evening after dinner, Timothy headed out to The Rusty Spike, hoping to find friends who might listen to his troubles. When he walked in the door, he was happy to see the place was packed. There were several tables filled with his buddies, so he had his pick of where to go.

He chose a table of fathers. They'd understand his woes. He signaled the barkeep to bring another pitcher for the table. They all cheered in appreciation and Maurice slapped him on the back.

"You look like you've been through the ringer!" he said.

Timothy nodded. "You don't know the half of it."

"Let me guess. It has something to do with your teenager. Am I right?"

The table erupted into knowing chuckles. It was clear that they all understood his plight.

"Yeah," Timothy said with a drawn-out sigh. "The boy's just not cutting it!"

"What did Charlie do this time?" Maurice said.

"Well, for one thing, he didn't show up to dinner last night. Made me half sick with worry."

"You mean your boy actually comes home for dinner sometimes?" a man from across the large circular table said.

Timothy furrowed his brows. "Yeah, I mean, that's what we normally do."

A large man next to Maurice burst out laughing. "Man, if I could get my three kids at the table at the same time, I think I'd call Mother Theresa over to have dinner with us. I mean, it would be a miracle."

There was a murmur of agreement among the others.

"OK, I get it, but you know, a kid's supposed to do what he's told, right?" Timothy said.

"Damn straight," a few of the fathers erupted in agreement.

"I don't know about all of you," Maurice said. "I'm just happy if I see my Gavin by the end of the day. And it's a plus if he's not drunk off his rocker."

Timothy inhaled sharply. "Your son drinks?"

"It's getting worse. And I think he's smoking weed, too."

A few of the other men around the table nodded their heads. "Ever since the stuff became legal, it's hard to keep it out of their hands," a large man said. "I found a stash in Gregory's closet last week and threw it away. But I know he'll replace it."

Timothy stared at them in dazed confusion. "Are you telling me all your sons and daughters are mixed up in drugs?"

There was silence for a moment. The men all took long drinks from their mugs and a few refilled theirs. Then Maurice said, "Pot isn't my only problem."

"It isn't?" Timothy asked.

"Gavin doesn't seem to be interested in anything but video games," he said with a shake of his head. "He and his friends all want to make money playing games all day."

Timothy shook his head. He must have heard wrong. "What?"

"Yeah, it's a thing," Maurice said taking a long swig of his beer. "They live-stream on a thing called Twig or something."

"Twitch," the large man corrected.

"Right. That's it. Twitch. Gavin's obsessed with it and plays all weekend."

Timothy looked around at the fathers. "So, you *let* him do that?"

Maurice shrugged. "At least it keeps him home, you know? I don't have to worry about him getting involved in gangs or serious drugs."

"Serious drugs?"

Maurice sighed. "A few of Gavin's friends are on probation for selling coke and other stuff."

Another man cleared his throat. "My daughter got picked up for shoplifting last month. We're lucky she didn't go to juvie."

Timothy whistled low. "I had no idea."

"It's not something I talk about a lot," the man said.

"Yeah," was all Timothy could say.

***

Sunday morning, Timothy got up quietly and read the paper downstairs in his armchair. When he heard Charlie's shower turn off, he waited a few moments before climbing the stairs and knocking gently on Charlie's door.

"Yeah?" Charlie said.

"Can I come in?"

"It's open."

When Timothy entered the room, he saw that Charlie was sitting at his desk reading. He had a document open on his laptop.

"What are you working on?"

"Nothing," Charlie muttered.

Timothy walked over and saw that he'd been writing an essay about the architectural differences between the beach community and the downtown. Many of the terms were foreign to Timothy, but he could tell at a glance that it was well-written.

"Doesn't look like nothing to me," he said.

Charlie looked up at him in confusion. "Huh?"

"Looks like you're writing a pretty good essay there."

Charlie continued to look dazed. "Thanks," he said.

"Look, I thought maybe you and I could go out for brunch. You know, so we could talk a bit. Man to man."

"I don't know. I've got a lot to do," he mumbled.

Timothy nodded and sat on the edge of the made bed. "So, when you were sketching on the beach, you were studying the designs of the buildings so you could write this essay?"

"Yeah. It's for my midterm project."

"Huh," Timothy said. "Can I see the sketches again?"

Charlie pulled the book out from his backpack and handed it to his father. Timothy looked through the sketchbook and could see the marked improvement from page to page. "You're really good," he murmured.

"Thanks, Dad."

Timothy sighed. "Sorry I never noticed. That's on me." He paused and really took a long look at his son. "You really like this stuff, don't you?"

Charlie chuckled. "By this *stuff*, I assume you mean architecture. Yeah, I like it."

Timothy knew that was an understatement. He returned his son's smile and said, "So, you're not so interested in becoming a mechanic, then?"

Charlie shook his head. "Not at all."

"OK."

"OK? Really?" Charlie asked.

"Really. I don't want you to do something you have no passion for. I can always sell the business."

"You know, Dad," Charlie said tentatively. "There might be someone else in the house who just might be interested in learning the ropes from you."

"Hm?" Timothy asked.

"Your daughter?" Charlie said with a laugh. "She keeps asking to go to the shop and learn. Heck, she keeps popping the hood of Mom's minivan to look at the water level and oil. Whatever she can get her hands on."

Timothy groaned. He'd missed all the signs. Of course, Elizabeth was showing an interest. "I'll talk to her. You're right. She'd be perfect."

Charlie closed his books, then stood up. "I *am* hungry. Is brunch still on the table?"

Timothy smiled and stood up. He walked over to his son and embraced him.

"Absolutely."

# Acknowledgements

This book is the result of a seed planted some forty years ago. I would like to thank my wife, Cathy, and our two wonderful daughters, Danielle and Devin, for their support. Without them, I do not believe this project would have happened.

The most enjoyable part of this process was collaborating with my talented writing partner, Laura Sherman, and publishers Mike Dauplaise and Bonnie Groessl at M&B Global Solutions Inc. Laura did a wonderful job bringing these characters to life, and Mike and Bonnie provided the finishing touches on a project for which we can all take pride.

I would also like to thank all the wonderful people I have encountered through the years that suggested I should write a book.

# About the Authors

Kevin J. Smith retired from a career as a Certified Financial Planner. He lives in De Pere, Wisconsin, with his wife, Cathy. They have two wonderful, grown daughters.

Laura Sherman, a.k.a. "The Friendly Ghostwriter," has authored and ghostwritten over thirty books during her 20-year career. She specializes in writing stories that uplift, educate, and inspire her readers.